WHO PAYS THE FERRYMAN?

Michael J. Bird

EFSTATHIADIS GROUP

EFSTATHIADIS GROUP S.A.
14, Valtetsiou Str.
106 80 Athens
Tel: (01) 5154650, 6450113
Fax: (01) 5154657
GREECE

ISBN 960 226 086 6

First published in Great Britain
by W.H. Allen & Co. Ltd., 1977

Printed and bound in Greece

WHO PAYS THE FERRYMAN?

A Star Original

Haldane knew he was staring but there was nothing he could do about it. There was such an air of unreality about this encounter, about her, about his reaction to her. It was almost as if this were some kind of magic moment; predestined and to be lingered over. And she did nothing to break the spell. Her eyes were on his. But then suddenly her frown deepened as though she were discomforted by his gaze and her own thoughts.

'What is it?' she asked.

'You remind me of someone,' he said and as he did so he felt certain that had to be the answer. But who?

She studied him. 'Are you lost?'

'In a way,' Haldane replied quietly.

The woman hesitated, but only for a second. And then she smiled gently and she was even more beautiful.

'You will take a glass of wine?' she asked.

He nodded, accepting the inevitability of the invitation; only now without question.

He crossed to the steps and began to climb them. And, as he did so, he was obsessed with the certainty that life had, at that moment, taken on a new beginning for him.

When Zeus ruled the universe and Hera was his consort and all men were the playthings of the Gods, Charon ferried the dead across the river Styx to the Underworld and the Elysian Fields beyond.

And for this service Charon demanded payment.

CHAPTER ONE

It had been drizzling when he had driven into the boatyard past the two men taking down the sign, HALDANE MARINE LIMITED. Now it began to rain heavily. Alan Haldane pulled up the collar of his coat and then, once again, ran his fingers over the recently varnished hull of the boat cradled in the slipway and remembered. It had rained on the day Ruth had been killed. And it had rained throughout the funeral too.

It had been difficult enough then, watching the coffin lowered into the grave. How do you say goodbye to anyone, to anything, to anywhere that has been a part of your life for so many years? But today, standing alongside the last *Sea Rover* to be launched from the yard, it was worse for him. Haldane felt it and did not even try to deny it. On this cold, wet January day his sorrow and his sense of loss were greater than they had been on that cold, wet January day six years earlier when he had buried his wife.

Momentarily he felt ashamed. But only momentarily. He shrugged, dismissing the twinge of guilt and retaining nothing more than a vague regret. There was no point in pretending. In twenty years of marriage the one thing Haldane had never doubted was his feelings towards the many boats which he had seen built to his designs; he had loved them all.

Frowning, he once more gazed along the sleek lines of the yacht in the slipway. Then he turned, walked across to his car, got into it, started the engine and drove slowly away. He did not look back.

Just inside the entrance to the boatyard the two workmen were sheltering in the doorway of the gatehouse with the sign they had removed leaning against the wall alongside them. Haldane did not even glance at them. He swung the car onto the road and accelerated up the hill towards the grey, wet town which Woolworthed and Kentucky Chickened the head of the estuary.

His house stood, detached and desirable, beyond the western straggle of bungalows and isolated from the last of them by three miles of open countryside. By the time he reached it and pulled into the drive his clothes were beginning to steam in the fan blasted warmth from the car's heater.

Haldane let himself into the house, took off his overcoat and dropped it on to a chair in the hall. As he did so he caught a glimpse of himself in the long mirror hanging on the wall beside the chair. He scowled. The fact that middle-age had brought with it no thickening of his waistline, no heavying jowls, only a rugged tracery of lines to his face and a hint of grey to his hair which, if anything, were an improvement on his youthful good looks, was little consolation at that moment. He crossed the hallway to his study.

As he pushed open the door his feeling of depression lifted a little. The rest of the house had always been Ruth's, the furnishings and decorations reflecting her taste much more than his and he had never really felt at home in any other room but this one. The study was his, inviolate to any whims brought on by the Sunday supplements or advertisements in *Country Life;* a bulwark of individuality against the tides of fashion and the dictates of good investment. Here, sitting either at the draughtsman's table by the window with its view of the front garden or behind the large, mahogany, Victorian desk, Haldane had known the deep satisfaction of hard work well done. Here, in the comfort of the scarred leather armchair drawn up to the open fire, alone, surrounded by his books and the litter of his personality and listening to his favourite music, he had known the absolute peace of mind and of spirit which elsewhere in the house had somehow always eluded him.

Haldane closed the door, moved over to the fire and

threw another log on to it. Then he took his pipe from his pocket, filled it and lit it with a taper which he took from a bowl on the mantleshelf and held in the flames in the grate.

As he was replacing the taper, Ruth, blonde, attractive, trim figured and forty-five, smiled at him from the framed photograph on the mantlepiece. Haldane winced. But it was the model on the shelf in the alcove alongside the fireplace which did most to totally depress him once more. It was a beautifully crafted replica of a *Sea Rover*, complete in every detail, under sail and mounted on a stand. Haldane picked up the model and read the inscription on the silver plaque attached to the base of the stand, needlessly because he knew it by heart. *Presented to Alan Haldane on the 7th May 1976 to mark the occasion of the sale of the five hundredth Sea Rover and as a token of the admiration, affection and esteem in which he is held by the staff and his fellow directors of Haldane Marine Limited.*

Still staring at the model, Haldane weighed it in his hand, as if to put a price on it. He sighed. And then, shaking his head and smiling a faint and bitter smile, he put the boat back on the shelf.

An hour later when he heard his brother's car pull up outside the house he was a long way away and in another time. And he had seen Melina again.

Haldane had come across the photograph album in a drawer in his desk while searching for an old address book. He had intended to check on the name of an hotel in the Austrian Tyrol, once recommended by a friend and which he had noted down but now forgotten. The album was in the bottom of the drawer lying under the case which contained his Distinguished Conduct Medal. He had not looked through it for years and, on a sudden impulse, he had taken it out of the drawer, sat down at his desk and opened it.

The first photographs, neatly mounted, had all bee

taken during his basic infantry training; a gallery of faces to many of which, to his surprise, he could no longer give a name. And there he was, in an ill-fitting uniform, holding a rifle and trying to look like a soldier. And, in another snap, posing on a football pitch with his arms around the shoulders of his best friends of the moment, both soon to die; one in the Western Desert, the other on the beaches of Normandy.

My God, he thought, was I ever that young? Were any of us? And then he had turned the page. More snapshots, on and off duty; drinking beer, learning to kill and clutching giggling, teasing girls. And then, pressed like wild flowers between official photographs of the Lofoten Islands raid of 1941, a commando shoulder flash and a faded set of sergeant's stripes.

Brushing aside the shoulder flash and the chevrons, Haldane had studied the battle-blackened face which had been his thirty-six years ago, gazed into his eyes and saw again and remembered how quickly and how brutally the adolescent on the football pitch had grown into a man.

Egypt next; in shorts, bare-chested on a beach somewhere, riding a camel, outside a mosque and trying it on with other girls and laughing.

And after Egypt, nothing. Just blank, grey pages. No glossy, monochrome records of the landing in Crete or of the hell of the straggling retreat and the bloody hand-to-hand rearguard actions. And no pictures taken during the years he had spent on the island with the Andarte. But then the partisans and those who had fought with them had tended to be camera shy. And with good reason. So no photographs, only the sights and sounds of memory which had come flooding back to him as he sat there at his desk for so long, lost in thought. Then he sighed deeply. So much and so many remembered, so much and so many forgotten.

It was as he was closing the album, the empty pages flicking through his fingers, that he had found the loose photograph tucked in between two of them. He had reacted to it with a start and a faint stab of pain. He'd taken the picture out and studied it. Why had he kept it, he asked himself, why? But then that was a bloody silly question, he thought. He knew why. The girl smiling up at him from the old snapshot was Melina. And whatever else Haldane might have forgotten he would always remember her.

The doorbell rang. Haldane slipped the photograph of Melina, face down, under a corner of the leather desk blotter, stood up and crossed the room.

David Haldane smiled nervously as his brother opened the front door. Although two years younger than Alan, with his plump body, thinning hair and stooped shoulders, he looked the older of the two men.

'Hello, Alan,' he said quietly.

Haldane nodded to him but did not return his smile. Gazing past David, he was aware that it had stopped raining but the heavy, grey sky held a promise of more.

'May I come in?'

Haldane hesitated for only a second or two. 'Of course,' he replied and stepped to one side.

David moved diffidently past him. Haldane closed the front door and led the way into the study. While his brother hovered just inside the room, he strolled over to the fireplace, cleaned out his pipe and then refilled it and lit it with a taper. Only then did he turn to David who gave him another nervous, discomforted smile.

'We're still speaking then.'

'What made you think otherwise?'

Faintly relieved but not entirely reassured, David moved further into the room. 'Well, you haven't been exactly communicative since the take-over. Not a word from you. And just before that there were moments when I thought you were going to hit me.'

Haldane studied him and realised that he had not even offered to take his coat. Still, no point really, he thought, I don't suppose he will be stopping long.

'I was angry then,' he replied.

'And now?'

Haldane shrugged. 'Well I'm not sulking anyway. Looking for a small victory somewhere.'

David gave him a puzzled, questioning look.

'That's what life's made up of, isn't it?' continued Haldane. 'Small victories and big defeats.'

David moved in closer to him. 'You put up a hell of a fight,' he said, managing a grin which could just have passed as an expression of admiration. 'But there really was no other course, Alan. We had to accept Aqua-Plastics' offer.'

'My mistake when we set up the company was not insisting on a majority shareholding. But then, of course, the one person I thought I could always count on for support was my brother.' Haldane laughed hollowly and shook his head. 'God knows why though,' he continued. 'Cain and Abel. There's a precedent for you.'

David flushed angrily. 'That's damned unfair!'

'Is it?' Haldane nodded. 'A bit extreme perhaps. Jacob and his brothers then. You sold me out.'

'And you said you weren't sulking.'

'I'm not. But that's the truth. A matter of record.'

'I didn't sell you out. Not just me anyway. Jack Hedges was in agreement. You were outvoted. That's business. There was nothing personal in it.'

Haldane gave him a hard look. 'No,' he said sharply. 'There was nothing personal in it. That's exactly my point.'

Things weren't going at all the way David had planned. He had seen this meeting as a reconciliation, a salve to his conscience with his brother all forgiveness and understanding. But here he was still on the defensive and with apparently no way out of the position. No point in getting angry though, he thought. Reason. I'll try reason.

'We couldn't have gone on the way we were going,' he said.

'We had a name. A reputation.'

'But too few customers. And debts. We'd priced ourselves out of the market.'

Haldane studied him closely. 'What you mean is that I'd priced us out of the market, don't you?'

David shrugged. 'If only you'd compromised on materials', he countered.

'I designed those boats to be carvel-built of wood. Mahogany on oak. The way a real boat should be built. I wasn't about to see them mass produced in ferro-concrete or fibreglass.'

'Ah, well!' sighed David. 'Water under the bridge. And you have to admit that AquaPlastics' bid was a good one.'

'You and Hedges thought so,' growled Haldane.

'Oh come on, Alan! You've done very nicely out of the deal cashwise. And you didn't have to sell. You could've held onto your shares.'

'A minority interest in a company I was once Managing Director of!' Haldane's tone was scathing. 'And see the yard where we once built class boats used to turn out plastic, car top dinghies. No thank you.'

He moved wearily over to his desk and sat down at it, his head lowered, his eyes on the blotter.

David watched him for a while and then turned to the mantelpiece and, to cover the lull in the conversation, picked up Ruth's photograph and studied it. He smiled. He'd always liked Ruth. She would have understood, she would've been on his side. Ruth had been practical. Especially about making money. Extravagant though when it came to spending it. Three hundred and eighty thousand pounds for Alan's shares in the company! That would've pleased her. I wonder what she was like in bed, he mused.

'So what are you going to do?' he asked absently, more to break the silence than out of any real curiosity.

Haldane raised his head and looked across at him. 'I'm not sure. Haldane Marine was only ever a sideline for you. You still have your estate agency. I'm pretty much out on limb. And at my age that's not really the ideal time to

13

start all over again.'

'Retire. You can afford it. You've only got yourself to consider. You've no ties.'

Haldane frowned. 'That's true,' he said quietly.

David looked up from the photograph, saw the expression on his brother's face, and realised his mistake. 'I'm sorry,' he mumbled. 'That was stupid of me. I wasn't thinking.'

'Forget it.'

Putting the photograph back on the mantelpiece, David walked over to the window to gaze proudly out at his new Rover parked in the drive. He frowned 'Damn!' he exclaimed, piqued. 'It's raining again.'

'Is it?' said his brother disinterestedly.

David turned to him. Now you're on the defensive, laddie, he thought with satisfaction. And vulnerable too you obstinate bastard. Time for magnanimity. Better get in quick.

'By the way, Barbara and I are giving a dinner party next Thursday. Nothing special. Just a few friends. Why don't you come along?'

Haldane shook his head. 'Good of you to ask. But I don't think so all the same.'

'Lorna Matthews will be there,' David said, smiling archly. 'On her own.'

Haldane had a momentary mental picture of Lorna lying naked on crumpled sheets and looking up at him and laughing. Dear, generous, understanding Lorna who had wanted to give him so much but who had been able to give him so little. Except her body. And that had never been enough. Of course she'll be on her own. Dear God! Why can't she just let go?

'Matchmaking?' he asked.

David laughed. 'Well maybe you should get married again. I'm told that can be a full time occupation.'

Haldane drew on his pipe. It had gone out. He laid it in the ashtray on the desk. 'Give Lorna my best and Barbara my regrets,' he said.

14

'Well, if you're sure. But if you change your mind just turn up.' David glanced at his watch. 'Got to go. Got a meeting at five. Looks like I've found a buyer for the old Hammond place.'

'Good for you,' murmured Haldane flatly. And then, as David crossed to the door, he reached out and picked up the snapshot of Melina from the edge of the blotter, turned it over and gazed at it.

In the doorway David paused. 'I'm glad there's no hard feelings,' he said cheerily.

Haldane looked up at him. 'I didn't say that. Just that I'm not sulking.'

'I see,' said David, subdued once more. 'So that's why you won't come to dinner.'

Haldane shook his head. 'No. The fact is I'm going away for a while. I won't be here.'

'Oh, I see.' David felt better again. He smiled. 'Holiday?'

'Not really. Stocktaking. For a week or two.'

David didn't understand. But what the hell? He didn't really want to know what his brother meant. Each to his own, he thought.

'Where are you going?' he asked. And he made it sound as if he cared.

Haldane looked at the picture of Melina again. Up until that very second he had had no idea where he was going. But he had now.

'Back,' he said.

CHAPTER TWO

The Boeing 727 came in out of a clear, blue sky and touched down at Heraklion Airport. The aircraft, on Olympic Airways flight 504 from Athens, taxied to dispersal and Alan Haldane was among the first passengers to disembark.

He paused in the doorway and looked across at the snow capped peaks of the Psiloritis Mountains, felt the gentle warmth of the January sun on his face, savoured the pungent scent of wild herbs which penetrated even the airport stench of kerosene and experienced an almost overwhelming sense of homecoming. He smiled and nodded to the doll-like stewardess standing just inside the door and then moved quickly down the steps and across to the terminal building.

The arrivals lounge was heavy with the smell of floor polish and the redolent aroma of Greek tobacco and Turkish coffee. No, thought Haldane, not Turkish coffee; Greek coffee. Here on Crete of all places. The coffee was Turkish of course and served in the same style; in a small cup, thick and usually very sweet unless, he recalled, you made a point of asking for it *metrios,* medium sweet, or *sketos,* without any sugar at all. But either way, as a point of national pride and honour, no Greek would ever call the muddy brew, Turkish. They hated the Turks too much to grant them even that. And with good reason, mused Haldane. 'Never trust a Turk,' he remembered one of the Cretan partisans advising him during the war. 'Even if he turns himself into a bridge don't walk over it.' And then the man had spat on his knife and dreamed a beautiful day-dream of cutting a Turkish throat.

There were few other foreigners among the passengers

who jostled into the small lounge. Only the German businessman who, throughout the flight, his table and the empty seat beside him strewn with papers, had endlessly checked and then rechecked column upon column of figures on an adding machine; a young couple who looked and sounded as though they were Scandinavian and the French woman who had protested so shrilly at being body searched before they boarded the aircraft in Athens.

The rest all appeared to be Cretans returning home from business trips or from visits to friends and relatives on the mainland. Peasants many of them; shiny suited, dark skinned and heavily moustached men and wizened, black shawled and headscarved women. For most, their luggage was nothing more than a wicker basket or a newapaper-wrapped bundle tied with string.

Others among them, though, were more smartly dressed, the men in well cut, expensive suits and carrying briefcases while a few of the younger women, with delicately shaped faces and beautiful eyes, were elegant enough to have stepped straight out of an ancient Minoan fresco. Only, instead of the many tiered, long skirts and bare breasts which were the fashion in 2000 BC when Crete ruled the Mediterranean, these modish, brassiered, bloused and sweatered descendants of the subjects of the Priest King Minos favoured, in the main, stylish trouser suits with high waisted slacks, close fitting around the cheeks of their small, tight and provocative backsides.

As each of the Cretans came up the steps from the dispersal area and into the building so those that had been waiting there for them surged forward to greet them with enthusiasm and exuberant emotion and Haldane soon found himself hemmed in on all sides by a kissing, crying, laughing, gesticulating mob of people all talking at once.

Until his luggage was unloaded there was nothing he could do to escape the hubbub and he had no wish to for strangely he felt a part of it and he was faintly saddened that there was no one there in the milling crowd to welcome him. But then, he consoled himself, no one knew

I was coming. Nevertheless he was grateful when the toothless old woman who had sat across the aisle from him and who had spent most of the time they were in the air praying, thrust a shopping bag and two dead chickens into his arms so that she was unencumbered while she embraced and cried over her numerous children, grandchildren and great grand-children. As Haldane handed her luggage back to her, one of the men in the group thanked him in Greek and shook his hand so that, if only for a moment, the Englishman was at least part of a reunion. And that pleased him.

It was only later, as the throng in the lounge thinned a little and he was edging his way towards the baggage counter, that the thought struck Haldane; what if he had let anyone know he was coming? What if he had managed to get in touch with anyone he had known thirty-six years ago and said that he was arriving today on flight 504? Would they have been there to greet him? Would anyone have cared?

'*Kalispera*,' said the barman, grateful for some customer so early in the evening and moving up behind the counter to take his order.

'*Kalispera*,' replied Haldane. He sat down on one of the bar stools.

'American?'

Haldane smiled ruefully. Did he really look like an American? And what had happened to his Cretan accent of which he'd once been so proud? 'English.'

The barman nodded and said proudly, 'I speak English. French and German as well.' He pulled a face and added hastily, '*Ligo, ligo,* you understand A little. You speak Greek?'

'I used to. Some. I seem to have forgotten most of what I knew though.'

'You stay a long time? '

'I'm not sure. A few weeks perhaps.'

'Then you will see. Your Greek. She will come back,'

18

the barman reassured him. 'What would you like?'

'Raki?' enquired Haldane hopefully.

The barman looked crushed. He made an apologetic helpless gesture. 'Sorry,' he said. 'No raki. Not here.'

'An ouzo then.'

'Water and ice?'

Haldane nodded. 'Please.'

As his drink was being poured he looked around the empty bar, proudly international in style and decor; all glass and chrome. I should have known that they wouldn't serve raki in this hotel, he thought. Only the more expensive drinks. There would be little profit to be made out of the fiery, local eau-de-vie so freely available in every household and taverna. Besides the management probably thought it would lower the tone of the luxury hotel. The Cretan peasants, he remembered, not only drank it but used it as an embrocation.

Haldane hadn't chosen the hotel. The taxi driver who had driven him from the airport had recommended it almost certainly because he got a commission for every uncommitted client he persuaded to stay in the place. And Haldane hadn't argued. Besides, despite its characterless modernity and its pretentiousness it suited him well enough; for a day or two anyway.

For one thing his room overlooked Liberty Square, the heart of the city; a noisy plaza shaded by eucalyptus trees set in a sea of traffic and almost surrounded by restaurants and tavernas. The square was the focal point, the pivot of Heraklion and if you were looking for anyone who lived or worked in the town sooner or later you were bound to meet them there.

Liberty Square itself appeared to Haldane to be the one part of Heraklion which had not changed a great deal. It was much as he remembered it. A new statue or two perhaps and many unfamiliar, hideous concrete façades among the buildings facing on to it. But otherwise the same. The tables and chairs were still there round the edge of the island where, winter and summer, people used to sit and drink and gossip. And, as he had already witnessed from the window of his room, that hadn't changed either. For the rest he would hardly have recognised the city. Not surprising really, he'd said to himself, since the last time he'd been there the place had been in ruins, the result of two savage invasions. Even so, while it was still largely intact and under German occupation he didn't recall it being the ugly place it was now. But perhaps he was wrong. Perhaps it had always been ugly and his memory, prompted by nostalgia, was playing tricks on him. One thing he was certain of though, because he'd already seen enough evidence of it on the drive in from the airport, was that Crete was now in the throes of another invasion; an invasion which it clearly welcomed, encouraged and was beginning to grow fat on; tourism.

The barman put the Englishman's drink down on the counter and placed a small bowl of olives beside it. Haldane smiled and nodded his thanks. 'Perhaps you can help me,' he said.

The barman grinned. 'Ask me. If I can I will.'

'There's a man I knew. He lived in Heraklion. Before the war.'

The barman looked doubtful. He shrugged. 'That is a long time ago. I was only a boy when the Germans came.'

'I was hoping he might still be here.'

'What is his name?'

Haldane sipped his drink. 'Spiridakis. Babis Spiridakis.'

'The lawyer?' suggested the barman, puzzled and hesitant.

Haldane was greatly encouraged by this. He leaned forward. 'Yes. Probably,' he said eagerly. 'He was studying law in Athens when the war started. He fought with the Andarte here in Crete. They called him 'The Eagle.''

The barman nodded gravely. 'Spiridakis the lawyer. And after the war he was in politics. A democrat.' And then he added just in case Haldane should be in any doubt. 'Like me.' He paused and sighed. 'And when the

20

Junta was in power he spoke out against them. And he was put in prison. He was tortured. He had a bad time.'

'You know him?' urged Haldane.

The man's grave expression gave way to a broad, beaming smile. 'Of course! Everyone knows Babis Spiridakis! He is a fine man.' Suddenly grave again, he crossed himself. 'More than that. A saint.'

'And where is he now?' asked the Englishman, half afraid to know.

'Where else?' The barman's face relaxed again into another broad smile and he spread his arms wide. 'Where he belongs. Here in Heraklion. He has an office on the Twenty-fifth of August Street.'

Haldane contentedly drank his ouzo, ordered another and then another, totally ignoring the old Greek saying that one ouzo is an aperitif, two ouzos are an aperitif but three ouzos are a disaster.

When he got up from his stool to leave, the bar was a lot busier. By then, though, he and Panos, the barman, were firm friends and he had learned not only that Babis Spiridakis was alive and well and practising in the city but also the name of the best taverna in Heraklion, a place where he should certainly go for dinner that night. And he had great difficulty in persuading Panos to accept such a generous tip.

The following morning Haldane went to Spiridakis' office. It was on the first floor of one of the old buildings on the Twenty-fifth of August Street, the road which ran down the gentle hill from the bustle of Venizelos Square and its famous Lion Fountain to the Venetian harbour.

An attractive woman in her late twenties looked up at him from her typewriter as he pushed open the door of the outer office.

'Kalimera,' she said without smiling.

'Kalimera,' replied Haldane glancing nervously at the closed door of the inner office beyond and to one side of her desk.

The secretary had him summed up in an instant. 'You wish to see Mr Spiridakis?' she enquired in more than passable English.

Damn, thought Haldane. She might at least have let me try my Greek. He smiled. 'If he's not too busy. I'm an old friend of his.'

The woman shook her head regretfully. 'I am sorry, sir. But Mr Spiridakis is in Athens. He will be away for four, five, maybe six days. I am not sure.'

Haldane was disappointed and it showed. 'I see,' he said lamely.

The secretary took pity on him and smiled. She picked up a pencil and her notebook. 'If you will give me your name and tell me where you are staying I am sure that he will telephone you there when he returns,' she assured him.

Haldane hesitated. 'That's difficult. I'm not sure what my movements will be over the next few days. Look, just tell him that Alan Haldane called, will you.'

The woman frowned. 'Aldine? she asked.

'Haldane.' He reached into his pocket, took out one of his old business cards and handed it to her. 'Here, I'll give you my card. And just tell him I'll be back.'

The woman nodded and Haldane left her staring at the card.

Back on the street again he paused in the doorway of the building. Somehow he had fully expected to find Babis in his office so he had not made any other plans. But now their reunion was to be delayed even longer. He had time on his hands. Maybe six days the secretary said. Six days in which to do what, he asked himself. He could, of course, try to track down some of the other men he had known during the war but he dismissed that idea as a course of action which very probably would lead only to other and perhaps wounding disappointments. No, he decided, he must make contact with Babis first. And it was, after all, Spiridakis who he most wanted to see again. Well almost. But trying to trace Melina was out of the question. If he found her he could only be an embarrass-ment to her. An intrusion. And almost certainly an unwelcome one. No, Babis would have to tell him about Melina.

He was still deliberating what to do when he saw the Hertz offices on the opposite side of the road just down from where he was standing. He knew then how he should spend the next few days.

Two hours later Alan Haldane, at the wheel of an Opel Kadett, was driving out of Heraklion and heading west.

CHAPTER THREE

Haldane spent three days in the White Mountains and touring through the wild southern province of Sfakia. It was in this part of Crete that he had spent most of the three years during which he had fought with the partisans and alongside Babis Spiridakis. And it was from their mountain strongholds that the Andarte had carried out their daring and often costly raids on German and Italian military establishments in other parts of the island. It was from here that Haldane had played no small part in the kidnapping of Major General Kreipe, the German Commandant who was later taken to Egypt by a British submarine. An audacious operation for which the Cretan people paid heavily in terms of the German reprisals which followed.

Haldane found that the countryside, so ideally suited to guerilla warfare, was hardly more accessible all these years later. To reach many of the more isolated villages he had to abandon his car and clamber up narrow, rock strewn paths. Not tourist country this, he had thought more than once. Not yet anyway. And he had found great comfort in that thought.

He had not stayed long anywhere and although the object of considerable curiosity in every village he had visited he had not once been recognised. Just occasionally, when he was enjoying the overwhelming hospitality for which the Cretans are renowned – in the more isolated areas particularly – and from which there is no escape without giving deep offence, had some of the men and women clustered around him who were of his own generation or older given him an odd searching look as if trying to rake up something from the past; as if trying to place a faintly familiar face.

And there had been faces equally familiar to him but none that he had immediately recognised and could name. But then most of the men he had been close to during the war were not of the mountains but had taken refuge in them after the German invasion and would now be once again scattered across the island if not around the world. Those among the people he had met on his travels and who troubled their minds to place him would all have played lesser, more peripheral, roles in his wartime experiences. So he had touched their lives again briefly but had remained unknown. And he was content to leave it that way. Leandros, the right hand of 'The Eagle' was of a distant time and part of another world and it was with no thought of a triumphant return to scenes of former glory that Haldane had decided to revisit Crete. Therefore he had said nothing, encouraged no recognition and passed quickly on from place to place, happy to be taken for a stranger and alone in his remembrances.

Early on the fourth day Haldane had turned eastward again and, whenever possible avoiding the new motorway and skirting Heraklion, he had made the tortuous cross-country drive, often along roads which at first glance appeared to be impassable, to the fertile Plain of Lasithi and the slopes of Dhikti Mountains which encircled it.

Haldane did not remember the house being there when he was last in the olive grove. It had been hidden from his view when he swung the Opel off the road, down the track and into the trees and coming on it had been a surprise to him.

It was an attractive, welcoming house built in the traditional Cretan style and standing on raised ground with a broad terrace and a garden around all four sides of it. Stone steps led up to the terrace.

He had parked the Kadett just off the track and for a while he had sat there looking at the house and admiring it, then he had got out of the car and walked closer until he was only a few yards from the base of the steps to the terrace. But now it was the olive grove which interested him more than the house and he turned and gazed into it and remembered.

He remembered the sounds of gunfire, the reek of death and the fear he had known that day. He remembered that, after four hours of bloodshed, often hand-to-hand, of the twenty-seven men trapped among the vast expanse of trees by the Germans only he and two others were still alive to break through into the open countryside beyond the grove and escape back into the relative safety of the mountains. And again he remembered Melina.

'Do you want something? Can I help you?' The woman spoke in Greek and from behind Haldane and at first he did not hear her. Then she repeated the questions and this time her voice penetrated and scattered his memories. He turned to her.

She was standing on the terrace at the top of the steps. She was not young. If, at that moment, Haldane had been challenged to guess her age he would have said that she was in her mid-thirties. A year or so older perhaps. It was difficult to tell. and anyway her age was unimportant. She was beautiful. Breathtakingly so. Her delicately moulded face was framed in light brown hair, immaculately cut in an elegantly casual style. Her mouth, finely sensual and half smiling, was set off by a strong, determined chin. Her eyes, sharp and intelligent under full, sweeping lashes, were now regarding the Englishman quizzically. The dress she was wearing was simple but expensive and the body beneath it was slim and well proportioned with firm, proud breasts, a well-defined waist and long, slender legs. She wore no make-up. And she did not need to.

Staring up at her Haldane found himself in the grip of a strange and oddly uneasy feeling that he had seen her before somewhere. But where? He racked his brains for the answer and knew then that it had to be an illusion. Nevertheless, he could not shake off the impression and it discomforted and troubled him.

'Who are you?' she asked him in Greek, frowning slightly and studying him thoughtfully.

Still trapped in the web of *déjà vu* and struggling to free himself from it, Haldane, unthinkingly, replied in English. 'I'm sorry,' he said awkwardly. 'Am I trespassing?'

She shook her head. 'Not really.' And her reply had only a slight accent to it.

Haldane knew that he was staring but there was nothing he could do about it. There was such an air of unreality about this encounter, about her, about his reaction to her. It was almost as if this were some kind of magic moment; predestined and to be lingered over. And she did nothing to break the spell. Her eyes were on his. But then suddenly her frown deepened as though she were discomforted by his gaze and her own thoughts. 'What is it?' she asked.

'You remind me of someone,' he said and as he did so he felt certain that that had to be the answer. But who?

She studied him. 'Are you lost?'

'In a way,' Haldane replied quietly.

The woman hesitated, but only for a second. And then she smiled gently and she was even more beautiful. 'You will take a glass of wine?' she asked.

He nodded, accepting the inevitability of the invitation; only now without question.

He crossed to the steps and began to climb them. And, as he did so, he was obsessed with the certainty that life had, at that moment, taken on a new beginning for him.

Side by side, slowly and not looking at one another, they walked across the terrace and into the house through open French windows. And they took the magic with them.

The large room was light and airy. The walls and the stone benches which were built into them were painted white. In the middle of the room there was a round fireplace with a canopy and chimney of beaten copper.

The furniture was modern but obviously made by

27

craftsmen to traditional Cretan designs, modified for contemporary comfort. There were three abstract paintings hanging on the walls alongside a genuine Byzantine icon and a filigree, wrought iron cross.

The stone benches around the walls were covered and backed with cushions of a bright, cheerful colour which blended with the curtains hanging at the windows.

Neither of them had said anything since they entered the room. Now they stood facing one another each holding a glass of the deep red, local wine. There was an air of intimacy between them which Haldane accepted but which he still could not explain.

The woman gave him another questioning look. 'Why are you here?' she asked.

'I fought a battle in that olive grove in nineteen forty three,' Haldane said. 'Men died there.'

She nodded. 'Men have died in battle all over Crete. Women and children too. This has been an island of slaughter. Throughout history. Our soil is the colour of blood.' She raised her glass to him. 'And so is our best wine.'

Haldane lifted his glass in acknowledgement and they both drank. 'The grove has changed,' he said.

She shrugged. 'Of course.'

'And now it belongs to you?' he asked.

'Yes. Or rather I hold it in trust. For the past.'

'The scars have healed.'

'Some of them perhaps.' They sipped their wine, each holding the other's gaze. Neither of them heard the sound of the car approaching the house and stopping at the foot of the steps to the terrace, nor of the car door slamming shut. 'Were you long in Crete?' she asked.

'Three years,' said Haldane. 'With the Andarte.' The woman gave him a curious, puzzled look. 'There were many British with the partisans,' he added.

'Yes, I know,' she said. 'When times were very bad my father would often speak of them. To remind us that we were not alone in our struggle.'

Haldane was surprised. 'But surely you don't remember those days?' he said.

'Little of them. I was only a child. The hunger. I remember that. But the fighting...' She shook her head. 'No. The village where my parents took me was not touched by that.' She took another sip from her glass and then looked up into his face again. 'The war. It now seems so long ago.'

'It was,' said Haldane.

'And you have not been back here since?'

'No.'

'So why now?'

Haldane shrugged. 'I'm not sure.'

She considered his reply, studying his face intently. And then she said, 'Interesting. All these years later. Like Theseus returning to the Labyrinth where he fought the Minotaur. In search of what?'

'A memory. A sense of purpose.' Again Haldane shrugged. 'I don't know.'

A man came in off the terrace through the French windows. He was in his forties, well built and handsome but with an air of arrogance and conceit which stemmed from something more than just *philotimo,* that sense of personal honour and pride so treasured by Cretan men and so characteristic of them. Under one arm he carried a sheaf of papers in a folder.

The man stopped abruptly when he saw Haldane and frowned. He glanced at the woman. 'Oh,' he said surlily in Greek 'Excuse me.'

'It is all right,' she replied, speaking in English. 'Come in, Matheos.'

The man moved further into the room, his eyes on Haldane.

'This is...' the woman continued and then gave the Englishman an enquiring look.

'Alan Haldane,' he said.

She smiled. 'My name is Annika. Annika Zeferis. And this is Matheos Noukakis.'

Noukakis gave Haldane an unenthusiastic nod. *'Herete,'* he mumbled.

'Herete,' replied Haldane, studying the man and sensing his hostility.

'Matheos is my right hand,' continued Annika. 'He manages the olive groves for me. And the factory where the oil is processed.' She looked at Noukakis. 'The *kyrios* was here during the war,' she explained.

'Oh yes,' said Noukakis flatly.

Annika looked into Haldane's face once more. 'Now he searches. But for what he is not sure.'

'I will know it when I find it,' said Haldane quietly.

She smiled wryly. 'That is a promise we all make to ourselves. To ensure against disappointment. And where do you go from here?'

'The monastery of Keras. We gathered there often. It was like a beacon to the Andarte.' Annika nodded. 'And if I'm to get there in good time I'm afraid I must go,' Haldane went on. He drained his glass. 'I'm sorry.'

'So am I,' said Annika. And Haldane knew that she meant it. She took his glass from him.

'Thank you for the wine,' he said. Then he looked across at Noukakis. *'Andio.'*

Noukakis had not taken his eyes off them since he entered the room and what he had seen had not pleased him. He did not reply.

Reluctantly Haldane crossed to the French windows. He paused gratefully and looked back when Annika spoke once more.

'Whatever it is you are looking for. I hope you find it,' she said.

'I'll let you know,' he replied with a smile.

'How long are you staying on Crete?'

'Two, three weeks.'

Annika nodded. 'If you have time then.'

Haldane studied her for a while, searching her face intently, then he turned and walked out onto the terrace.

Annika crossed to the French windows and watched

him move away. He did not look back.

'He interests you?' asked Noukakis, crossing to her side and with a sour note in his voice.

Annika ignored the question and turned back into the room. 'What is it you want, Matheos?' she asked.

He strode over and stood close to her. 'The Kalogeridis contract. It requires your signature.'

Finding her alone with the Englishman had made him even more aware of how desirable she was, of how much he needed to possess her. And for so many reasons.

'Annika!...' he said and there was entreaty in his voice. And he would have continued if she had not interrupted him. Her smile was friendly, her expression pleasant but her tone cool and matter of fact.

'Leave it with me, will you?' she said. 'I would like to study it.'

CHAPTER FOUR

It was late in the afternoon of the next day that Matheos
Noukakis returned to Annika's house to pick up the
contract. He found her in a strange mood; edgy, distant
and preoccupied. Several times during their discussion she
walked across to the windows overlooking the olive grove
and stared out at the track which led to the road, lost in
thought. But, as he had expected, she had read through
every clause of the Kalogeridis deal thoroughly and she
went through it with him line by line and there were many
questions for him to answer before she was satisfied and
she finally approved it. And by then it was evening and
the sun was beginning to set.

Noukakis hoped that she would ask him to stay on for a
while and have a drink as she invariably did when he came
to the house on business but she did not. She merely
thanked him politely, apologised for keeping him so long
and then walked with him to the French windows and said
goodnight.

And it was only as they were crossing the room that
Noukakis noticed for the first time that the table in the
dining alcove was already laid for the evening meal and set
for two.

He was still wondering who her dinner guest could be as
he drove the pick-up truck slowly back through the trees.
Her mother? That was a possibility but an unlikely one, he
thought. The old lady seldom left her house in Neapolis.
A woman friend perhaps? But then, as far as he could
recall Annika had no close friends among her own sex and
she had confided in him once that female gossip bored
her. Her brother? No, Petros lived in Athens and he was
too busy making money to spend much time visiting his

mother and his sister. If Petros Matakis was dining out anywhere tonight, Noukakis reflected, it would almost certainly be somewhere expensive overlooking the Acropolis or in the Grande Bretagne Hotel. And he would be in the company of some influential politician or a likely business prospect. Besides Noukakis was certain that he would have heard if Petros was in Crete again. Her niece then? But she was married and, quite rightly, her husband would never allow her to go out alone at night; even to have dinner with her aunt. And there were only two place settings on the table. So who had Annika invited to eat with her? Noukakis frowned.

And then, as he approached the head of the track a car turned on to it from the road and the question which was nagging him was answered.

Haldane had spent the night in the guesthouse at the monastery of Keras but he had not slept well. The two monks he had found living there had greeted him warmly and had insisted that he stay but neither of them was old enough to remember the war and they assumed his interest in the monastery to be no more than that of any other discerning tourist. And Haldane had said nothing to correct their impression. They talked until late and of many things but never once was the war mentioned. And when finally he excused himself and went to his room it was not his wartime recollections of the place which disturbed Haldane's rest, it was the image of a woman, smiling.

He had left early the next morning and driven higher into the mountains to a place where there had once been a village but where there were now only ruins, overgrown by a wilderness of thorn bushes and juniper scrub and a carpet of herbs and tall grasses. With dynamite and flame throwers the Germans had razed every building in 1942 because they had claimed that the villagers had given shelter to men of the Andarte. And they were right. They had. And Haldane had been among those whom they had

33

fed and then watched over while they snatched a few hours sleep.

Sitting on a mound of rubble, smoking his pipe and deep in thought, Haldane had taken the photograph of Melina out of his wallet and gazed at it.

'Were you long in Crete?' he heard Annika say again and he snapped his head around sharply to look over his shoulder, willing her to be there. But he was alone.

For almost an hour he sat here, his mind a turmoil of questions without any answers. Then he had slipped the photograph back into his wallet, got to his feet and pushed his way through the tangle of bushes to where he had left his car.

It was no use fighting it any longer and he knew it. He was going back. He had to. Back to the woman whose smile had haunted him during the night.

As the Kadett edged past the pick-up, Haldane recognised the driver and waved to him but Noukakis did not wave back. He stopped the truck, put on the hand brake and watched the Opel in his rearview mirror as it accelerated away from him and towards the house. Then he spat out of the window and cursed.

Haldane parked his car, got out and looked up at the terrace. Annika was standing at the top of the steps, the sun setting behind her. He was only faintly surprised.

'I was waiting for you,' she said simply when he stood facing her. 'I was expecting you. As I think I was expecting you yesterday.' And then she turned and led the way into the house.

They had said little during dinner. Now, still sitting opposite one another at the table, they lingered over coffee and brandy.

'So tell me,' said Annika, not looking at him. 'Did you find anything?'

'Only the memory. Ghosts.'

Annika lifted her head and their eyes met. 'They are always with us,' she said.

'There was nothing else.'

She shook her head. 'Of course not. Not among phantoms. You will have to look elsewhere.'

'Among the living?'

She nodded. 'In today anyway. Not in yesterday.'

Haldane drank from his coffee cup and studied her thoughtfully. 'You said you were expecting me,' he said.

'Something. Someone. And then you arrived. But this evening I knew that it was you I was waiting for.'

'I had to come back,' he said. 'I don't know why.'

'Yes you do,' Annika said quietly. She picked up her glass and sipped her brandy. 'You are married of course?'

Haldane shook his head. 'No. I was. But my wife was killed in a road accident six years ago. And you?'

'Divorced.' She saw the look on Haldane's face. 'You are surprised?' she asked. 'Ah yes, but then of course you know something of Cretan attitudes from the time you spent here. Well, little has changed. In that respect at least. Here a woman is still not expected to divorce her husband. No matter what cause he gives her. It offends his masculinity, his pride. Here a woman is born to walk behind the donkey. But I am one of those who have broken that pattern.'

'I imagine that hasn't made life easy for you,' he said.

She shrugged. 'That is not important. Only dignity is important. And giving. When you can.'

'You have a family?'

'I have two children. A boy and a girl. They are both studying in France. And I have a mother and a brother. So I am not alone.'

Again their eyes met and each held the other's gaze. 'Aren't you?' he asked.

'Alone I said. You speak of loneliness. They are different things. I think you know that.'

'Yes,' said Haldane. 'And the man who was here when we first met?'

35

She frowned. 'Matheos? A business associate. A friend. Nothing more.'

His eyes still on hers, Haldane slowly reached out across the table and gently laid his hand on hers. 'I want you,' he said.

Annika showed no shock, no surprise and she did not avert her gaze nor did she move her hand from under his but she shook her head sadly. 'You *need* me. As I *need* you. That is why you came back. That is why I wanted you to come back. But think about it, Englishman. As I have. What would it mean? What would it be? An interlude? A holiday affair?' She shook her head again and sighed sadly. 'We are both too vulnerable. We have spent a pleasant evening together and when you leave we shall have that memory.' Now she slid her hand from under his. 'But neither of us will have invested anything in our meeting. And it is better that way. Because there is no future in tonight. And that is your real need. And mine.'

And Haldane knew that she was right. And the thought saddened him.

The secretary smiled at him when he went back to Babis Spiridakis' office at eight thirty the next morning.

'Yes,' she informed him. 'Mr Spiridakis has returned from Athens. Late last night. But he is not yet in his office.' She indicated the bench to one side of the outer door. 'If you wish to wait.'

Haldane nodded and sat down.

Ten minutes later the door was thrown open and Babis Spiridakis exploded into the fusty office like a violent blast of fresh air. He was carrying a briefcase.

'Andreas Phokakis is a fool,' he exclaimed vehemently in Greek as he strode across to his secretary's desk, unaware of Haldane's presence. 'Get Tzortis on the telephone for me.' Then he frowned and looked puzzled as the woman, somewhat embarrassed by his outburst, gave him a cautionary look and nodded in Haldane's direction.

Spiridakis turned with a questioning look. Haldane stood up. The two men gazed at one another.

He hasn't changed that much, thought Haldane, taking in the big, broad shouldered and powerfully built man opposite him. And he doesn't look his age. He must be, what? Fifty-eight? Or was it fifty-nine? He was a little fleshier perhaps and the lines on his rugged face were now cut deeper around his mouth and still penetrating eyes. But there was not even a hint of grey in his dark, black hair and thick moustache. And his movements were still as bold and positive as ever.

Spiridakis recognised Haldane instantly and, once he had recovered from the surprise, for a moment his face broke into a broad, beaming smile. He took a step towards him but then checked himself and his smile faded until it was only a faint, polite curve to his lips. It was as though a light which had suddenly been turned on inside him had instantly burned itself out.

He acknowledged the Englishman with a nod. 'Leandros!' he said quietly.

Haldane frowned. He had imagined this reunion many time since his decision to return to Crete and always differently but always with enthusiasm in it, on both sides. And it had been there, in Spiridakis, for a second. He had seen it. But now there was only reserve and he had not prepared himself for any show of coolness. He made a great effort to hide his disappointment but his smile was now as awkward as he felt.

'Hello, Babis.' And then he added lamely. 'You remember me then?'

'Of course,' replied the lawyer.

Haldane shrugged. 'It's been a long time,' he said.

Spiridakis nodded. 'Yes. A long time.' He walked to the door of his office and opened it. 'Come in,' he said.

Feeling very foolish and somehow cheated, Haldane followed him into the room.

Spiridakis closed the office door and then crossed to his desk and put his briefcase down on it. He turned and looked across at Haldane and it was clear from his expression that he was perplexed and troubled. He studied him searchingly for a while and then he moved over to the window and stood with his back to him, staring down into the street below.

Haldane was at a loss to understand. 'You are not pleased to see me, Babis?' he asked.

Spiridakis did not turn to him. 'I have often wondered,' he said softly. 'Is he alive or is he dead, my English brother. He who fought alongside me in the war. He who was my right hand.'

Was that it, thought Haldane. Is that the reason for his coolness? Because I didn't keep in touch? Surely not.

'I meant to write,' he said. 'But always tomorrow. You know how it is.' Spiridakis nodded. 'And then, as the years passed, I thought perhaps now it is too late. Babis will have forgotten.'

The lawyer shook his head and turned to him. 'Never.' And he meant it. He smiled; but it was a smile which did nothing to dispel the atmosphere between them. 'So, Leandros, what have you been doing with your life?' he asked.

Haldane shrugged. 'Too little I think. Building boats. And losing money. Lately anyway.'

'You still build boats?'

'No.'

Spiridakis gave him another faint smile. 'Well, that is a saving then,' he said.

'And you?' said Haldane. 'From what I have heard there have been times since I last saw you when things have been difficult for you, eh?'

'For all honest Greeks. There are always barbarians who would oppress other men. Fighting them is never easy. You know that. From the old days.'

'From the old days, yes. From those days when each time we met we embraced as friends,' said Haldane.

'As brothers.'

Haldane nodded. 'So tell me, Babis,' he asked. What's

happened? Are we no longer brothers?'

Spiridakis winced. 'Always,' he said. 'Believe me. Nothing could ever change that.'

Haldane made a helpless gesture. Now he was totally confused. 'You say that,' he exclaimed. 'But yet here we are, after all these years, almost like two total strangers making polite conversation. What's wrong?'

Spiridakis' eyes searched his face. 'Melina,' he said at last.

This was a surprise. 'Melina!' said Haldane.

Spiridakis nodded. 'Do you ever think of her, Leandros?' he asked.

'Often. A great deal lately. Is she well?'

Spiridakis shook his head. 'She died. Four years ago.'

The news came as a stunning, almost physical blow to Haldane. He stared at Spiridakis. 'Melina's dead?' he said dully. This was something he had never expected. A possibility which had never even entered his mind.

'A brain tumour. It was very sudden. She did not suffer.'

Haldane found it difficult to accept the fact. She had been so young, so vital when he had last seen her. 'I can't believe it,' he said. And then he sighed deeply and crossed slowly to stand beside Spiridakis and stare out of the window but seeing nothing, only remembering. After a while he said, 'I wrote to her, you know. When I got back to England. Three times. But she never replied.'

Spiridakis looked at him. 'Well if that is so,' he said quietly, 'I can tell you for certain, Leandros, that those letters never reached her. And she did write to you. Once at least. I helped her with the English.'

Haldane turned to him with a look of surprise. 'Where did she send the letter?' he asked.

'To the War Office in London. We had no other address.'

Haldane swore silently and shook his head. 'And they didn't forward it. Or if they did it must have followed me from posting to posting. Either way I never received it.'

Spiridakis studied him closely. 'And that is the truth?' he asked gravely.

Haldane felt himself bridling. 'What do you mean?' he protested. 'Of course it's the truth. Why should I lie about a thing like that, for God's sake?'

To his utter amazement Spiridakis' expression slowly changed to one of relief and joy and sadness all intermingled. 'Then you don't know about . . . You really never knew!' he said.

Haldane looked at him blankly. 'About what?' he asked with a note of irritation in his voice. 'Tell me.'

Spiridakis hesitated but Haldane was insistent. 'I want to know,' he demanded. 'About what?'

The lawyer shrugged resignedly. 'Soon after you were sent back to England in nineteen forty-four Melina found that she was pregnant. She was carrying your child. That is what she wrote to tell you.'

CHAPTER FIVE

'Oh my God!' said Haldane. Then came the sickening realisation. 'And she heard nothing from me in return.'

Spiridakis shook his head. 'She thought you had abandoned her.'

'But I'd never have done that, Babis,' replied Haldane urgently. 'I loved her. You know how much. I was coming back. And then, when I didn't get any reply to my letters I thought she had changed her mind about us. I took her silence to mean that what she really wanted was not to see me again. I never knew about the child. You have to believe me.'

'I do,' said Spiridakis. 'Now.'

Haldane frowned. 'And before? What did you think then?'

Sprirdakis looked away from him, unable to meet the challenge in his eyes. He walked slowly over to his desk. 'It was wartime,' he said. 'These things happen. In a war a man seeks consolation and moments of forgetting wherever he can find them. But when the fighting is over . . .' He shrugged. 'A foreign wife, a woman already carrying a child, that is something different.'

The hurt went deep. 'Did you really see me like that?' asked Haldane, sadly.

The lawyer swung round to face him again. 'I saw you as my brother. I knew you as the man you are. But where there is strength there is also weakness. I was disappointed, yes. But I did not judge you.'

Haldane turned and stared down out of the window once more. The street below was a noisy river of traffic. 'Little has changed,' Annika had said. and he knew that she was right. He saw it in the faces of the men and

41

women passing by on the opposite pavement. The Cretans always had been and always would be proud and generous. But where honour was involved they could be cruel and seldom forgiving.

'What happened?' he asked. 'How did she manage alone? Here of all places.'

Spiridakis read his mind and nodded. 'Fortunately she was not alone,' he said. 'Do you remember Stelios Papadakis?'

Haldane remembered him well. 'Yes of course. He was in our group. A good man.'

The lawyer corrected him. 'A very special man. Only Melina and I knew that she was pregnant by you. But then, when Papadakis saw how distressed she was, he must have guessed the truth. He knew the shame and disgrace she would have to suffer here if she had a child and no husband so he asked her to marry him. Melina accepted of course. She had little choice. Papadakis went to her family and took the blame for what had happened. As you can imagine Melina's parents, although they were angry, were anxious to see them married and quickly.'

'Papadakis must have loved Melina very much,' said Haldane pensively.

Spiridakis nodded. 'Yes, he must have done. To give her his name and take on the responsibility of another man's child. And she was fond of him and very grateful. She was a good wife in the little time they had together.'

Haldane turned from the window and gave him a questioning look.

'Stelios was killed in nineteen forty-nine,' Spiridakis continued. 'During the civil war. Fighting with the army on the mainland.'

'And the baby?' asked Haldane.

'A girl. They named her Elena.'

There was a gentle tap on the door of the office and then it was opened and Spiridakis' secretary stood in the doorway. She looked apologetically across at Haldane and then spoke to the lawyer in Greek. 'Excuse me,' she said,

'But Mr Vandoulakis is here.'

Spiridakis glanced at his watch. 'Ask him to wait a minute, please.'

The secretary nodded and retreated back to the outer office, closing the door behind her.

Spiridakis turned to Haldane. 'Forgive me,' he said. 'A client. On urgent business.'

'But there are so many questions, Babis,' Haldane protested. 'So many things I want to know.'

'Later,' replied Spiridakis. 'There will be time. For now all that matters is that you are back. After so many years.' He smiled. 'And among friends. So.' He opened his arms and crossed to the Englishman. 'As it should be with brothers.' He swept Haldane into a warm, loving and firm embrace.

'Welcome home, Leandros,' he said. 'Tonight we celebrate.'

'I am grateful to you, Matheos, for bringing the olive oil to me,' Katerina said as she ushered Noukakis into the sitting room. And her tone was gravely polite.

Apart from the rugs on the tiled floor, the room had little colour in it and the furniture was bulky and severe; much of it old pieces made of dark, intricately carved wood. There were hand-made lace antimacassars and doilies on the backs and arms of the sofa and the two upright armchairs. The walls were hung with framed photographs and yellowing tintypes covering many generations of the Matakis family. Noukakis noted that even in the winter the old woman kept the windows which overlooked the front garden and the street shuttered against the midday sun and the resultant gloom only enhanced the atmosphere of solemn, respectable discomfort.

Katerina Matakis was seventy-two; a handsome, grey-haired woman of peasant stock who carried the scars of age and of her early struggles in life well and with great dignity. She was dressed entirely in black, as she had been

43

for the past three years, in mourning for her husband, Georgios, who had died leaving her a wealthy woman, respected and, by some, feared. Noukakis both respected and feared her.

'Annika said you were in need of it,' he said.

'And that is true,' replied Katerina as she moved across to a large, ornate cabinet on the far side of the room. 'And tell her I thank her for it. But you should not have bothered to come yourself. You are a manager. A busy man. You should have sent someone with it.'

Noukakis waved away her mild admonition with a quick movement of his hand. 'It was no trouble, *Kyria* Matakis.' he assured her, casually but with deference. 'I had to be in Neapolis anyway. And it always gives me such pleasure to see you.'

Katerina acknowledged the compliment with a gracious nod and opened the door of the cupboard above the two wide drawers in the cabinet. 'You will take a glass of raki?' she asked.

Noukakis nodded. 'Please,' he said. And then he turned to examine the antique, bas-relief plaque hanging on the wall beside the doorway. The plaque depicted the three Moerae, the Fates of ancient Greek mythology; Clotho, the spinner of the thread of life, Lachesis, chance and Atropos, the ultimate fate against which there is no appeal. This was the one thing in the room which appealed to Noukakis and which he coveted, for quite apart from any aesthetic appreciation he had for it he knew its value.

Katerina took a silver tray from the cupboard on which there were half a dozen small glasses in silver filigree holders. 'And how is my daughter?' she asked.

'She is well, *Kyria,*' replied Noukakis his eyes still on the plaque, and then he scowled, 'As far as I know. But I am not sure if she would tell me if things were otherwise.' things were otherwise.'

Katerina carried the tray across to the table and set it down. She glanced at Noukakis and smiled quietly to

44

herself. 'She is a headstrong woman,' she said, returning to the cabinet and this time taking from it a delicate, glass decanter half filled with raki. 'But she is free and you are a good man. A woman is nothing without a husband. Do not give up easily.' She crossed back to the table and opened the decanter. 'If you were to marry her it would be with my blessing. You know that.'

Noukakis turned to her, a sullen expression on his face. 'Unfortunately, at the moment there is someone who it would seem interests her much more than I do,' he said. And then he added scornfully. 'An Englishman.'

Katerina was about to pour the raki. She hesitated and frowned. 'An Englishman?' she said quietly.

'Yes. She entertained him to dinner at her house last night. They were alone together.'

The old woman shook her head in a gesture of disapproval and despair. 'I will speak to her about that,' she said sternly. She sighed. 'Not that she will listen of course.'

Very carefully and with a steady hand she began to pour raki into one of the glasses. 'This Englishman,' she queried. 'What is he like?'

Noukakis shrugged dismissively. 'He did not impress me when I met him,' he said sourly. Then he remembered and scowled again. 'But strangely Annika acted as though she had known him for many years although I know that is not possible. He is here on holiday. A tourist. His name is Alan Haldane.'

Katerina Matakis reacted with a violent start as though in the grip of a sudden, searing pain. The colour drained from her face, her head jerked up and the decanter slipped from her fingers and shattered on the tiled floor.

Pavlos. the school teacher, and Leonidas, the taxi driver, had made the long journey from Chania. Manolis, the bootmaker, had driven in from Anoyia and Vassilis, the policeman, from Mires in the south. The others were farmers from villages nearer to Heraklion or professional and businessmen from the city itself. There were more than a dozen of them, all veterans of the Andarte. And they were there to welcome and honour Leandros who was among them once more.

They sat at a long table in a taverna on the outskirts of Heraklion close to the trio of musicians, two of whom played *bouzoukis* and the third a guitar. The old comrades had already drunk many glasses of raki between them and they had danced, insisting that Haldane join them and they had laughed goodnaturedly when he had difficulty remembering the steps. And when they had danced the *pentozali*, the wild dance of the Cretan warriors, Haldane had found the leaps and high kicks beyond him and he had been grateful when the music had stopped and, to the applause of his companions, he had been able to collapse, exhausted and breathless, back on to his chair.

Now they ate and laughed and talked and drank a heady, red wine, a speciality of the taverna and poured into jugs from a large cask. And, after thirty-six years, their undisputed leader was still Babis Spiridakis who sat at the head of the table with Haldane on his right; The Eagle and Leandros side by side as they always had been in the old days.

Pavlos raised his glass to the Englishman. *'Stin iyassou,'* he shouted above the laughter and the excited, animated conversations going on around the table.

Haldane smiled and lifted his glass to him. *'Episis,'* he shouted back and then drank.

Leonidas, the taxi driver, who was sitting beside Haldane, pulled a worn leather wallet out of his pocket, extracted a photograph from it and handed it to him. 'See, Leandros,' he said with a hesitant smile. 'My children, six. Four boy, two girl.'

Haldane examined the photograph politely, smiled and nodded. 'A big family, eh, Leonidas,' he said, mustering his Greek. 'Very nice. The girls are beautiful and the boys are handsome. Just like their father.'

Leonidas beamed proudly and slapped Haldane on the

46

back. 'How many children you have, Leandros?' he asked.

Haldane hesitated and shot a look at Spiridakis.

Leonidas shouted to the assembled company. 'Quiet! Leandros is going to tell us about his family.'

There was a sudden silence at the table. All eyes were on Haldane. His companions were genuinely interested and they waited expectantly. He frowned slightly and then looked at Leonidas. 'I have no children,' he said quietly.

'No children!' exclaimed Leonidas, aghast. 'Your wife has cheated you. Better you should choose another.'

Spiridakis stepped in quickly to save Haldane from any further embarrassment. 'The wife of Leandros is dead,' he announced in a low tone. 'She died six years ago.'

There were murmurs of sympathy and condolence from among those around the table.

Leonidas looked crushed and ashamed. He reached out and put a hand on Haldane's seeking forgiveness. Haldane smiled at him. An atmosphere of sadness threatened the table.

Pavlos shook his head sadly. 'Six years,' he said. 'That is a long time. It is not good for a man to live alone. You should marry again. Leandros.' Then, inspired, he smiled. 'We must find someone for you here on Crete.'

This declaration was greeted with nods of agreement, laughter and cheers. The atmosphere lifted a little.

Haldane was as anxious as the others not to dampen the proceedings. He picked up his cue. 'Very well,' he said. 'You find someone for me, Pavlos. But two things I insist on. She must be beautiful.' He paused for effect. 'And, above all else, she must of course have a good dowry.'

There was a great burst of cheering at this and every man raised his glass and drank to the prospect. The air of gloom was totally dispelled.

At three o'clock in the morning they were the only customers left in the taverna. And, while the waiters sat patiently playing cards, the musicians played on. The guitarist was singing a melancholy, nostalgic song to his own accompaniment and that of the two *bouzoukis*. Haldane and Spiridakis sat alone at the table and watched while their companions danced, no longer in an exuberant group but separately, each man in a world of his own and expressing the music individually.

Spiridakis had his worry beads in his hand and was absently toying with them. Both he and Haldane were very subdued, caught up in the mood of the moment. Then the lawyer stopped flipping his *komboloi,* caught the beads in the palm of his hand and looked at them. He showed them to Haldane who saw that attached to the tail of them were two flattened and distorted bullets.

'See,' said Spiridakis quietly. 'The bullets that you took from my chest. That day when you alone refused to accept that I had to die. Here on my *komboloi* they are with me always so that I shall never forget.'

'I couldn't afford to let you die,' said Haldane lightly and smiling to cover his embarrassment. 'You owed me a hundred cigarettes.'

Spiridakis grinned. 'That's right,' he said. 'Did I ever repay you?'

'Yes. So you see you are not in my debt.' He sipped his drink. 'In any way.'

Spiridakis turned his head to watch the dancers again.

Putting down his glass, Haldane reached into his pocket and took out the photograph of Melina. He studied it for a while and then glanced up to find Spiridakis watching him thoughtfully and frowning. 'Where is the child, Babis?' asked Hadane.

Spiridakis shook his head. 'No longer a child, Leandros,' he said. 'She is a woman now. Married and with a son of her own.'

'Where does she live?'

'In Elounda. She and her husband, Nikos, run a taverna there.'

'I must see her,' said Haldane.

The lawyer's face took on an expression of alarm. 'No,' he said sharply. 'No, Leandros. Leave it. Perhaps I should

48

have said nothing. But then I thought you already knew. Please though, do as I say. It can do no good. Besides, what would be the point? As far as Elena is concerned, Stelios Papadakis was her father. After all these years you cannot turn up, a stranger from England, and tell her otherwise.'

Haldane shook his head. 'Of course not. I just want to see her. That's all.'

'Don't,' pleaded Spiridakis. 'It would be a mistake. Believe me.'

'But you don't understand, Babis. Earlier I had to say that I have no children. But I was wrong. I do have a child. A daughter. Here on Crete.' Haldane nodded thoughtfully. 'I have to meet her. Talk to her. That at least.'

CHAPTER SIX

Haldane stopped the car on the top of the hill and looked down on Elounda. He had taken the motorway from Heraklion and had turned off at Aghios Nikolaos to approach the village from the east on the narrow, asphalt road which undulated along the coast.

As he had driven through Aghios Nikolaos he had seen how it had changed from the quiet and remote fishing port which he remembered into a busy and sophisticated tourist resort. Not unlike St Tropez, he had reflected, just before the final rot had set in and while it had still retained some of its charm and character. But the writing was on the wall for Aghios Nikolaos and he had seen plenty of evidence of it; new hotels, pizzarias, superior arts and crafts shops, boutiques, discotheques and, where once there had been simple tavernas there were now smart, new restaurants and bars. Most of these attractions were closed, shuttered and desolate now but all would soon be opening their doors as the present trickle of tourists swelled to a river at Easter and then finally burst over the town to flood it with marks, dollars, francs, kroner, yen and pounds sterling throughout the height of the season.

And the tentacles of commercialism, development and exploitation reached out beyond the town. The road to Elounda was littered with a straggle of holiday villas and only a short distance from the village a private road branched off to a luxurious hotel and bungalow complex which clearly catered for the upper price bracket of the package tour market.

Looking down from the hill, though, it seemed to Haldane that Elounda itself had, so far anyway, escaped the worst effects of the tourist invasion. Its white houses rose in steps up the slope of the hill behind the village which faced a wide and sheltered lagoon, at the northern end of which loomed the island fortress of Spinalonga, once a Venetian and then a Turkish stronghold and finally, early in the present century, a leper colony which had only been cleared of the last of its wretched exiles in the late nineteen fifties.

He put the car into gear and drove down the hill and into the village where he parked on an already dusty, tree-dotted open space, one side of which was open to the sea and served as a quay and moorings for the local fleet of fishing caiques, three of which had been hauled up out of the water for repainting or minor repairs.

Haldane got out of the car and looked around. There were few people about, only three men sitting grouped around the foot of one of the trees close to the water's edge mending fishing nets and, beyond them, some children playing on a spit of sand. Otherwise the place appeared deserted. Then he glanced at his watch and saw that it was ten minutes past two and he remembered how, even during the winter months, the majority of Cretans and certainly those in the villages retired to their homes for a three-hour siesta at one or two o'clock in the afternoon.

To his left was an ugly, two-storey concrete building. It was obviously a taverna and it was open for business. But it was not the taverna he was looking for. Then, from Spiridakis' description, he spotted it across the open ground and facing on to it and separated from it by the road. It was an old, attractive building flanked and backed by a large garden and an expanse of orange, lemon and olive trees. Outside the entrance was a small forecourt on which there were three or four tables shaded by a canopy of bamboo.

Haldane moved slowly away from the car, crossed the road and entered the taverna.

Stepping in out of the broad sun, he paused just inside the doorway to adjust this eyes to the shuttered twilight of the place. He found himself in a medium-sized bar with tables and chairs ranged along two sides of it leading down to a counter at the far end. In front of the counter stood a half dozen or so tall stools and to one side of it there was an archway hung with a beaded curtain.

Built into the right wall, about two thirds of the way down the length of the bar, glass doors stood open revealing a tree shaded patio. The patio was ringed with more tables and chairs and there was a flight of steps leading up from it to the balcony and the rooms which overlooked it and which Haldane decided must comprise the *en pension* accommodation.

The taverna was bright and clean and welcoming but sparsely furnished and with few frills. It clearly catered mainly for the local people and the few concessions which had been made for the tourist who stayed there were a display of replica Minoan pottery standing on a shelf, four original but amateurish paintings of local scenes hanging on the walls and a rack of picture postcards on the bar counter.

The place was empty. The only sound was of a man and a woman arguing indistinguishably in Greek somewhere beyond the curtained archway. The argument was fierce and voluble.

Haldane moved down the bar to the counter, looked around and waited. He realised that he was sweating a little and that he suddenly felt faintly sick. He took out his handkerchief and wiped his forehead.

The argument reached a peak of ferocity. The man shouted something and then the woman responded with equal vehemence. But both outbursts were unintelligble to Haldane.

Then the beaded strands of the curtain in the archway were brusquely swept to one side and a woman flounced into the bar, looking backwards over her shoulder and shouting defiantly in Greek.

'I don't care! Whatever they say! Whatever you say! I still say no,' she cried out in her anger and she was close to

52

tears.

She was slim and, despite a somewhat petulant mouth, attractive. She had uncharacteristic fair hair and she was the right age. Haldane knew that this had to be Elena; that here before him was his daughter.

Elena swung round and saw the Englishman standing at the counter. She reacted with a start of surprise and then looked embarrassed.

'Oh, excuse me,' she stammered in Greek. 'I did not know there was anyone here.'

Haldane watched her as, struggling to regain control of herself, she moved behind the counter.

'What would you like?' Again she spoke in Greek.

He stared at her until, disconcerted by his gaze, she frowned.

'A beer? An ouzo? What?' she asked.

Haldane was suddenly aware of what she had said. He smiled. 'A coffee please,' he replied in Greek. 'Medium.'

Elena nodded and began to prepare the coffee on the gas burner at the back of the bar. Haldane found that he could not take his eyes off her but she was too intent on what she was doing to notice. He abandoned his Greek. 'Do you speak English?' he said.

Elena looked at him. 'Yes,' she replied haltingly and with a marked accent. 'A little. You are English?'

'Yes. You are surprised?'

The woman shrugged . 'I knew you were not Greek. French I thought. Or German perhaps.'

'This is your place?' Haldane asked. She nodded. 'Then you are Elena,' he said.

Her face took on a puzzled expression. 'Yes. I am Elena. But how did you know that?'

'A friend told me about this place. And about you.'

'Oh! What friend?'

'Babis Spiridakis,' said Haldane. 'You know him?'

Elena nodded. 'Of course. Ever since I was a child. He comes here often. He has a house here. He is a good friend of yours?'

'I knew him during the war,' replied Haldane.

'I see.'

'Your English is very good. Where did you learn it?'

Elena poured the medium-sweet coffee into a cup. 'At school.' she said. 'I did not want to.' She put the cup down on the counter in front of him. 'I wanted to speak French. French is beautiful, do you not think? But my mother said 'No, you learn English.' So I did. But it is not easy for me. I do not get much . . .' She groped for the word. 'How do you say it?'

'Practice?' suggested Haldane.

She nodded. 'Yes. Practice.'

'Elena!' a man called angrily from beyond the archway.

Elena frowned and her mouth hardened. Haldane paid for his coffee.

The man called again. Louder this time. 'Elena!' And then he thrust his way through the curtain and into the bar.

He was in his mid-thirties, tall, muscular, good-looking and deeply tanned. He had the appearance of someone who spends most of his time out of doors. He was carrying a letter in his hand and his bad temper showed in his expression. He saw Haldane and pulled up sharply, his scowl momentarily deepening, then he made a visible effort to check his temper, for the time being at least. His pride would clearly not allow him to continue the argument in front of a customer. And a stranger too.

Elena looked at him and said icily in English. 'The *kyrios* is English. We were talking.'

'Excuse me,' the man muttered.

'My husband,' said Elena.

So this is Nikos Vassilakis, thought Haldane. He smiled. 'Hello.'

Nikos acknowledged the greeting with a curt nod and then looked at Elena and spoke to her in Greek, trying hard to make his tone sound conversational. 'That cannot be the end of it. We must discuss it,' he said.

'We have discussed it,' she snapped, uncertain as to

how good Haldane's command of their language was and discomforted by the possibility that he might be able to follow every word of the exchange.

Nikos shot a meaningful look at the Englishman. 'Further. Please!' he continued, tight-lipped and in Greek. 'And now. Come into the back.'

Elena sighed and moved out from behind the counter. 'What is there to discuss?'

Nikos held up the letter. 'This has to be answered.'

'Well, answer it then,' said Elena, beginning to flare again. 'You know what to say.'

Nikos took her arm and reluctantly she allowed him to hustle her back through the archway.

Haldane watched them go. Then he picked up his coffee, crossed to one of the tables and sat down. He could still hear their voices but again indistinctly and within seconds Nikos and Elena were quarrelling again. Then a door slammed violently and there was a sudden silence.

Haldane frowned and sipped his coffee. When, after nearly half an hour, neither Nikos nor Elena had put in an appearance again he got to his feet and slowly walked back out into the afternoon sunlight. He paused outside the taverna to fill and light his pipe and then, deep in thought, he crossed the road and strolled across the open space towards the three beached caiques.

It was as he was standing alongside one of them studying it with a critical eye and admiring the craftsmanship that had gone into the building of it that the boy collided with him. He was playing a game and being chased by two friends who he had out-distanced and, head down, he had come round the bow of the caique and run full tilt into the Englishman.

The boy stumbled and almost lost his balance but Haldane grabbed him so that he did not fall. 'I'm sorry,' the boy said in Greek, gazing up at Haldane abashed and repentant.

Haldane smiled. He judged the child to be about ten

years old. 'It's all right.'

'Alexi!' someone called and both Haldane and the boy turned to look in the direction of the taverna. Nikos was standing on the forecourt and beckoning. 'Alexi,' he called again. 'It is time to eat.'

The boy gave Haldane a grateful smile and then ran off towards the road.

Nikos opened his arms to his son as he came near to him and, laughing, picked him up and swung him round. Then, side by side, they disappeared into the taverna.

The Englishman, his eyes still on the building, gently tapped out his pipe on the hull of the caique and slipped it back into his pocket.

'Yes, Leandros,' sighed Spiridakis,. 'Sadly they have quarrelled a great deal lately, I think.'

Haldane had gone to the lawyer's office immediately on his return to Heraklion. 'Are they in some kind of trouble?' he asked.

Spiridakis leant back in his chair. 'They have a problem,' he said.

'Is it money?'

Spiridakis shook his head. 'No. Or at least not the lack of it. They have the taverna and Nikos owns four fishing boats and some land which he farms very profitably. They make a good living.'

'They are not happy?' pressed Haldane.

'They were. Very happy. But now they disagree. And that perhaps threatens their happiness.'

'What do they disagree about?'

'The future,' replied Spiridakis. He took a cigarette out of the box on his desk and lit it. 'You see, the taverna and the land around it belong to Elena. It was part of her inheritance from her mother. And she has kept the title to it. It is hers. Not theirs. Nikos has always been resentful of this. As you know,' he continued, 'in Crete it is usual for the husband to control everything.'

Haldane snorted. 'So Elena struck a blow for Women's

Liberation. Good for her. But that's in the past. You said they quarrel about the future.'

The lawyer nodded. 'Yes,' he said quietly. 'Because now a development company is most anxious to buy the taverna and the land For them, it is the ideal site for a new hotel. They have made a very handsome offer.'

'And she won't sell.'

'Exactly. And that angers Nikos. He is very ambitious. There are many things he thinks they could do with the money.'

Haldane frowned. That had been his brother's argument he remembered when they had first discussed AquaPlastics' offer for Haldane Marine and he had told David that he wasn't interested. 'And to hell with the village,' he growled. 'It's a beautiful place. Good God, if it's more cash in the bank Nikos wants, there's enough potential there as it is without spoiling it with yet another damn great hotel. Elena obviously cares about preserving the character of the place.'

'To be truthful I am not sure what her motives are,' replied Spiridakis.

'Has she consulted you? Asked your opinion?'

'Both of them have talked to me about it. But it is difficult for me to be objective. As you said, Elounda is a beautiful place. And I have a small house there where I spend some time each year. I do not wish to see the village changed any more than it has been already.'

'Well, so long as Elena refuses to sell,' said Haldane.

'I suppose so,' Spiridakis said with another sigh. 'But meanwhile life will go on being difficult for her. The quarrelling will continue.'

'So what's the answer?'

The lawyer shrugged. 'I think it is inevitable. Sooner or later she will no longer be able to resist the pressure.'

'Maybe if she's stubborn enough the developers will give up trying,' suggested Haldane.

'No. They see the profits that are to be made there. They are a big company. A Greek/German consortium.

They will not be put off easily. They have the patience and they have the money. They have already twice increased their offer. And one day Nikos will forsake argument for an ultimatum.'

'The taverna or me,' said Haldane, thoughtfully

The lawyer nodded. 'Something like that. And Elena loves her husband.'

'So she can't win?'

'I doubt it.'

'Maybe if she had some help?' said Haldane.

'There is nothing one can do,' replied Spiridakis, with a shrug. 'It is a family affair.'

Haldane turned and looked out of the window. 'Yes,' he said softly. 'You're right. It is. A family affair.'

It took more than an hour for Haldane to get his call to England. Twice he rang down to the hotel switchboard and asked what was happening and each time the operator told him tetchily that she was doing her best. At last he was connected and it was a good line.

'David... It's Alan... No, I'm calling you from Crete... No, I'm fine... That's just it, I'm not. I'm staying on here... I'm not sure, indefinitely... Well, something's come up... No, business. I can't tell you much about it now. It's early days. The point is I may want to invest out here... Exactly. That's why I'm ringing you. So get on to Jack Bainbridge at the bank for me, will you? Find out what the form is... Everything I've got if that's possible... Well, it could be that big. And something else. Put my house on the market, will you?... Well, the best price you can get for the quickest possible sale... Yes, I understand... Yes, I understand that... No, I'll phone you again in a couple of days... Of course, I've thought about it... Yes, I am. Very involved.'

He hung up. And that night he slept soundly, confident that he had made the right decision. And not just about Elena.

The following morning Haldane got up late, ate a leisurely breakfast and then checked out of the hotel. It was a beautiful day and he enjoyed the drive to Annika Zeferis' house. He was bitterly disappointed, however, when he got there to find that she was not at home. Still, no hurry, he consoled himself as he descended the terrace steps and returned to his car. Tomorrow. She'll probably be here tomorrow. I'll drive out again then.

He negotiated the tight bends of the steep mountain road with care and once back on the coast again turned east on the motorway. He stopped at Mallia for lunch and then spent three hours wandering through the ruins of the Minoan palace just outside the village. The air of timelessness which hung over the excavations fitted his mood perfectly.

From Mallia he continued driving eastward again but then, at the slip road signposted to Neapolis, he turned off and took the tortuous but scenically much more attractive old road through the mountains to Elounda.

It was early evening when he entered the taverna. There were several customers in the bar and his entrance caused a brief flurry of curiosity and interest. Elena and Nikos were both behind the counter and Elena, watching the Englishman approach them, first regarded him with a puzzled look on her face and then placed him. '*Kalispera*,' said Haldane, returning her smile.

'*Kalispera*,' replied Elena. She glanced at her husband. 'You remember,' she prompted. 'This is the Englishman who was here yesterday.'

Nikos nodded. '*Kalispera*,' he said.

'*Kalispera*.' Haldane surveyed the row of bottles on the shelf behind the counter. 'An ouzo I think, please.'

Nikos reached for a bottle and poured his drink.

'You like Elounda, eh?' said Elena.

Haldane smiled again. 'Very much. That's why I have come back. To stay.'

Elena frowned a little. 'You want a room?' she asked. 'We have one. But only for a week and then we are all booked I am afraid.'

Haldane shook his head. 'Thank you', he said. 'But I am planning on being here longer than that. And Babis Spiridakis has kindly lent me the house he has here.' He smiled, remembering the lawyer's reluctance to do so and the lengthy argument it had taken to persuade him. 'So you see,' he continued. 'We shall almost be neighbours.'

Nikos put Haldane's drink down on the counter. 'Good. Then we shall see much of you. Yes?' Elena said with a polite smile.

Haldane studied her. 'Yes. You will. That's a promise.'

'I am glad,' she replied. 'But you must excuse me now. I have to see that things are going well in the kitchen.' She moved out from behind the counter and disappeared from view through the archway.

Haldane watched her go and then looked at Nikos and took out some money to pay for his drink. Nikos waved it away. 'Please,' he said. 'To welcome you to Elounda.'

'Thank you.' Haldane was touched by the gesture. He raised his glass. '*Stin iyassou.*'

Nikos nodded. '*Episis.*' Then he left Haldane to take the order of a customer at the far end of the counter.

Sipping his drink, Haldane turned to study two men who were playing tavli at a nearby table. They were locked in fierce and dedicated combat, each man with his own loud supporters and critics.

Haldane smiled and then glanced in the direction of the doorway to the patio and reacted with a start and straightened up. Annika Zeferis was standing just inside the bar. She saw him and it was obvious from her expression that she was as surprised as he was. And just as pleased.

Haldane put his glass down on the counter and crossed to her. 'Hello,' he said quietly.

She smiled. 'Hello.'

'I drove out to your house this morning,' he said. 'But you weren't there.'

'No. I was at the factory.' She frowned. 'Why did you

60

want to see me?'

'To tell you that I am staying on Crete. For some time.' He shrugged. 'Perhaps forever. I wanted you to know that it's no longer just a holiday for me.'

Annika studied him. 'I see,' she said. 'That is a big step to take. What made you decide on it?'

'I think I may have found what I was looking for.'

Annika studied his face, only partly misinterpreting his expression.

'I was going to come and see you again tomorrow,' he went on. 'I certainly didn't expect to meet you here. Quite a coincidence.'

She shrugged. 'Not really. I come here often.' And then she told him and he knew why he had felt as he did when he first met her. And just who it was she had reminded him of. The chill realisation was saddening and forbidding. 'You see the taverna belongs to my niece,' she said. 'Elena's mother was my sister.'

Katerina Matakis sat in one of the upright armchairs in the sitting room of her house in Neapolis, staring into space. Ever since Noukakis had told her that Alan Haldane was back on Crete she had been deeply troubled and she had not been able to dismiss the thought from her mind.

Wearily she got up from the chair and crossed to the ornate cabinet. She opened one of its drawers and lifted from it a wooden box which she carried over to the table and then she unlocked it with a key which she took from her pocket. She removed a bundle of documents from the box and then reached into it again and produced three letters. She stared at them. There were English stamps on all three envelopes and they were postmarked 1945. The envelopes were all addressed to Melina Matakis and they had all been opened.

Katerina's hand closed round the letters in a savage grip and when she looked up from them her normally serene face was contorted with hatred.

CHAPTER SEVEN

Haldane clambered up through the hatch and back onto the deck of the caique again. He wiped his hands on his handkerchief and stamped on the planking, testing its soundness. Topside, the woodwork was in a surprisingly good condition but below deck it was a very different story. The hull was badly holed in four places and much of the straking was rotten. Still, with the modifications, that would all have to go anyway, he thought.

He'd spotted the old boat shortly after his arrival in Elounda. It was lying, beached and derelict, on a patch of rough ground above the small beach which edged the curve of land beyond the moorings where the local fishing fleet tied up. Haldane had reckoned that it must have been built fifty years ago and abandoned for at least five. It had interested him then and, during the two weeks he had been in the village, nearly every day he had taken another look at it. And over that time he'd come to see the possibilities in it and a positive and exciting picture had formed in his mind of how it could be rebuilt, retaining its traditional lines but refashioned to his own design.

He heard Nikos calling him and looked up to see him approaching across the open space in front of the taverna.

'He is here, *Kyrie* Haldane,' he said, as he came up alongside the caique. 'Waiting at the taverna.'

'Good,' said Haldane. He swung his legs over the rail and dropped down onto the ground.

Nikos was studying the boat critically and with disdain. 'Do you really want to buy this?' he said.

Haldane nodded. 'If the price is right.'

'It is a wreck,' said Nikos scornfully.

'Not quite. The frame and beams are sound enough. And the keel.'

'It has no engine.'

Haldane shook his head. 'She was built to have sails, Nikos. And she'll have them again if I buy her.'

'But that is the way it used to be,' Nikos replied contemptuously. 'Today caiques have engines. That is progress.'

'Is it?' said Haldane thoughtfully. 'For you perhaps. But I wonder.'

Together they turned and walked away from the caique towards the taverna.

As they approached the doorway Alexis came running out. He saw Haldane and smiled but he did not stop. *'Kalimera, Kyrie* 'Aldane,' he called out.

'Kalimera, Alexis.'

Nikos grabbed his son, checked his flight and pulled him towards him. 'Where are you going?' he demanded in Greek.

'To play,' said the boy.

'Does your mother know?'

'Yes.'

Nikos released him. 'Well walk. Don't run.'

'But I am late,' pleaded Alexis. 'The others are waiting.' And he ran off.

Nikos looked at the Englishman and raised his eyes in despair.

'He is a real boy. Your son, eh Nikos?' said Haldane with a smile as he watched the boy run down the street. And he's my grandson, he thought. And intermingled with his secret pride was feeling of sadness and loss.

Nikos shrugged. 'I think sometimes that his mother spoils him,' he muttered. He led the way into the taverna.

Elena was standing behind the bar counter wiping the top of it with a cloth. She looked up and smiled at Haldane. *'Kalimera.'*

'Kalimera, Elena,' said Haldane, returning her smile.

Sitting on a stool at the counter was a dour-looking man

in his seventies, a peasant with skin the colour and texture of cracked leather and a heavy, unkempt moustache. There was a cup of coffee and a glass of water on the counter before him. His eyes were on Haldane's face as the Englishman followed Nikos down the length of the bar.

'This is Andreas Hagieleftheris,' Nikos said to Haldane. 'He owns the boat. He speaks no English so I will speak for you, yes?'

Haldane nodded. It would probably be easier that way.

'A coffee?' asked Elna.

Haldane shook his head. 'No thank you. Later perhaps.'

Nikos spoke to the old man in Greek. 'This is the *kyrios* I told you about,' he said. 'The Englishman who is interested in that old caique of yours.'

Still studying the Englishman intently and thoughtfully, Hagieleftheris nodded. Nikos turned to Haldane and said in English. 'You must not accept the first price he asks. You must bargain.'

'Of course. So ask him how much he wants for it.'

Nikos turned back to the old man. 'The *kyrios* wants to know what price you put on the boat, Andreas.'

Hagieleftheris hesitated. Haldane was beginning to feel slightly embarrassed by his unwavering stare. Not once had the old man taken his eyes from his face.

'Well,' Nikos demanded 'How much?'

Hagieleftheris said something in reply but his accent was too thick for Haldane to understand. Nikos looked surprised and glanced at Elena. Then he turned to Haldane again. 'Andreas says that the caique is not worth any money,' he said. And he was clearly at a loss. This was certainly not the way Cretans normally did business.

'Yes it is,' insisted Haldane. 'It needs a lot doing to it but it can be made to sail again. And I know about boats. It's my work. So I would like to buy it. At the right price.'

Nikos shrugged and spoke to the old man once more. 'The *kyrios* says...'

Hagieleftheris, continuing to gaze at Haldane, interrupted. Again Haldane did not understand what he said but Nikos reacted to it and so did Elena. When Nikos turned to the Englishman there was a stunned look on his face. 'He wants to know,' he said, 'If you are the one who fought with Babis Spiridakis and the Andarte in the war. He asks if you are Leandros.'

Haldane nodded. 'Yes. That is what they called me.'

Nikos was impressed and it showed. Both he and Elena regarded Haldane and their expressions betrayed a new interest in the Englishman and a greatly increased respect for him.

'Yes,' Nikos said to the old man. 'He is Leandros.'

Hagieleftheris nodded solemnly. He spoke again. Nikos translated. 'Andreas says that he remembers you. And what you did during the war. The caique is yours. For no money. As a present.'

'No, that's not possible,' Haldane protested. 'I can't accept . . .'

'You will hurt him if you refuse,' Elena said urgently, breaking in on him. 'He says he would give more. Everything he owns to such a man as Leandros. You must accept.'

Nikos nodded. 'Elena is right,' he said quietly.

Haldane studied the old man and hesitated. And then, for the first time, Hagieleftheris smiled. '*Endaksi*, Leandros?' he asked.

Haldane saw that he had no choice if he were not to give offence. He nodded his agreement. '*Endaksi*, Andreas,' he replied with a smile. '*Efharistopli*.'

The old man waved away his thanks. '*Parakalo*.' Then his smile faded. Not without difficulty he got to his feet and then impetuously he took Haldane into his arms. The Englishman responded to the embrace. And this time when Hagieleftheris spoke he understood him. 'It is I who thank you,' said the old man. He released Haldane, gazed into his face once more and then turned from him and moved slowly away down the bar. In the doorway he paused and looked back. '*Andio*, Leandros,' he called.

Haldane waved. *'Sto kalo.'*

Hagieleftheris looked at Nikos and Elena and his farewell words were again too thickly accented for Haldane to follow them. Then the old man stepped out onto the forecourt and lumbered away out of sight.

Nikos gazed after him nodding thoughtfully. When he spoke it was in a low tone. 'He said that we are honoured by your presence here.' He looked at Haldane. 'And he is right. We are.' He smiled. 'But why did you not tell us? For two weeks you have been here in Elounda and you said nothing.'

Haldane shrugged. 'It was a long time ago. The war is best forgotten. And it can have meant little to you and Elena.'

'Perhaps not,' replied Nikos. 'But the story of Leandros is known to everyone in Crete.'

'And my father also fought with Babis Spiridakis,' said Elena proudly.

'Ah, Babis!' said Haldane. 'Now his is a name that must be remembered. Always. As a true patriot. And a great fighter. He was The Eagle.'

Nikos laughed. 'And Leandros was the steel in his . . .' He looked at Elena and demonstrated, holding his fingers like claws. 'How do you say it?'

'Talons,' said Elena.

'Yes,' nodded Nikos. 'You were the steel in The Eagle's talons.'

Haldane smiled. 'Well, I helped to sharpen them anyway.'

'Did you know my father? Stelios Papadakis,' asked Elena eagerly.

'Yes,' he said quietly. 'I knew him, Elena. Babis told me that he was killed in nineteen forty-nine.' Elena nodded. 'He was a fine man.'

Nikos moved round behind the bar and poured two rakis.

'I was only a child when he was killed,' said Elena. 'But my mother often spoke to me about him. She is dead now also. Four years ago.'

'I'm sorry,' Haldane said lamely.

Nikos picked up one of the glasses of raki and slid the other across the counter to Haldane. '*Kyrie* Haldane.'

Haldane corrected him. 'Alan.'

''Leandros?' enquired Nikos hesitantly. 'May we call you Leandros?'

Haldane nodded. 'I'd be very pleased,' he said with a smile.

'Our house is your house.'

'Thank you.'

Nikos raised his glass in salute. '*Yassou*,' he cried.

'*Yamass*,' said Haldane, and he downed his drink in one swallow.

Babis Spiridakis' house was less than three hundred yards from the taverna and when Haldane left Elena and Nikos he made straight for it.

He had much to do. The things he had asked David to send him from England by air freight had been delivered late the previous afternoon and he had not yet unpacked them. And he knew that he had to have some of his personal possessions around him before he would feel truly at home in the village. Then he would have to start work immediately on developing and costing the counter-proposition which he intended to put to Elena and Nikos, a proposition which had only been a hazy notion a fortnight ago but which had now taken on a more or less positive shape in his mind. But he had to have it all cut and dried and everything down on paper before he could even make the first approach to them with it. And that was going to take time. Quite a lot of time. And meanwhile he could only hope that Elena would continue to resist the pressures on her to sell. It was going to take a lot of concentrated effort on his part before he would be in a position to make his move but at least he now had the caique to work on as relaxation and that pleased him.

And then there was Annika. He pictured her in his

mind but then hastily dismissed the image. He must not think about Annika and suddenly he was grateful for all the demands on his time and preoccupation which lay ahead of him.

Spiridakis' house faced the sea across the road which ran through the village. It was a three-storey building erected at the turn of the century and more Turkish than Cretan in style. The ground floor had once served as a vast storeroom and still fulfilled that purpose but was now also the garage. A stone stairway ran up the side of the house to the front door on the floor above where a balcony fronted on to the road and overlooked the sea. At the rear of the house there was a terrace and a small, walled garden.

As Haldane climbed the steps a car pulled up at the kerb and the driver tapped the horn. He paused and looked round. It was Babis Spiridakis.

The lawyer smiled and waved and then got out of his car and mounted the steps. Haldane was surprised but pleased to see him.

'I have been to see a client in Aghios Nikolaos,' Spiridakis explained. 'At the office there is nothing but work. But here in Elounda is my brother, Leandros.' His smile broadened. 'It was not a difficult choice to stop on my way back to Heraklion.'

'I'm glad you did,' said Haldane. 'Come on in.' He led the way up the rest of the steps and into the house.

The first floor had been skilfully and tastefully converted into an open-plan living area on two levels. Against one wall a wooden staircase led up to the two bedrooms and the bathroom on the floor above and to one side of the staircase was a doorway through to the kitchen and the terrace beyond it.

The single spacious room, warm in winter and cool in summer, was alive with colour. The friendly furniture consisted of a mixture of antique Cretan pieces and twentieth-century discernment. There was an open fireplace in a stone surround, stacked against which was a pile of logs. Wall-length windows opened on to the balcony at the front of the house.

Haldane closed the front door. 'Coffee? A drink?' he asked.

Spiridakis shook his head. 'No thank you. Nothing. Unfortunately I cannot stay long. I'm flying to Athens this afternoon.' He moved further into the room and looked around.

'Oh? How long will you be away?' enquired Haldane.

Spiridakis shrugged. 'Four, five days. I have a case which comes up in court tomorrow. And I must also meet with those who try to persuade me to go back into politics.'

'That's a possibility?'

'No. And they must know that. Once and for all.'

'Perhaps they'll change your mind,' Haldane said with a smile.

'No,' replied Spiridakis firmly. 'To be worth anything a politician must at least believe that he can alter things. For the better. I no longer do. It is no mere coincidence that both democracy and tyranny are Greek words. In this country there is an inevitability about the way one follows on the heels of the other.' He sighed. 'It is a drama I do not wish to play a part in any more.' Then, pointedly, he changed the subject. 'So. How is it with you, Leandros?'

Haldane pulled out his tobacco pouch and his pipe and began to fill it. 'Fine. I've bought a caique. Or rather I was given one. By a man called Andreas Hagieleftheris.'

The lawyer thought for a moment and then nodded. 'I know him,' he said. 'His two brothers were among the hostages taken after the Kreipe kidnapping. They were both executed.'

'It's a generous gift.'

'But one which will have given him much pleasure, believe me,' Spiridakis assured him.

'I'll have a lot of work to do on the boat. But I'll enjoy that.' Haldane saw his friend glance enquiringly at the two large packing cases which were standing at the foot of the stairs. 'Things I asked by brother to send from England,' he explained. 'They arrived yesterday evening. Some clothes, a few books, some records, my drawing board. Things like that. I'll unpack them later.'

Spiridakis smiled. 'And then you will be really at ease here.'

'Yes. But I'll still feel guilty.'

'About what?'

'Taking your house away from you.'

'Nonsense,' exclaimed Spiridakis. 'I told you. I only use this place in the summer. Occasionally. And recently less and less.'

Haldane nodded. 'Well, thank you anyway. And just until I find a place of my own.'

He crossed to the mantelpiece; picked up a box of matches and lit his pipe. Spiridakis studied him and frowned. 'You do intend to stay on then. Indefinitely.'

'Yes.'

'Do you really think that is wise?'

'Probably not.' Haldane blew out the match. 'But it's what I want to do. And there can be no harm in it.'

'Not unless Elena discovers the truth. Then there could be.'

'How can she?' asked Haldane. 'I am not going to tell her. And you're not. Melina and Papadakis are both dead. There is no one else who knows.'

'Then why stay?'

'To be near her. To help her if I can with this problem between her and Nikos.'

Spiridakis regarded him sadly. 'And what if she sees that as only the interference of a foreigner and not the concern of a father for his child. As she must. And, without knowing the truth, resent it. As she so easily might.'

Haldane gazed into the bowl of his pipe. 'I hope she'll see it as the interest of a friend. Of someone she can trust. That at least.'

'And that will be enough for you?'

Haldane looked at him. 'It has to be, doesn't it?' he said. Slowly he crossed to the windows with their view of the sea and stood looking out of them thoughtfully.

Spiridakis watched him, his expression one of great concern.

'I never knew that Melina had a sister,' Haldane said at last.

The lawyer nodded. 'Yes. Annika. A remarkable woman.'

'Truly,' Haldane agreed.

'And very attractive.'

'Very.'

'You have met her?' Spiridakis said, frowning.

Haldane nodded. 'Shortly after I returned. And it was like meeting Melina all over again. Feeling the same things I'd felt then. Emotions I thought I'd lost forever. And I believe it was that way with her too. But then, later, I found out who she was. I haven't seen her since.'

Spiridakis shook his head. 'Do not unpack, Leandros,' he said quietly. 'Go home. Before someone is really hurt by all this.'

Slowly Haldane turned to him. 'If I keep silent. If I keep my distance. Who can be hurt?'

The lawyer regarded him thoughtfully. 'You, he said.

CHAPTER EIGHT

Matheos Noukakis parked the pick-up truck outside the taverna, got out of the driving cab and moved around to the other side of it to open the door for Annika. She stepped down onto the road, looked around and then walked to the back of the truck with him where he unfastened the tailboard.

'There is someone I want to see,' she said.

Yes, thought Noukakis, of course. And I know who. He scowled.

'Wait for me here. I won't be long,' she added.

He grunted and let the tailboard fail noisily on its chains. Then he reached for one of the two 20-litre drums of olive oil standing in the back of the pick-up and edged it towards him.

'Nikos will help you with those,' Annika said.

'I can manage,' replied Noukakis sulkily and without looking at her. She shrugged.

Still scowling, Noukakis watched her walk away down the street. You are making a fool of yourself, Annika Zeferis, he said to himself as he manoeuvred the second drum to the sill of the truck. And treating me as though I were one. And it was more than just a passing petulant reflection. He carried the two drums of oil into the taverna.

Nikos was serving two men who were sitting at a table just inside the door playing tavli. He looked up and greeted Noukakis. 'Yassou, Matheos.' Noukakis nodded.

'Here,' Nikos went on. 'Give me one of those.' He took one of the drums from him and carried it down towards the counter where Elena was polishing glasses. Noukakis followed him. Elena looked puzzled.

'You are making deliveries now, Matheos?' she asked.

Noukakis flushed. 'Your aunt needed an excuse to come to Elounda,' he muttered.

Elena glance in the direction of the doorway. 'She is with you?'

'She has gone running along to see the Englishman, Haldane,' said Noukakis scathingly.

Nikos shot a look at his wife, grinned and raised his eyebrows. Elena shrugged and looked at Noukakis.

'He is Leandros. Did you know that?' she asked.

'Yes, I have heard.' He was clearly unimpressed. 'Who has not?'

'It looks as though he is planning to stay here for a long time,' said Nikos.

Noukakis snorted.

Elena smiled mischievously. 'And if my aunt always uses such an excuse to see him,' she said, 'soon we shall be swimming in olive oil.'

Nikos laughed but Noukakis was not amused.

Haldane had left the front door open after he had returned from seeing Spiridakis to his car and Annika stood in the doorway and watched him.

He had already emptied one of the packing cases and distributed the contents around the room. The half dozen LPs which had been racked alongside the record player when Haldane had moved in had now grown considerably in number and there were books on shelves which had previously been bare. A drawing board and an array of draughtsman's equipment was set out on a table which the Englishman had placed in front of the long windows to the balcony so that when he was working he would have a view of the sea.

Now, surrounded by sheets of crumpled, discarded newspaper, Haldane had turned his attention to the second packing case. He had not heard Annika approach and, with his back to the front door, he was unaware of her presence. He prised off the lid of the packing case with the blade of a screwdriver and threw away the layer of wood shavings beneath it. Then he lifted out a package wrapped in corrugated cardboard and opened it. It was the framed photograph of Ruth which had stood on the mantlepiece in his study in England. Haldane gazed at the picture.

'Hello, Leandros,' said Annika quietly and, startled, he swung round, surprise giving way first to pleasure and then, just as quickly, to a feeling of consternation. She held his look.

'Hello,' he said.

'I am disturbing you,' Annika said with a slight note of apology. 'You are busy.'

Haldane shook his head. 'No, it's all right. Just unpacking a few bits and pieces. Come in. Please.'

He stood the photograph on the dining table beside him. Annika moved into the room. 'Getting settled?' she said.

'Yes.'

Haldane was aware that there was an awkwardness between them that had not been there before. And he knew that it was generated by him. Annika felt it too but she ignored it. She looked about her and smiled.

'It is a nice house, isn't it? I have always liked this room.'

'You've been here before?' Haldane was surprised.

'Often. Babis Spiridakis is my friend too. A family friend. He is Elena's godfather.'

Haldane frowned. 'I didn't know that. About him being Elena's godfather I mean.'

'Yes.'

'Of course, I knew he was a friend of your sister's. And he has spoken to me about you.'

'Oh?' asked Annika with a faint smile. 'What did he say?'

'That you are a remarkable woman.' She gave him an enquiring look. 'I agreed,' he assured her.

She picked up the photograph from the table. 'Your wife?' she asked.

'Yes.'

'What was her name?'

'Ruth.'

'A road accident you said.'

Haldane nodded. 'A lorry ran into her car.'

'How long had you been married?'

'Twenty years,' replied Haldane.

Annika put the photograph back down on the table again. 'You have children.'

He hesitated and then shook his head. 'No. No children.'

'That is sad.'

'Yes, I suppose it is. But then living's a pretty sad business, isn't it?'

Annika studied his face. 'Often,' she said. 'But then perhaps because we expect too much.'

'Perhaps.'

'And,' she went on, 'because we do not value happiness enough when we have it, or are offered the chance of it.'

Haldane nodded thoughtfully. 'That too.'

He reached into the packing case again and took out another bundle of books and started to undo the string around them.

'Would you marry again?' Annika asked.

Haldane fumbled with a knot. 'I might. For the right reasons.'

The string untied, he carried the books across the room and slipped them into a space on one of the shelves.

'Yes, there are many wrong reasons, aren't there?

Haldane turned to her. 'At twenty-five or fifty-five,' he said. 'More at fifty-five though. Then it's too often a challenge. Or an insurance policy.'

'Against loneliness.' Annika nodded. 'But a challenge! Surely that is a good thing.'

Haldane returned to the packing case. 'It depends on what you're trying to prove,' he said. He looked at her. 'Would you marry again?'

'Not to prove anything. But if I loved. If I was loved. To

share. To be a part of a secret again. Yes.'

'A secret?'

She nodded again. 'That is what marriage is. When it works. A secret shared by only two people. A conspiracy against the world.'

Haldane gazed at her and then he said simply. 'It's good to see you again.'

She smiled. 'Thank you. Then why have you been avoiding me?'

Haldane, taken off guard by this, floundered. 'I haven't been avoiding you,' he said. 'It's just that... Well, I've been busy. There's been a lot to do.'

'Of course,' she said, understandingly. 'Well then, if that is the only reason I haven't seen you for the past two weeks I am happy. And in that case I accept.'

Haldane frowned. 'Accept?'

Annika was pleased with herself and it showed in her eyes. 'Your invitation to have dinner with you tonight.'

Haldane looked at her, still frowning slightly. He was pleased to see her; more than just pleased. And the idea of having dinner with her was a tempting one. But he remembered Spiridakis' warning. Oh, what the hell? Why not? What harm could there be in it? So long as he kept his distance. He smiled.

'Good. I'm glad I asked,' he said.

Her mother's tone on the telephone had been peremptory and Annika had resented that. But, nevertheless, she had driven to Neapolis to see her. Now, as she stood across the sitting room from her, she felt her temper rising and she had to force herself to control it.

'You saw him again today.' Katerina hurled the accusation at her. 'In Elounda.'

'Do you expect me to deny it?' Annika's anger gave a chill edge to her voice.

'He is an Englishman. A foreigner.'

'Not quite, mother. He is Leandros. Did you know that?'

Katerina nodded gravely. 'He is still a foreigner,' she insisted. 'What is he doing in Elounda?'

'He has come back to Crete. He plans to live here for a while.'

'But why in Elounda?' demanded her mother.

'Babis Spiridakis lent him his house.'

Katerina studied her. 'He spends much time with my grand-daughter?' she probed.

'Elena!' exclaimed Annika, puzzled by the question. 'Some time I imagine. When he goes into the taverna. Why should that trouble you? Or do you think she is also in some danger because of him?' Katerina frowned darkly. 'Well you clearly believe that I am,' Annika went on. 'Why else did you send for me?'

'Because I do not want you to make a fool of yourself again. You have already made one mistake with a foreigner.'

Despite her anger Annika could not resist a smile. 'Hardly a foreigner. My ex-husband was born in Athens.'

'He was not a Cretan,' countered Katerina stubbornly. 'I want you to re-marry. But you must choose wisely. Matheos is a good man. And he loves you. Why do you treat him so badly?'

Annika sighed. They had been through this before. Many times. And in this same oppressive room.

'Matheos is an excellent manager,' she said, summoning up all her patience. 'He works for me. He is also a friend. And as a friend and an employee I do not treat him badly. But I do not love him. And I would never marry him.'

Katerina was not to be put off. 'Such a marriage would have my approval,' she said. She crossed herself. 'As your father would also have approved of it.'

'I am sorry, mother. But if and when I marry again, it will be to someone of my own choice,' replied Annika, still managing to keep her voice level and her tone reasonable.

'As it was before,' snapped Katerina.

'Yes.'

'You did not choose very wisely then, did you? And because of that you brought the shame of a divorce to the name of Matakis.'

Annika knew only too well the pain her mother had suffered at that time. 'Yes,' she said sadly. 'And I regret that. For your sake. I really do.' She smiled gently. 'But why all this talk of marriage? The Englishman and I have known each other for a little over two weeks. And during that time we have only been together for a few hours.'

'But you find him attractive,' her mother said reproachfully.

'Yes. I do.'

'And you entertained him at your house. Alone.'

Annika's temper began to flare again. She sighed and shook her head. 'Matheos!' she muttered angrily.

'That was not wise,' said Katerina.

'Times have changed.' Annika was already weary of this conversation. 'And I am not a child, a virgin who must be chaperoned. I am a woman. I have two grown children of my own.'

'Yes. And you should think of them also. They would not wish you to become involved with someone who was not even Greek. With a foreigner.'

'With this particular foreigner you mean, don't you? You have never even met him.' Katerina shook her head. 'So what is it then that you have against him?'

The old woman crossed slowly to the table and gazed at the wooden box which was standing on it. She was tempted to open it, to show Annika the letters and tell her everything. But that was not possible. And she knew it. She looked up at her daughter again.

'Promise me that you will not see him any more,' she pleaded.

'Why?' demanded Annika, totally bewildered. 'I don't understand.'

'Because I ask it. That should be enough.'

'Not without a good reason. Can you give me one? Other than because he is not a Cretan?'

78

'Promise me,' urged Katerina.

Annika felt sorry for her. 'Mother, try to understand,' she said quietly. 'It is a different world today from the one you grew up in. Here, when you were young, those who lived in Heraklion were foreigners to those who lived in Chania. And that is the way you still see it. But now, in three hours, someone from Heraklion can be in London. In ten in New York. There are no foreigners any more. Just people. Some good. Some bad.'

'Promise me.' Now Katerina was begging and it was as if she had not heard a word that had been said to her.

Annika shook her head. Clearly she was just not getting through to her and now she could no longer restrain her impatience.

'No, I am sorry,' she said sharply. 'But I won't do that. I cannot give you such a promise.' She turned on her heel, walked over to the sitting-room door and opened it. Then she looked back at her mother. 'I am seeing him again tonight. We are having dinner together,' she said unequivocally. 'And you have heard that from me. So I will tell Matheos that there is no need for him to pass on the information to you.'

She closed the door quietly behind her.

CHAPTER NINE

By the end of the first week in March, Haldane had achieved a great deal and he was feeling pleased with himself. There had been very little rain during February and although there had been quite heavy snowfalls west of Heraklion and the peaks of the Dhikti Mountains behind Elounda were now even more thickly blanketed by deep drifts and often obscured by clouds, along the eastern coastal strip there had been only occasional chill winds and the exceptionally mild winter had been the principal topic of conversation among the villagers.

It had delighted Haldane because it had meant that almost every day he had been able to put in at least four or five hours of work on rebuilding the old caique and the restoration was well advanced. What had been even more satisfying to him was the fact that, with the exception of some weekend and evening help from young Alexis who had eagerly volunteered his services and who he had welcomed the chance of being with, he had done it on his own. Invariably he had laboured under the critical eyes of at least two or three of the older men of the village who would sit at a discreet distance from him, turning their worry beads between their fingers and nodding their approval whenever he glanced across at them. But never once had anyone other than Alexis offered to help and he had never asked for it. The general feeling in Elounda seemed to be that if the Englishman was crazy enough to want to put so much of his time, energy and sweat into repairing a wreck when, if he wanted a caique that badly, he could so easily obtain one in good condition and at a fair price then that was his affair and he was best left to it. And Haldane understood those feelings and was content with the villagers' polite interest but total lack of involvement.

And while work on the boat had progressed well, so had the development of the idea which he intended to put to Nikos and Elena. Much research, many discreet enquiries and a daily stint of several hours at his drawing board had resulted in his finishing a fully detailed and attractively illustrated proposition much earlier than he had anticipated. And now he was ready to present it to them. And not before time either for, in conversation with Babis Spiridakis, he had learned that the hotel group had set the 6th May as the deadline on their final offer. And that must mean that Elena would already be under even greater pressure from her husband to agree to the sale. And, as the lawyer had said, if she still refused then Nikos, pushed to the limit, might well resort to emotional blackmail. So Haldane had good cause to be pleased with his efforts.

And he was pleased too that, despite his workload, he had still managed to spend time with Annika. After the evening they had had dinner together he had seen her often but, true to his resolve to keep a distance between them, never alone. Each time she had accepted his invitation to have lunch or dinner with him he had always taken her to some crowded restaurant or taverna. They had watched the Independence Day parade together from the balcony of an hotel in Heraklion and afterwards visited the grave of Nikos Kazantzakis on the Martinengo bastion of the old Venetian wall. And they had been to Knossos and Phaestos. But on each of those occasions Haldane had persuaded Babis and his wife, Sia, to accompany then. He had never once entertained Annika at his home and, using fatuous excuses, he had politely declined when twice she had suggested preparing a meal for them at her house. And it had not been easy for him. For each time he had seen her not only had he rejoiced more and more in her company but he had felt increasingly drawn towards her; had known that she felt the same way towards him and had said and done much to make

81

him aware of this. And he had often seen the look of hurt surprise in her eyes at his reserve and his rejection of her warmth and her need for him.

On the morning that he received Lorna Matthews' letter, Haldane had got up early as usual and, after breakfast, he had gone to the boat intending to finish caulking the deck seams. But he did not get much work done. His mind was not on it. This was the day that he had decided to talk to Nikos and Elena and, although he had every confidence in his idea, he had no way of knowing how they would react to it. After two hours he gave up and headed home again to shower and change before strolling down to the taverna.

Christos, the postman, saw him approaching and waited gratefully for him at the foot of the stairway to the front door. They exchanged greetings and agreed that the weather was truly remarkable. Christos handed Haldane four letters and then shuffled away down the road. Without even glancing at his post, Haldane climbed the stairs and entered the house. Tossing the letters on to the table, he went upstairs.

Spiridakis' secretary smiled and nodded Annika through into the inner office. The lawyer was sitting at his desk. He was delighted to see her. He stood up, moved to meet her and kissed her on both cheeks.

'You're looking well, Annika,' he said.

'Thank you.'

'And even more beautiful.'

Annika laughed. 'Such a welcome! I am glad I called in to see you.'

'So am I.'

'On an impulse. I had to be in Heraklion. I was passing. I am not disturbing you?'

'Happily, yes,' replied Spiridakis, with a smile. 'Which only proves that I am not yet as old as I so often feel.'

Annika gave him an ironic look. 'Now you search for compliments in return.'

The lawyer laughed. 'Of course. So feed my conceit. Flatter me a little.'

Annika studied him and then nodded. 'Very well, Babis Spiridakis,' she said. 'You are the most handsome and wisest of men.'

Spiridakis shrugged and made a gesture with his hands. He hugely enjoyed this game which they played from time to time. 'Unquestionably,' he agreed.

'The cleverest lawyer in all Greece.'

'Without doubt.'

'And the most expensive.'

Spiridakis laughed. 'Naturally.'

Suddenly Annika's expression changed and she looked at him with great affection in her eyes. Now she was no longer playing the game; her tone was no longer bantering. 'But only to those who can afford to pay,' she went on quietly. 'The champion of those who cannot and who are in need. A loving and faithful husband and a proud father.'

Spiridakis held her look, catching her mood but resisting it. He smiled wryly. 'Well, no man is entirely without faults.'

But Annika was not to be deflected. 'You are also my dearest and most trusted friend.'

The lawyer took her hand. 'Now you really compliment me,' he said sincerely. 'And I thank you.' Then he lightened the mood once more. 'So then, when will you come and have dinner with us?' he asked. 'Only yesterday Sia told me to remind you that you have a standing invitation.'

'How is Sia?' enquired Annika.

'Very well, thank God. But neglected I fear. And taken too much for granted. As always. Fortunately for me, however, my wife is a woman of great tolerance and understanding.'

'She adores you. As you adore her.'

Spiridakis nodded. 'Yes. That is true.' He looked into her eyes. 'A light and a warmth we all need, eh, Annika?'

Annika nodded. 'But not easy to find. And even when one does strike the sparks, the torch does not always light.'

The lawyer considered her and then said almost casually. 'Perhaps because one chooses the wrong kindling. English oak for instance.'

Annika frowned as he turned from her, moved back behind his desk and sat down again. She took a cigarette from the box on the desk and Spiridakis lit it for her. Then she crossed to the window.

'So tell me about Alan Haldane,' she said.

The lawyer regarded her thoughtfully. 'What do you want to know?'

'Everything. Who else can I ask. He is your friend.'

Spiridakis shook his head. 'More than that. My brother. I owe him my life.'

'So tell me about him.'

Spiridakis shrugged. 'He fought here in Crete during the war. With the Andarte. With my group. He was my right hand. We called him Leandros. And then, in nineteen forty-four, when the island was liberated he was sent back to England.'

Annika drew on her cigarette and then exhaled. 'Go on.'

Spiridakis picked up the pen lying on the desk in front of him and toyed with it. 'I know little about his life after that time. Except that he built boats. That he married and that six years ago his wife was killed in an accident.'

'All this I already know.'

Spiridakis studied the tip of the pen and nodded. 'Of course. He would have told you.' Annika turned to him. 'So what is there I can tell you about him that you do not know?'

'Of the man that he is,' she said. 'As you see him.'

'He is brave. And honest. A man who has made his share of mistakes and suffered for them.'

'And what is it that he is afraid of?' Annika demanded quietly. 'Can you tell me that?'

Spiridakis looked surprised. 'Afraid of! Little I think.'

Annika nodded. 'He is afraid of me. Of what I offer. Of what he knows I am offering. Freely and without reservation. Or even conditions.' She met Spiridakis gaze unflinchingly. 'Do I shock you?' she asked.

'No,' replied the lawyer quietly. 'Because I know you. And because I admire your independence. And those things in you which others fear and resent. And because I know also that love is a gift that you would not give lightly.' He stood up again and crossed to her. 'Perhaps he doesn't wish to hurt you' he said.

'But for him it is the same way, Babis.' Annika's tone was urgent. 'He needs me as I need him. He cannot hide that. I see it in his eyes; know it in his presence.'

'Of harming you in some way then.'

Annika nodded. 'Yes. I think it is possible that he does fear that.' She examined Spiridakis' face searchingly. 'But how could he do that?'

'There are many ways in which one person may harm another. And not only by intent. Sometimes by default.'

'You know, don't you?' insisted Annika, her eyes still on his face. 'You know what it is that he fears.'

Spiridakis hesitated. 'I know only this,' he said, choosing his words carefully. 'Leandros is a man I would trust with my life but you would trust him with your happiness. You would place it in his hands. And that is a terrible responsibility. One which he may feel he cannot accept.'

'Because I am wrong?' asked Annika, frowning at the possibility. 'Because what I have read in his eyes is only what I have wanted to read?'

Spiridakis put his hands on her shoulders and shook his head. 'No,' he said. 'Because you are right.'

Haldane descended the stairs, his hair still wet from his shower, and moved quickly over to his drawing board, scooping up the letters from the table as he passed. The taverna would be quiet now and there would be time before the first customers began to drift in for lunch for him to go over his scheme with Nikos and Elena at least in outline. And then he would go into Heraklion and meet Babis as they had arranged. It will be good to have some transport again he thought. For more than a week he had been without any having surrendered the Kadett when it had finally dawned on him just how expensive car hire was on Crete. And buying one was even more prohibitive he found. It was Babis Spiridakis who had come up with the answer; Babis who knew everyone, Babis who could fix almost anything. Leave it to me. I will find a car for you, he had told him. And he had. Only the night before he had called Haldane on the telephone and said that there was a car in the Customs yard in Heraklion, impounded by the authorities for non-payment of duty, which he felt sure would suit him admirably. And if he wanted it it was his for a very reasonable price. Haldane had not hesitated and they had agreed to meet at the Customs House at one thirty. Haldane glanced at his watch. Plenty of time.

He perched himself on the stool in front of the table on which his drawing board stood and flipped through his post. The first two letters were bills and the third was from his bank in England. He tossed them aside. The fourth letter with its handwritten envelope and English stamp intrigued and mystified him. The writing was familiar. He opened the envelope and took out the letter inside and read it. It was from Lorna Matthews. By the time Haldane got to the last page his expression was thoughtful and troubled. He frowned and read the letter through again. Then he sighed, shook his head sadly and slipped the letter and its envelope under a pot containing pencils standing on a corner of the table. He would answer it later.

Opening the long drawer in the table, he took out a sheaf of notes and a rolled-up sketch. He slipped the notes into his pocket, closed the drawer again, stood up and, with the sketch in his hand, made for the front door.

He was still some distance from the taverna when he saw Nikos storm out of the doorway. He was clearly very angry. Puzzled and concerned, Haldane pulled up and watched as Vassilakis got into his car, started the engine, slammed it into gear and drove away heedlessly and at speed. Haldane stood watching until the car was out of sight and then walked on again.

The bar was empty. Haldane waited for a minute or two and then, when there was still no sign of Elena, he strolled out onto the deserted patio. Elena was half way down the steps which Haldane now knew led not only to the guest rooms but also to the Vassilakis' own apartment. Her eyes were scorched and inflamed by tears. Lost in her thoughts and cloaked with misery, she did not notice the Englishman standing there until he spoke.

'*Kalimera*, Elena,' he said gently.

She reacted with a start of surprise and tried for a smile. But with little success. '*Kalimera,*' she replied flatly, as she crossed the patio towards him. 'You are not working on the boat today?' There was no real interest in her enquiry, she was merely making conversation.

'I have been,' replied Haldane. 'But I have to go into Heraklion.'

Elena nodded. 'Do you have time for a coffee?' she asked listlessly.

'Thank you.'

She moved away from him towards the bar. Haldane followed her. He settled himself on a stool and watched as she prepared the coffee. When she turned and set it down in front of him he said, 'Matter of fact I was hoping that if Nikos was going into Heraklion he'd give me a lift. But there's something I wanted to talk to you both about first.'

'Nikos is not here,' she said.

'No,' said Haldane, his eyes on her face. 'I saw him leave.' She shot him a worried look. 'What's wrong, Elena?' he asked gently.

'Wrong?' she countered defensively.

'Something is. Nikos was upset. Anyone could see that. And you've been crying, haven't you?' Her expression took on the semblance of a scowl. Haldane nodded. 'Yes, you're right,' he said. 'It's none of my business. But I'm fond of you.' He paused. 'Of both of you. And if I can help.'

Elena looked at him and her expression softened. 'You are a kind man, Leandros,' she said. 'And I thank you.' She shook her head. 'But there is nothing you can do. It is between Nikos and me.'

'A quarrel.'

She nodded. 'And we both said things to hurt the other.'

'I'm sorry.' Haldane picked up his cup and sipped his coffee.

'So am I. I do not wish it. It was never so before but these days we quarrel too often.'

'About what?'

Elena waved dismissively. She had no wish to continue this conversation. 'Please do not concern yourself. I have said. There is nothing you can do.'

'The taverna,' sighed Haldane.

Elena looked surprised. 'You know about that?' she asked. Haldane nodded. 'How do you know this?' Elena was beginning to brindle again. 'Who told you?'

'Babis Spiridakis.'

'Why?'

'Because it was necessary for him to tell me once he knew what was in my mind.' Elena frowned. Haldane went on, 'I told you I wanted to talk to you and Nikos, didn't I?'

'About the taverna?'

'Yes.'

Elena made an exasperated gesture and shook her head. 'You also wish to buy it?' she asked bitterly. 'Is that it?'

'No.'

'Then I do not understand.'

'I'll explain,' said Haldane. 'But first tell me this. Why won't you sell, Elena?'

Somewhat taken aback by this, Elena groped for

justification. 'Because . . . Because there is no reason to sell. We have what we need for a good life. We are not without money. Nikos has his fishing boats. And this is not only our home it is also a good business.'

Haldane nodded. 'And one which you worked hard together to build up.'

'Yes,' agreed Elena, building on her case. 'To sell would mean many changes I think. And I do not want changes. Already there are many hotels on Crete and not all of them are beautiful. This taverna has been here more than a hundred years. It is part of Elounda. It belongs here. As we belong here. Nikos and me. And our son.'

'And you have said all this to Nikos?' asked Haldane.

'I have told him how I feel.'

'But he still wants you to sell?'

Elena pouted angrily. 'Those who would buy from me have offered a great sum of money. Nikos says it would mean a new life for us.' Her eyes filled with tears again. 'But I do not want a new life, Leandros. I am happy with what I have. And so was Nikos before these people came to us and talked in many millions of drachma.'

Haldane felt desperately sorry for her. He knew only to well how she felt. He looked at her and gave her an encouraging smile. 'What if there was a way for you both to make more money?' he asked. 'Not millions. But a lot more than you do now and for you still to own the taverna. Would that make Nikos happy? Would that end the quarrelling?'

Elena nodded. 'If Nikos was happy there would be no quarrelling.' Then she regarded him searchingly. 'But how is that possible?'

'Simple,' replied Haldane. 'By realising the full potential of this place and capitalising on it. That's how. It's an idea I've had since I first came here. I've been working on it for the last few weeks.' He took the sheaf of notes from his pocket. 'It's all here. Facts and figures.' He tossed the notes down on to the counter and then unrolled the sketch. 'Look at this.'

Elena leaned forward, bewildered but interested.

Noukakis got out of the pick-up truck and looked up at the house. In the back of the truck, the top half resting on the roof of the cab, was an old wooden mast, badly in need of revarnishing.

With a disgruntled expression on his face, Noukakis slowly climbed the steps to the front door and rang the bell. There was no response. He rang again. Still getting no reply, he opened the door and peered in. 'Hello,' he called. 'Are you there?' Silence.

Noukakis stepped into the room and looked around, curious and interested. He saw the framed photograph of Haldane's wife, crossed to it, picked it up and studied it critically.

Setting the photograph down again, he strolled across to the drawing board and examined the sectional drawing of Haldane's modifications to the caique which was pinned to it. He snorted contemptuously. It was as he was turning away from the drawing board that he saw the letter under the pot of pencils. Casting a look over his shoulder to make certain that he was unobserved, he moved the pot to one side. He checked the postmark on the envelope and then picked up the letter and read it. When he had done so he stood staring thoughtfully at it for a while and then very carefully he put the envelope and the letter back where he had found them.

And when he looked up again he was smiling.

CHAPTER TEN

Elena was impressed and Haldane had been delighted to see her mounting enthusiasm as he had outlined his scheme to her. She pored over the meticulous, colour washed, pen and ink drawing which lay unrolled on the bar counter between them. It showed the taverna as Haldane envisaged it if his plan were followed through.

'You did this?' she asked.

Haldane nodded. 'Yes.'

She gave him an admiring look. 'You are a very clever man, Leandros.'

'It's just a sketch,' he replied deprecatingly. 'An impression. We'd need an architect to prepare the proper plans. So what do you think of the idea?'

'I think it is a good one. As you said, more money but without many changes. I would like that.'

'And Nikos?' he asked.

Elena's face clouded with doubt. She shrugged. 'Who can say?' she sighed. 'For myself I think Nikos would need much convincing.'

'If you like the idea then between us we will persuade him,' said Haldane encouragingly.

She shook her head. 'Oh, no. Nikos will not listen to me in matters of business. And as for you, Leandros.' She paused. 'Well you have only been here for a few weeks. He likes you but he doesn't know you well enough for you alone to convince him.'

Haldane frowned. She was right of course. Then he had an inspiration. 'What if Babis Spiridakis were on our side,' he said. 'What about that?.'

Elena gave this idea some thought and then she nodded. 'Yes,' she said, but there was doubt in her voice.

'Perhaps.' Then she smiled, encouraged by an inspiration of her own. 'But even more so if it were my aunt who spoke in favour of the plan.'

'Annika! ' exclaimed Haldane, surprised.

'Yes. Nikos admires her very much. He would never say so because for a woman in Crete she is . . . How do you say it in English? '

'Unconventional? Different?'

'Yes,' said Elena. 'She is different. She does not obey the rules. And many people speak against her.'

'Because of her divorce? ' asked Haldane.

She nodded. 'Because of that. And because of the way she thinks. Of what she says. Because she does not believe that she has to answer to any man. But she has made a big success of her own business. And when she speaks she speaks only the truth. Nikos knows these things and when she talks he listens.'

'Right,' said Haldane. 'Then first I'll speak to her.'

'Good,' said Elena. And then she smiled and went on. 'That will please her I think.'

Haldane gave her a questioning look. Elena's smile broadened knowingly. 'She welcomes seeing you. But then I do not have to tell you that.'

Haldane was not going to be drawn on that subject so he ignored the implications behind her smile. He glanced at his watch and then gathered up his notes and re-rolled the sketch. 'I must go if I'm going to catch the bus to Heraklion,' he said. He took out some money to pay for his coffee but Elena raised her hand in protest and gave him a hurt look.

'Please Leandros,' she said.

'But Elena!' he protested. 'Every day it is the same.'

'And every day it is our pleasure.'

He smiled. 'Thank you,' he said and then stood up. 'I will let you know what your aunt says. If she is in favour of the scheme maybe it would be a good idea for all of us to get together and talk about it.'

'Yes,' agreed Elena. 'I think it would.'

He turned and started for the doorway.

'Why, Leandros?' said Elena.

Haldane turned back to her with a puzzled look on his face. 'Why?'

'The drawing. The calculations. Everything. Why did you do this? Why did you bring your plan here to us?'

Haldane studied her. He had to have a reason. One which would satisfy her. He shrugged. 'Perhaps because I know how you feel. I once had something I built up from nothing. Something I loved. And in the end I lost that to money.' He smiled. 'And then again perhaps because it's just a damned good idea. And there's profit in it.' He hesitated and then added. 'For everyone.'

He swung round and Elena watched him walk out on to the street.

Outside Haldane's house Noukakis was leaning against the side of the truck, smoking a cigarette. He straightened up as the Englishman approached him. Haldane was surprised to see him. He glanced at the mast and then gave him a questioning look. Noukakis regarded him contemptuously.

'A mast. For your caique. It is a gift from *Kyria* Zeferis,' he said, making no attempt whatever to disguise his scorn. 'She found it in a boatyard in Heraklion. It is old.'

Ignoring the man's manner, Haldane examined the mast and ran a hand down it feeling the strength of the seasoned wood. 'It's marvellous,' he exclaimed delightedly. 'Exactly what I've been looking for. But a present!' He shook his head. 'She shouldn't have done that.'

'No,' said Noukakis flatly, flipping his cigarette end across the road.

He climbed into the back of the truck and untied the mast. Haldane helped him to unload it and together they carried it into the garage. When they came back out on to the street Haldane closed the garage doors and turned to look at Noukakis to find the Cretan regarding him with only thinly veiled hostility. My God, but you really do hate my guts, don't you, thought Haldane. I've trodden on your toes, haven't I? But how? Then he realised. It had to be Annika. He smiled at Noukakis.

'Are you going back to Heraklion now?' he enquired innocently.

'Yes.' Noukakis' reply was cautious.

Haldane nodded. 'Good,' he said pleasantly. 'You can give me a lift.'

Noukakis frowned. He got into the driving cab and started the engine. Haldane climbed into the seat beside him.

Throughout the forty-minute drive, Noukakis said nothing but occasionally he would grin quietly to himself and Haldane had the feeling that he had something on his mind. And that whatever it was it both pleased and amused him.

Spiridakis was waiting outside the Customs House and so was the car. It was a Fiat 850 drop head sports coupe, several years old but in very good condition. Haldane examined it gleefully. It had covered a lot of kilometres in its time but, with a thorough overhaul and treated with respect, the engine still had a lot of life left in it.

'Everything is in order,' said Spiridakis, handing him a sheaf of documents. 'The car is yours, Leandros.'

'It's ideal,' enthused Haldane. 'And for such a good price.'

He reached for his cheque book but Spiridalis raised his hand and shook his head. 'Later,' he said. 'You can settle with me later. Tomorrow I am having lunch with the Chief Customs Officer.' He smiled. 'He is the cousin of a cousin of mine. And it is possible that he might yet be able to improve on the price. You know how these things are done here.'

Haldane laughed. He knew only too well. Everyone on Crete seemed to be related in some way and a blood tie, however remote, carried obligations with it. And those obligations were, in turn, repaid with favours.

'Yes, I know,' he said. 'Thank you, Babis.'

Spiridakis shrugged dismissively. 'For what?'

'For finding the car for me,' replied Haldane. 'For taking care of all the formalities.'

'It was nothing. You need a car of your own.' He fixed Haldane with a penetrating look. 'If you are really going to stay here for some time that is.'

'I am,' Haldane said.

'Still?'

'Still,' said Haldane firmly.

The lawyer sighed and shook his head sadly. 'You know what I think, Leandros,' he said.

Haldane nodded. 'Yes. That it's a mistake.' And then he added reassuringly. 'But don't worry. As far as Elena's concerned, well that's not going to be any problem. I promise you.'

'And what about Annika?' asked Spiridakis.

'A good friend. Nothing more. And I'll see it stays that way,' said Haldane lightly. But he could see from the doubtful, troubled look on Spiridakis' face that his friend's fears were in no way allayed.

He got in the Fiat and started the engine. 'Follow in your car and we'll take a glass of raki together somewhere,' he said.

Spiridakis looked at his watch and shook his head. 'Forgive me, Leandros. I would like to but sadly I cannot. I must get back to the office. There will be a client waiting for me there. You are returning to Elounda?'

'Not right away,' replied Haldane. He smiled. 'There's a lady I have to thank for a present. And I need her help.'

The lawyer reacted to this with a disapproving frown. Haldane shook his head. 'I told you,' he went on. 'A friend. That's all.' He waved. '*Yassou*, Babis. And thanks again.'

He put the car into gear and drove off.

He took the road along by the harbour and then up the 25th of August Street. Pulling away from the traffic lights and turning into the main shopping thoroughfare, he headed for Liberty Square. Had he not had his full attention on the traffic he would have seen Matheos Noukakis. As it was neither saw the other for Noukakis' mind was elsewhere too. He was standing by a tobacco kiosk staring at a piece of paper on which he had written a name and address. And Haldane's car was already out of sight by the time Noukakis looked up, turned and walked off quickly in the direction of the Telegraph Office.

Haldane parked the Fiat close to the foot of the terrace steps. It was the first time he'd been to Annika's house since he had had dinner there the evening after his visit to the monastery of Keras, and on the journey up through the mountains he had begun to wonder if calling on her was such a good idea after all.

For a time he sat in the car gazing up at the terrace and debating whether he should turn round and head back to Elounda. But if Annika had seen him arrive he knew that he would have difficulty in explaining to her the next time they met why he had not gone up to the house. And already there were too many things which troubled her and which he could not explain. To add to them by turning tail now could only further complicate matters. Besides, he wanted to see her. There was no doubt in his mind about that. He picked up the bunch of flowers and the rolled drawing from the seat beside him and got out of the car.

Annika had not seen him drive up. That was obvious from the expression of astonishment and sudden pleasure on her face as she came into the sitting room and found him standing just inside the French windows.

'Leandros!' she exclaimed.

Haldane smiled. '*Kalispera*,' he said quietly.

She crossed to him. 'I was not expecting to see you today. What a wonderful surprise. How are you?' she asked.

'I'm well.' Haldane grinned sheepishly. 'Very well in fact. It's been a good day for me so far.'

'I'm glad,' Annika said.

'I'm now the owner of a car and this morning something very special was delivered to me in Elounda.'

She smiled. 'You like it? It is what you needed?'

'It's perfect. But I really can't let you. . .'

Annika did not let him finish. She put a finger to her lips and then said, 'The joy in what is given is in how it is received. Would you rob me of happiness, Leandros?'

Haldane looked into her eyes. 'Never. If I can prevent it.'

'You can,' she replied softly. 'At this moment. Accept my gift.'

'It's a handsome present.'

Annika shrugged. 'Things are easy to give,' she said. 'They show only that you are in someone's mind.'

Haldane held out the bunch of flowers to her and she took them from him and savoured their perfume. 'They are beautiful.'

Haldane pulled a face. 'But there is no comparison.'

Annika frowned, studied him for a moment and then held out the flowers as if to hand them back to him.

'A gift is not a debt,' she said. 'And neither is it something to be weighed or measured.'

Haldane recognised his mistake and regretted it. He shook his head and smiled. 'I would have brought you them anyway.'

'Because you were in my thoughts,' he said. 'To please you. To please myself.'

'Because?' you were in my thoughts,' he said. 'To please you. To please myself.'

Annika smiled again and gently hugged the flowers to her. 'In that case, thank you. Excuse me while I put them in some water.' She turned from him and crossed back into the kitchen.

Haldane looked around the room. It pleased him no less now than it had on his first visit. He walked over to admire one of the paintings and then began a slow perambulation. There was a photograph standing on one of the side tables. He picked it up. It was of a good-looking young man in his early twenties and a strikingly attractive girl of a year or two younger. They were unmistakably Annika's children and, if any confirmation were needed, the signed inscription on the photograph read: *In case you have forgotten what we look like and with our love, Andreas*, and then in another hand, *Katerina*.

Haldane replaced the photograph on the table and moved on to study the long playing records standing on the shelves above the expensive hi-fi unit. Pulling out some of the record sleeves and examining them, he was impressed and pleased to find that Annika's taste in music was as wide-ranging as his own and included the works of many of his favourite composers.

Annika returned with the flowers now tastefully arrnaged in a vase. She stood for a moment with her head cocked on one side looking for a place where they would be seen to their best advantage. Finally she decided on the chest standing between the two windows which overlooked the olive grove and she crossed to it and put the vase down on to it. Then she turned to Haldane with an enquiring look, seeking his approval. He smiled and nodded. 'Perfect.'

'Good.' She crossed to him. 'You said that you now have a car?'

'Yes. It's only a small one. But big enough for two.'

She laughed. 'I'm glad. And also because you will now have no excuse for not visiting me.'

'You think I've been finding excuses?' he asked.

'Well, haven't you?'

Haldane shrugged. 'You're a busy woman. You have a business to run. And I've been hard at work on the caique.'

'It goes well?'

'Yes, very well.'

'Good.' Annika smiled. 'Only today you have forsaken it for me.'

'I had to come and thank you for the mast. That

wouldn't wait,' he said. 'And. . .' He hesitated.

'And?' she prompted him hopefully.

'Because I need your help.'

He saw that she was disappointed and even a little hurt. She moved away from him and took a cigarette from a box which stood beside the photograph of her children. She lit the cigarette and when she turned to Haldane again she was smiling once more, if a little ruefully.

'Well that is something at least,' she said. 'It has to be a good thing that you come to see me for help, doesn't it?' Her smile broadened and she indicated the settee on the far side of the copper-canopied, stone fireplace. They sank down into the comfort of it together.

'So what is it that I can do for you?' she asked. 'You have a problem?'

'Elena and Nikos do.'

Annika gave him a puzzled look. 'I do not understand.'

'Well, you must know how things are between them,' Haldane said. 'About the offer that has been made for the taverna I mean.'

'Oh that!' She nodded. 'Yes, of course I know. It has caused much unhappiness. For Elena particularly.'

'And how do you feel about it?'

'That Elena is probably right. That, in the end, the decision must be hers alone anyway. The taverna belongs to her.'

'But you are not happy about the situation,' he suggested.

'Of course not.'

'And you'd like to see it resolved?'

Annika's face took on an even more puzzled expression. 'Yes I would, Leandros. But it is between them. Only they can find the answer. I cannot interfere.'

'And meanwhile the arguments and the quarrelling will continue. They will go on being unhappy.'

She gave a helpless shrug. 'Until one of them puts the feelings of the other above their own ambitions.'

'Or a compromise is found,' he said.

Annika drew on her cigarette and looked at him with interest. 'You have something in mind?'

'Yes. I've spoken to Elena about it already and she approves. But she says we'll need an ally to persuade Nikos. Or even to get him to listen. And, according to Elena, ideally that ally has to be you.'

Annika laughed quietly. 'Really,' she said. 'I never realised that I had any influence over Nikos.'

Haldane nodded. 'Apparently. A great deal. And understandably I think.'

She settled back into the sofa, a wry smile on her lips. 'So first I have to be persuaded. Is that it?'

'Yes,' said Haldane. 'Well, that's what we're hoping anyway.'

'Very well, Leandros,' Annika said, her eyes on his. 'Persuade me.'

Haldane took the sheaf of notes from his pocket and unrolled the drawing.

CHAPTER ELEVEN

'I think it's a wonderful idea,' Annika said with the same genuine enthusiasm she had shown when Haldane had first explained the proposition to her that afternoon. Now, sitting out under the stars at a table on the patio of the Vassilakis' taverna, she had listened attentively, along with Elena, as he had once more gone over the scheme in detail, this time with Nikos.

During dinner nothing had been said about Haldane's plan but once the table had been cleared and the women had sat sipping their coffee and the men their brandies, prompted by Annika, Haldane had introduced the subject into the conversation. Nikos had at first been sceptical about it but he was impressed when Haldane presented him with his sheaf of facts and figures. And he had leaned forward with interest to study the drawing as it was unrolled before him on the table.

'It is a scheme which has many advantages,' Annika went on. 'And one which you and Elena should consider very seriously, Nikos.'

Annika's judgment also made an impression on Nikos but his *philotimo* would not allow him to betray the fact so he nursed the knowledge privately to hold and then weigh along with his own opinion. He scrutinised the drawing carefully. 'Sailing holidays,' he mused.

'Based on the taverna,' said Haldane. 'With the place suitably enlarged to cope with the number of guests that would be needed to make a go of it.'

'Mmm,' reflected Nikos, without taking his eyes from the drawing. 'That would mean a lot of rebuilding.'

'Some,' said Haldane. 'Not a lot. And all in keeping with the original architecture. Just like it is there. As I

101

said, I've estimated for another twenty-five double bedrooms but it'd be modification and enlargement mostly. A residents' lounge. Shower and changing rooms. A bigger kitchen. More bar space. That kind of thing.'

Nikos picked up Haldane's calculations and leafed through them. 'And the boats?' he asked.

'Fifty of them. Sailing dinghies. An entirely new class specially designed for these waters.'

'Designed by you,' said Nikos.

Haldane nodded. 'Yes. And built here in Crete. A boat that's easy for beginners to handle but really exciting for someone who's experienced.' He glanced at Annika who smiled encouragingly. 'Of course,' he went on. 'There'd be the offer of full instructions for novices. That would be part of the attraction.'

Nikos looked at him. 'It all sounds very good,' he said. 'And if you are right about the profit which is to be made. . .' He shrugged.

'And those figures are conservative ones,' Haldane assured him. 'I tell you. It can't miss, Nikos.'

Nikos studied Haldane's figures again. 'It would need a lot of money to do all this. For the building. For the changes. For the boats.' He sighed. 'And it is not so easy now to get money from the Bank. And even if we succeeded they would demand much in return in interest.'

'But you wouldn't need to go to any Bank,' said Haldane quietly. 'I'd put up the capital.'

Nikos shot him a look of surprise. 'You, Leandros!'

'Of course. I have money to invest. Not a fortune but enough. And there's nothing I'd rather have a stake in than this. We'd be partners. The three of us.'

Nikos turned to Annika trying hard not to appear as though he was seeking advice but the questions were there in his eyes and she saw them.

'Of course it is up to you but that would seem like a good offer to me, Nikos,' she said casually. 'And I think there are few men in whom you could put greater trust.'

Nikos nodded graciously to show that he had noted her

views. Then he said to Elena. 'You would like this?'

'Yes,' she replied, holding her breath.

Once again Nikos turned his attention back to the sheaf of notes which Haldane had prepared. And while pretending to read them once more he turned the proposal over in his mind.

'I will need to think about what is written here,' he said at last. 'All that you have said also.'

'Naturally,' agreed Haldane.

Nikos dropped the notes down onto the drawing. 'You know perhaps that another proposal has been made to us on which we have yet to give an answer.'

Haldane nodded. 'So I believe.'

'That must still be taken into consideration.' He reached for his glass and leant back in his chair. 'But I will say this now. I have a feeling that maybe you are pretty smart, Leandros.'

'Of that I do not think there can be any doubt,' said Annika quietly.

No longer able to hide his very real interest, Nikos straightened up in his chair once more. Then, his head bent over the drawing, he pointed to a feature on it and said to Elena with a note of excitement in his voice. 'The taverna. It would look good with these alterations, wouldn't it?'

Elena gave Haldane a happy, grateful smile. 'Yes, Nikos,' she said humbly. 'It would look very good.'

Haldane was feeling very satisfied and not a little pleased with himself. He looked across at Annika and saw that she was regarding him and smiling quietly. He raised his glass to her in salute.

The music filled the softly lit room. Haldane sat on the settee while Annika, curled up on a large cushion lying at his feet, rested her back against it. A small log fire burned in the stone fireplace and, caught up in the sweeping, melancholic magic of Elgar's *Violin Concerto*, they both gazed into the flames, each cradled in the soaring ecstasy of the work and with the brilliance of Menuhin's interpretation as the background to their thoughts.

Haldane had driven Annika home after their dinner with Nikos and Elena. He had opened the car door for her and he had thanked her.

'For what?' she had asked.

'For being there. For your support. For everything.'

'I did nothing more than speak the truth,' she'd replied. 'What I truly believe.'

And then she had asked him in for a drink. Haldane had hesitated but only because he knew the dangers there were in accepting her invitation. Alone with her in her house, with the doors and shutters closed against the world and sheltered from reality would he, as he must, still be able to maintain that degree of distance which so far he had managed to keep between them.

But then, seeing his hesitation, she had said, 'Please, Leandros.' And it was almost a plea and he had known that he could not refuse her; that there was no excuse he could make. But more than anything else he wanted to be with her and hold on to the comfort and joy of her presence and cherish being with her for just a little longer. Whatever the risk. So he had accepted, and gratefully.

While he had chosen the music she had poured brandy for them both and then they had settled down before the fire to listen to it.

Now, as the concerto soared to its end through the meditative but naked emotion of the accompanied *cadenza*, they were lost in its beauty; each carried away into another dimension beyond space and time and each in a web of their own dreams; separate but together. And at peace.

The music stopped and the record player switched itself off but for a long time the spell remained unbroken.

It was Annika who spoke first. 'Such longing, Leandros,' she said quietly, still staring into the fire. 'Such passion. No Greek could have written that.'

Haldane was faintly surprised by this. 'With all their

passion,' he said. 'With all the longing they know. What about your *mantinades* here on Crete. They are so full of both.'

Annika nodded. 'Yes. And in a *mantinade,* in all real Greek music, we express those things. But wildly, heedlessly, recklessly. And by so freely spending passion and longing it has become our common currency. That concerto is the anguish of a more disciplined soul. A lonelier one. And more moving perhaps because of that. It is the cry of a Northern European soul.' She looked at him. 'It is your music.'

'But it speaks to you,' said Haldane.

'Because it is universal. That is its genius. And each time you hear it, it is a new revelation of yet another truth. But even the best *mantinade* is the same truth told over and over again. That concerto is a well. Greek music is a spring.'

She looked back into the fire again. Haldane regarded her thoughtfully. He sipped his brandy and then he asked, 'Could you live in Northern Europe, Annika?'

'I have,' she said. 'For more than one year I was in England. Studying.'

'And were you happy there?'

'No. Because my life was empty.' She picked up a poker and stirred the logs in the fire. 'There was nothing shared in it. If there had been, yes I would have been happy.' Again she looked up at him. 'And if there was now I could live anywhere. Places are not important, are they?'

'No,' said Haldane softly and without taking his eyes from hers.

'Only people.'

He nodded. 'Yes. Only people.'

Unable to resist the impulse which suddenly swept over him, Haldane leant forward, gently tilted her head to him and kissed her. Then, angry with himself and frowning, he pulled back a little from her but their faces remained close. He started to say something but Annika placed a finger across his lips. 'Do not say you are sorry,' she said.

'Please.'

Haldine's frown deepened. She nodded. 'I think you were going to. I would not want that.' She took her finger from his lips. And Haldane managed a quiet smile while he searched in his mind for justification and all he could come up with was: 'You are a very beautiful woman.' It sounded weak and unconvincing, and he knew it.

'If that is how I am to you then I am glad,' said Annika. 'For you are a very special man.' She put out a hand and drew his face to hers and again they kissed. And this time Haldane felt her lips part beneath his.

Oh my God, how I want you! How I need you! The thoughts raced through his mind and threatened to tear him apart but then, even as he put his arms around her, he knew that he could not, he dare not, follow through. What she was offering had a price which he could not afford. Her future. And his peace of mind. Abruptly he drew his lips away from hers and got to his feet. Annika gazed up at him, hurt and bewildered. Feeling foolish but unable to explain, Haldane moved slowly round to the far side of the fireplace and stood there staring into the flames.

Annika watched him for a while then she stood up and went to him. 'What is it?' she asked. 'What is wrong?'

'There's nothing wrong.' He glanced at his watch. 'It's late that's all. I must go.'

Frowning again and confused, she searched his face anxiously. 'You do not have to leave,' she said softly. 'You know that, don't you? I do not want you to go.'

Stricken and unable to bear the entreaty in her voice and the look in her eyes, he turned away from her. 'Good night, Annika,' he said.

Feeling exposed and wounded by his reaction, and with nothing to explain it, Annika watched him as he walked across to the French windows. Then she turned her back to him. But she could not let him go like this. She had to know why. And the questions which, over the past few weeks, his calculated reserve had raised in her mind had to be answered.

'There is something, isn't there, Leandros?' she said quietly. 'Something that is a barrier between us. Is it a ghost?'

Haldane, about to open the French windows, swung round, startled. 'Why do you say that?' he said sharply, with a note of anxiety in his voice.

Annika turned to him. 'Because there are times I think I see it in your eyes. That you are haunted. By something. By someone.'

Haldane studied her thoughtfully and then he said, 'Annika, what would you say. . .' Perhaps this was the moment for the truth. 'What if I were to tell you. . .' Then he knew that he could not do it, dare not risk it. He broke off and shrugged helplessly.

'To tell me what?' she begged.

He shook his head. 'Nothing,' he said. 'There is nothing to tell. Goodnight.'

He opened the French windows and walked out into the night.

'Where do I put my name?' asked Katerina Matakis wearily.

She was seated at the table in the sitting room of the house in Neapolis.

'There,' said Babis Spiridakis, indicating the place on the official form spread out on the table in front of her. Laboriously, Katerina signed her name. The lawyer moved it aside and put a duplicate in its place. 'And this one.'

Katerina signed and then sighed as Spiridakis presented her with the triplicate. 'And now this. It is the last,' he added encouragingly.

With another sigh, Katerina put her name to the form. 'Taxes, taxes,' she grumbled. 'Thank God I have an honest lawyer.

Spiridakis smiled and gathered the forms together. 'A friend,' he said.

Katerina shook her head. An honest lawyer. I have

known one friend to cheat another in business.' She looked up at him. 'And so have you.'

Spiridakis laughed. Katerina studied him and then smiled. 'But yes, Babis. A friend also. A good friend. To me and to all my family.'

'I hope so.' The lawyer put the documents into his briefcase. 'And for many years to come I trust. As to the property in Anoyia, I will write to Prevelakis. I am sure that he will be reasonable.'

Katerina stood up and crossed to the window. 'Good,' she said absently, staring out through the slats in the shutters.

Spiridakis had sensed Katerina's strange, uneasy mood from the moment she had let him into the house and she had been distracted throughout his visit. Her mind had never really been on the business which he had called to discuss with her. He regarded her with some concern. 'You are looking tired, Katerina,' he said.

She turned to him and nodded. 'I know. I am. I do not sleep easily. I have much on my mind.'

'What is it that troubles you?' he asked.

'Many things. My daughter.'

The lawyer gave her a look of surprise. 'Annika!' he said. 'She is well. You have nothing to worry about there.'

'She is a foolish child.'

Spiridakis smiled and gently corrected her. 'A woman, Katerina. Foolish perhaps, yes. At times. But then which of us is not?'

'She has been spoilt by the world outside Crete,' muttered the old woman. 'She is stubborn and headstrong.'

'Spoilt?' Spiridakis shook his head. 'No.' Then he continued. 'Stubborn and headstrong, yes. She goes her own way. She always has. But when the path she chose has been difficult and she has stumbled not once has she complained. And when she has fallen she has picked herself up again. She has great courage.'

'Perhaps,' Katerina admitted grudgingly. 'But she is obstinate. And her obstinacy has already once ruined her life. And now . . .' She broke off. She had no wish to pursue the subject any further Not with Babis Spiridakis anyway.

The lawyer frowned. 'And now?' he probed.

Katerina shrugged. 'She does not take my advice,' she replied offhandedly. 'She does not listen. And Elena. I am also concerned about her. From what I hear she still refuses to sell the taverna.'

Spiridakis gave her a wry smile. 'You seldom leave this house, Katerina. But is there anything that happens in Crete that does not reach your ears?'

'Little. Of importance. And nothing that concerns the family.' Again she sighed. 'Elena should not humiliate Nikos so. She must show him more respect,' she insisted. 'He is her husband. She should follow him in all things. That is the duty of every woman. Why does she not agree to the sale, Babis? Is the price offered not a good one?'

'Very good.'

'Then why?'

Spiridakis shrugged. 'I am not sure.'

Katerina crossed to him and put a hand on his arm. 'Talk to her, Babis,' she pleaded. 'Persuade her. As my friend. As her godfather. For her own good.'

Spiridakis smiled sympathetically at her. 'If I was convinced of that,' he said. 'But in any case that may not be necessary.' Katerina gave him a questioning look and again he smiled. 'You see,' he went on, wagging a finger at her. 'You do not hear everything after all. Another offer has been made. One which pleases Elena. And Nikos I think.'

Katerina scowled, displeased at having been caught out as not being up to date on this new development. 'Oh,' she enquired stiffly. 'And what is this offer?'

'A partnership. Capital to invest in the taverna and turn it into a very profitable business.'

'Partnership,' repeated the old woman, intrigued 'Who makes this offer?'

'He is a friend of mine,' said Spiridakis. And then added to reassure her. 'A good man. His name is Alan Haldane. The one who fought with us during the war and who we named Leandros. You must know him.'

Slowly Katerina turned from him, moved back to the window and stared out of it once more. Her face was drawn and her mouth set in a hard, tight line. 'Yes,' she said almost in a whisper. 'I know him.'

Haldane hurried down the stairs to answer the front doorbell. He had not seen Annika for three days. And, although she did not normally ring the bell, it was just possible that after their last meeting she would be hesitant about entering as informally as in the past. And understandably too. He opened the door and reacted with an expression of stunned shock and surprise. The woman standing on the doorstep was not Annika. It was Lorna Matthews, a bulging carrier bag from the Heathrow duty free shop in one arm and a suitcase at her feet.

'Hello, Alan,' she said quietly and with a shy smile. 'Well, here I am.'

CHAPTER TWELVE

Lorna kissed Haldane lightly on the lips, picked up her suitcase and stepped into the room.

She's looking good, thought Haldane. Chic as always and with her blonde hair cut short in a style which suited her so well, her well-rounded and voluptuous body as desirable as ever. But what the hell is she doing here?

He followed her into the room, leaving the front door open. Lorna turned to him, put down her case and thrust the carrier bag into his arms.

'Here,' she said. 'I've brought you something. Two bottles of scotch and some of that tobacco you like.'

It was then that Haldane saw how keyed up and diffident she was. She did not give him a chance to thank her for the gifts but, looking about her and admiring the room, she continued without pausing.

'What a charming place! It's lovely! It really is. You know I couldn't believe it. Not at first. Not when your telegram arrived.'

Haldane frowned and set the carrier bag down on the table. She spun round to face him, smiling exitedly. 'But it was true. And here I am. Let me look at you. You look marvellous.'

Still totally bewildered, Haldane nevertheless managed to smile. 'You too,' he said weakly.

'Living in Crete is obviously good for you.'

The words tumbled from her in a flow which allowed for no interruption. She pointed to the carrier bag.

'Well, let's have a drink, eh, darling? To celebrate. Frankly I can do with one. I'm all butterflies. And I'm talking too much. I know it. But I can't help it. I'm happy. Happy but just a little bit embarrassed. And this'll give you a laugh. Shy!' She nodded. 'It's true. Shy! Silly isn't it? But don't worry, it'll pass. A drink would be nice though.'

'Of course,' said Haldane. He took the carrier bag over to the sideboard, removed one of the bottles of whisky from it and, while Lorna watched, poured two drinks.

'Staight?' he asked.

'You've forgotten,' Lorna said with a smile and teasing him. 'Water. The same again.'

'I'll get some,' he said. 'Ice?'

She shook her head. 'No thanks.'

Haldane went into the kitchen and took a jug from a shelf. Oh my God, he thought as he filled it from the tap, she can't have got my letter.

Lorna was studying the photograph of his wife when he returned. She looked across at him, smiled and put the photograph down again. He added some water to the whiskies, picked them up, crossed to her and handed one of them to her.

'Thank you, darling,' she said. She toasted him. 'Cheers.'

'Cheers.'

Lorna sipped her drink. 'I bet you were surprised to get my letter, weren't you?'

Haldane nodded. 'Yes. Very.'

Still very nervous and sipping her drink, Lorna started on a tour of the room, picking things up from time to time and examining them but without really seeing them and all the while keeping up an incessant flow of bubbling talk. 'I got your address from your brother. Had to really persuade him. He wasn't keen to give it to me. And he could have been so right.' She briefly studied the drawing of the caique on the drawing board. 'I see you're still working on boats.' She looked at him and smiled. 'I'm glad. You wouldn't be happy doing anything else.' Then she continued on her slow tour of the room. 'Yes, David could have been so right. I said to myself when I wrote to you, 'Lorna Matthews, you're crazy, do you know that?

112

Crazy. He might just not want to know. Maybe he couldn't care less. All he'll think is that you're being pushy and that'll put him right off.' She glanced at him and her expression was serious. 'But I had to let you know.' And then she was off again, an uninterruptible torrent of chatter. 'You see, this feller who's asked me to marry him, he's nice, he's kind, he's considerate. And he loves me. I'm not in love with him but he'd make a good husband. Emotional security and all that bit. And, well,' she shot him a wry look, 'I'm forty-three for God's sake. And with two marriages on the rocks already I'm not exactly the woman-of-the-month choice. Could be that someone like Philip isn't going to come along again. But with us it was different, wasn't it? We really had something going for us, didn't we? Something special. And for four whole years. Four wonderful years I can't forget. Years I'll never forget. And all I could hope was that you hadn't forgotten them either.'

She stopped pacing and turned to him. 'I've stored up those years, Alan. I've lived off them ever since. Like a squirrel through a long winter. And they had to have meant something to you. It wasn't just an affair, was it? It was much more than that. We...' She shrugged. 'Well, we really sort of blended, didn't we? You know,' she went on with a laugh, 'I can't think of a damned thing we didn't agree about. And we were good for each other, weren't we? In every way. That's why, when Philip asked me to marry him, before I said yes I had to know. I had to be sure that there wasn't a hope in hell of us ever getting together again.' She held up her glass. 'So with my pride suitably anaesthetised by scotch, I wrote you that letter. I can tell you I regretted it the next morning when the anaesthetic had worn off. I thought, you damned fool! What the hell have you done? Coming straight out with it like that. Suppose you just embarrass him out of his mind. Suppose he doesn't care.' She paused and studied him, still wounded by the thought. 'Suppose he laughs.'

She shrugged and, smiling once more, crossed to him.

'But it was too late,' she continued. 'The letter had gone by then. All I could do was pray that I hadn't made a complete fool of myself and bite my fingernails.' She put her glass down on the table, opened her handbag and, with a theatrical flourish, took out the telegram. 'And then I got this.' She read it triumphantly. 'Seat booked for you on Olympic Airways flight OA 206 on 11th. All my love. Alan.'

Haldane took the telegram from her and looked at it. He frowned.

'Now you didn't have to do that, Alan,' she scolded him. 'The ticket I mean. It was good of you. Generous as always. But just a telegram saying get out here. That would have been enough. But I. . .'

This has gone far enough, thought Haldane. He put a hand on her arm and interrupted her. 'Lorna, stop. Please. Listen to me.'

She looked at him, still smiling but puzzled. He guided her over to the settee. 'Sit down,' he said. She hesitated and her smile faded a little. 'Please,' he said firmly.

She sat down on the settee. Haldane regarded her sadly. 'There's no easy way of saying this,' he said gently. 'But you have to know. This can't go on. I didn't buy a ticket for you.' He held out the telegram. 'And I didn't send this.'

Lorna stared up at him, bewildered. There was silence in the room for a moment and then she said, 'You didn't send it?'

'No.'

'And the ticket. You didn't . . .'

'No,' said Haldane.

She examined his face, desperately searching for some sign that he way playing a game with her. She shook her head disbelievingly and tried to smile. 'I don't believe it,' she said. 'You are joking, aren't you?'

Haldane sat down beside her. 'No,' he said. 'I'm not joking. It's the truth.'

'But it can't be,' Lorna cried out desperately. 'It just

can't be.'

'It is,' Haldane assured her as kindly as he could.

Lorna's face crumpled. Again she shook her head. 'But I don't understand. If you didn't send the telegram. If you didn't buy the ticket. Who did?'

'I don't know,' replied Haldane grimly. 'But I'll find out I promise you. And when I do I'll bloody well break their neck.'

Lorna was close to tears. Her expression was piteous. 'But who would do such a thing?' she asked. 'Who would be so cruel?'

'I have no idea. Not at this moment.'

'And why?'

Haldane shrugged. 'I can't imagine. I really can't explain it. I didn't tell anyone about your letter. No one else could have read it.'

Lorna frowned. 'So it has to have been you.'

'Only it wasn't,' said Haldane. 'I got your letter. I thought about it. I was touched. I wrote back to you yesterday.' He paused, and studied her face. 'To wish you luck and every happiness.'

'I see,' she said flatly.

Haldane took her hand in his. 'I'm sorry, Lorna. And even sorrier about this. And angrier than you'll ever know.'

Lorna drew her hand away from him, stood up quickly and crossed to the table. She picked up her glass of whisky and drained it. Then she turned to him and smiled weakly. 'I think I could do with another one of those,' she said. 'A large one.'

Haldane got to his feet, took her glass from her and crossed to the sideboard with it. 'This fellow, Philip,' he said, as he half filled the tumbler with whisky. 'The man who wants to marry you. Did you say anything to him before you left?'

Lorna shook her head. 'No,' she replied in a whisper. 'I wanted to see you first. To be absolutely sure.'

'Well, that's something I suppose,' said Haldane quietly, as he moved back to her with her drink.

'Is it?' she said. She began to cry. 'Is it?' Her expression was suddenly wild and anguished. 'Oh my God,' she cried, and now she was sobbing. 'No, it isn't. Not after this. Not after I thought . . .' She looked at him, her face a mask of despair and hurt. 'Oh Alan! Alan! Whoever did this? Why? Why? To let me believe . . . To let me make such a complete fool of myself.

Haldane put the glass down on the table and took her in his arms. 'Lorna, don't. Please,' he said. He held her close to him and let her cry it out. Slowly her sobs subsided than she looked up at him again and put on a brave but faint smile. 'And now I'm making an even bigger fool of myself, aren't I?' she said, wiping her face with the back of her hand.

Haldane shook his head. 'No.' He held her away from him at arms' length. 'Oh, Lorna,' he said. 'I wouldn't have had you hurt like this for anything. Believe me.'

She nodded. 'I do. It was a bastard thing to do. And that's not your style. Maybe that's why I love you.'

They studied one another and Haldane saw in her the desperate need for consolation, some kind of comfort. He drew her to him again and kissed her, gently at first but then, as she responded, with a hunger that matched her own.

It was as he lifted his face from Lorna's that Haldane was suddenly aware that they were no longer alone. He shot a look in the direction of the front door. Annika was standing in the open doorway, her expression one of pain and embarrassment. She had stood there watching them. She had seen the kiss and she had wanted to run away but somehow she could not move. Deeply concerned, Haldane frowned.

'I'm sorry,' Annika said quietly. 'I had no idea . . . Forgive me.' She turned and moved quickly away down the steps.

Lorna gave Haldane a questioning look. He broke from the embrace and ran for the door. 'Annika!' he called.

She was almost at the bottom of the steps by the time he reached the doorway. He called again and more urgently this time. 'Annika, wait!'

She took no notice of him. She got into her car and, without looking back, drove off. Haldane watched the car until it was out of sight and then he turned and went back into the house. He closed the door behind him.

'Who is she?' asked Lorna. She was now much more in control of herself and genuinely concerned about Haldane's reaction.

'Her name's Annika Zeferis,' replied Haldane dully. Then he picked up his glass, moved to the sideboard and refilled it.

'And she's important to you?'

'She's a friend,' Haldane said dismissively. He turned and saw the disbelieving look on Lorna's face. 'I just wouldn't want her to think . . ' He shrugged. 'But it doesn't really matter.'

'Doesn't it?' she asked quietly and seeing in his eyes just how much it did matter to him. 'Do you know where she'll go now?'

'Home probably.' Haldane swallowed some of the neat whisky from his glass. He felt it burn the back of his throat.

'Then follow her,' said Lorna. 'Explain. Tell her why.'

He shook his head. 'No. There's no point. And maybe it's better this way.'

Lorna frowned. 'You want her to misunderstand?'

'It's one way out,' replied Haldane wearily.

'And that's what you're looking for? A way out.'

'Its a situation I can do nothing about.'

'Complications?'

'One or two,' said Haldane.

'Is she married?'

'Worse. But that's my problem. Or it was.'

'Was?'

'I'd say so,' said Haldane. Lorna frowned. 'Believe me, he said. 'It's best it happened like it did.' He emptied his

117

glass and put it down on the table and then he looked at her. 'Now then, what about you?' he said, changing the subject. 'What are you going to do?'

Lorna smiled wanly. 'What else? Go back to England. To Philip. He wants us to get married next month. No frills. Just a quiet affair. Is there a flight from Athens tonight?'

'I imagine so,' said Haldane. 'But that's ridiculous. You've only just arrived. You've done enough travelling for one day.'

She nodded. 'Tomorrow then.'

Haldane crossed to her. 'Stay for a while,' he said, putting on a smile. 'Have a holiday.'

Lorna studied him and then shook her head. 'No,' she said. 'I don't think that would be a good idea. And neither do you really. Tomorrow.'

She was right and Haldane knew it. He nodded. 'I'll take you to a hotel.' He started to turn from her, intending to pick up her suitcase but she put a hand on his arm and checked him. 'No, Alan,' she said quietly. He looked into her eyes. 'Not a hotel. Please.'

CHAPTER THIRTEEN

Bathed in moonlight, Haldane stood at the bedroom window and stared out into the night.

He had made love to Lorna and with passion but in a strangely detached way. Practised, used to one another and sharing a mutual need, they had reached a climax together as they had always done from the first time they had been to bed together. He had heard her cry out and he had been aware of her fingernails scoring his back. But for him it had meant little more than a release of pent-up animal desire. Afterwards he had said the things that he knew she would want him to say. And he had held her in his arms until she closed her eyes and he thought that she was asleep. Then he had carefully eased himself away from her and got out of bed and slipped on his dressing gown. Standing at the window he had been conscious for a time of her gentle breathing. And then she had gone from his mind completely and his thoughts were filled by Annika.

'Alan,' Lorna said quietly.

He heard her distantly when she said his name a second time and he pulled himself out of his reverie and turned to her. 'I'm sorry,' he said with an apologetic smile. 'I didn't mean to wake you.'

She sat up in the bed. 'I wasn't asleep. I've been watching you. You've been standing there for almost an hour.'

'That long!' said Haldane, genuinely surprised. 'It seems like only a few minutes.' And then he added by way of explanation. 'Something on my mind.'

'Someone,' she corrected. 'It's Annika, isn't it?'

Haldane walked slowly over to the bed and sat down on

the edge of it. Lorna reached for a packet of cigarettes on the bedside table, took two from it and lit them. She handed one to Haldane and then rested the ashtray on her lap.

'Tell me about it,' she said.

'There's nothing anyone can do,' he assured her.

'Perhaps not. But just the same, it might help.'

Haldane gazed into the shadows on the far side of the room. He drew deeply on his cigarette and then slowly exhaled the smoke. Then he told her. About Melina, his new found daughter and about Annika. Everything. She listened to his story without interruption and without once taking her eyes from his face. When he'd finished he picked up the ashtray from the bed and stubbed his cigarette into it and sighed. Lorna regarded him thoughtfully and sadly. 'And you really can't tell her?'

Haldane shook his head. 'If I did I'd lose her. I'm certain of that. And she'd be hurt even more. Her sister and I were lovers. Elena is my child. And how could I ever convince her that I didn't abandon Melina? She'd hate me for that alone.'

'So it's better that she thinks there's someone else, eh?'

'Well isn't it?' he said. 'There's no way she can be told the truth. That would be too cruel. I couldn't face her.'

Lorna reached for the ashtray and extinguished her cigarette. Then she looked at him again. 'My poor, poor Alan,' she said.

Haldane was still asleep when Lorna left the house the next morning. The taxi driver put her suitcase into the boot of the old Mercedes and, not without some difficulty, she told him where she wanted to go.

More than an hour later and after the driver had stopped at the police station in Neapolis to confirm his fare's destination, the taxi pulled up outside Annika Zeferis' house. Lorna got out and the driver nodded to show that he understood from her signs that he was to wait. Then she climbed the steps to the terrace.

Annika has seen the taxi arrive and she was standing in the open French windows, surprised and unwelcoming, as Lorna approached.

'May I come in?' asked Lorna without flinching under her hostile looks.

Annika frowned. 'Are you alone?' she asked.

'Yes. I have to talk to you.'

Annika hesitated and then turned and moved back into the house. Lorna took this if not as an invitation at least as permission to follow her.

'I cannot imagine what we have to talk about,' said Annika icily.

'Yesterday,' replied Lorna. 'When you found Alan and me together. We have to talk about that.'

Annika regarded her stonily. 'That is hardly any of my business, is it?' she said.

Lorna nodded. 'Yes. It is. Because you made a mistake. A big one.'

'Did I?' Annika's tone had lost none of its frigidity.

'Listen,' said Lorna. 'Alan Haldane and I had an affair. It lasted a long time but it ended three years ago. We were lovers. Were. Past tense.'

Annika studied her disdainfully. 'Oh, really,' she said with a faint and bitter smile. 'And the present indicative?'

'He was kissing me. I was upset. Close to hysteria. And yes, we went to bed together.'

Annika winced mentally but her expression did not betray her pain. 'I am sorry,' she said. 'But I do not understand. Are you here to boast? Or for confession? Either way you have come to the wrong place. I am not in the market for spice. Nor am I a priest. And it is none of my concern.'

Lorna nodded. 'Oh, but it is,' she said quietly. 'Very much so. Because Alan's in love with you.'

Annika appeared unimpressed. 'I see,' she said. 'Neither to boast nor to confess. You are a messenger, is that it?'

'No. Alan doesn't know I'm here. But that's the truth. He is in love with you. I thought it might be important to you to know that.'

Annika continued to regard her coldly and then she crossed to the side table, took a cigarette from the box and lit it. 'If it was of any interest to me, you must forgive me if I doubt it,' she said. She turned to Lorna. 'In view of what you have told me.'

Lorna sighed. 'You don't understand. Alan took me to bed last night because he was saying goodbye the way he knew I wanted him to say it. Because he's that kind of person.' She shrugged. 'That's all.'

Annika frowned. 'Goodbye?'

'Yes. I'm leaving today,' replied Lorna. 'The only reason I came in the first place is because of a very cruel and sick joke that someone played.' Annika's frown deepened. Lorna went on. 'I wrote to Alan. Out of the blue. To ask him if there was any chance of us picking up where we left off three years ago. The reply I got was a telegram saying that he'd booked me a seat on a flight yesterday. But when I arrived I found that he wasn't interested, that he didn't want to know and that he had written to me to say so. Though not quite as brutally as that I'm sure. And I also found out that Alan didn't send the telegram. Nor did he buy the ticket. And I can tell you, Crete's a helluva long way to come to get kicked in the stomach.'

Annika, who had been studying her closely, suddenly realised that she was telling the truth. 'I am sorry,' she said, her expression softening. 'Forgive me. I think I understand now. But the telegram. The ticket. Who? Why?'

'Good questions,' said Lorna bitterly. 'Alan swears he'll find out. And if he does God help whoever did it.' She glanced at her watch. 'Well, that's all I wanted to say. I must go or I'll miss my plane. And Alan will be wondering where the hell I've got to. The idea was that he'd drive me to the airport.'

Annika studied her visitor thoughtfully. 'You have to love him very much,' she said. 'To do this for him.'

'You're damned right I do,' replied Lorna defiantly.

'What is your name?'

'Lorna.'

Annika smiled. 'You have a great heart, Lorna,' she said, 'and much courage. I wish we were friends.'

Lorna laughed hollowly. 'No way,' she said. 'You've got what I want.'

'He has told you this? That he loves me.'

Lorna nodded. 'Yes. And I only came here to confirm it to you.' She paused and then continued. 'Just in case you were in any doubt.'

'There have been times when I have thought it,' said Annika.

'Well, you were right. And if you love him hold on to that thought. No matter what cause he gives you to question it. No matter what happens.' She crossed to the French windows, hesitated and then turned back to Annika. 'Be good to him. He's a fine man. And a rare one. Someone worth hanging on to. I wish to God I'd been able to.'

And then she was gone.

Haldane was at the airport searching for her in the terminal building when Lorna arrived. He spotted her and strode over to her, frowning. 'Where the hell have you been?' he demanded. 'I looked all over Elounda for you. I said I'd drive you in, didn't I?'

'Yes, but I took a taxi instead. There was something I had to do.'

Haldane gave her a puzzled, questioning look but it was clear from her expression that she was not prepared to elaborate.

'Good thing the plane was late arriving from Athens,' he muttered. 'It's only just unloading.'

And as he spoke the first of the incoming passengers came through the glass doors from the dispersal apron and into the lounge.

'Don't wait,' said Lorna. 'Please.'

Haldane was about to make a polite protest but she cut him short. 'No. I'd rather you didn't. Really,' she insisted.

He looked at her and understood. He nodded. 'Take care of yourself, Lorna,' he said quietly. He kissed her on the cheek. 'Be happy.'

'And you,' replied Lorna. She studied his face for the last time. 'But all things considered,' she went on, 'I think I'm the one with the better chance.'

Haldane shrugged and then turned and moved quickly away from her and into the rapidly swelling throng of incoming passengers.

Lorna picked up her suitcase and carried it over to the check-in desk.

It was as he was leaving the building that Haldane collided with the man. He was in his late forties, well built and good-looking but with a somewhat surly face. He was wearing an expensive and conservative business suit and carrying a briefcase. Haldane judged him to be an Athenian who had been on the plane which had recently landed.

'*Signome*,' Haldane excused himself. Without even glancing at him the man nodded his acceptance of the Englishman's apology and hailed a taxi.

As Haldane walked across to the car park, Petros Matakis settled himself into the back seat of the cab and gave the driver his mother's address in Neapolis.

'I checked.' Annika had difficulty in controlling her anger. 'It was not difficult. I went to every travel agent in Heraklion. And also to the office of Olympic Airways. It has been confirmed to me. You bought the ticket. So it was you who sent the telegram.'

Immediately on her return she had summoned Noukakis to her house and the moment he had stepped into the room from the terrace she had confronted him, inwardly seething. He looked at her sullenly.

'And your scheme almost achieved its purpose,' Annika continued. 'It would have done if it had not been for a ruly remarkable woman.'

'It was for your own good,' Noukakis countered sulkily.

Annika shook her head. 'No. It was not done from any concern for me. You did it because you are a jealous and piteful man. I thought you were my friend. I was wrong. t is true that you have always managed the refinery well or me. I shall miss you for that at least.' Noukakis cowled. 'Do not go back there,' she went on. 'Whatever money there is due to you I will see that you receive it.'

For a moment Noukakis considered giving her an argument but then he decided against it. She would not isten to anything he might have to say in his defence. And what defence did he have? Abruptly he turned on his heel and strode over to the French windows.

'This Leandros,' he said, pausing and looking back at her. 'He is the wrong man for you.'

'That must be my decision,' said Annika coldly. 'One way or the other. It was never your right to make it. And I will give you this advice, Matheos. Light a candle against Leandros ever finding out that it was you who did this to him.'

Noukakis spat out onto the terrace and then looked at her scornfully. He laughed. 'I am not afraid of him,' he snarled. 'Let him come looking for me. Better he should ight candles. And pray. Not matter what he was or what he did in Crete in the past, remember he is still a foreigner. And I have many friends. It could be that if I sneeze he catches cold. And that if I spit, he drowns.'

He was pleased to see, briefly at least, a look of concern on her face. He swaggered away across the terrace.

Petros Matakis sat across from Katerina, the wooden box standing on the table between them.

'So what is it that is so urgent, mother?' he said petulantly. 'So dark, so secret that it can not be spoken of on the telephone.'

'It is a matter of honour,' replied Katerina gravely. 'It concerns your sisters. Melina,' she crossed herself, 'may

125

her soul be at peace, and Annika. A man has come to Crete who threatens the good name of one and the happiness of the other. Who threatens us all.'

She unlocked the box, opened it and took out the three letters which Haldane had written so many years before.

CHAPTER FOURTEEN

Haldane worked on the caique until eleven o'clock, revelling in the warmth of the sun which every day grew stronger and which had already coaxed the first of the spring flowers into bloom on the slopes of the hills behind the village. Easter would see all the countryside carpeted with bright red anemones, yellow ranunculi and a host of other plants and sweet smelling herbs, so closely interwoven as to make it impossible to walk anywhere without stepping on them. But Easter was still more than two weeks away.

Haldane packed up his tools and walked slowly to the taverna, pausing as he crossed the square to buy a three-day-old copy of the *Times* from the tobacco kiosk. The price was exorbitant but it was a luxury which from time to time he allowed himself. He was disappointed to find, when he got to the taverna, that Nikos was not there. It had been a fortnight since he had put his plans for the sailing centre to him and not once had Nikos mentioned it since then and that disturbed him vaguely.

Elena welcomed him and, grown used to his daily routine, made him a cup of medium-sweet coffee without his having to ask for it. Nikos was out fishing, she told him, and would not be back until the evening. I'll talk to him then, thought Haldane, as he carried his coffee out on to the patio, see if I can't sound him out. But gently. He settled himself down at one of the tables, filled and lit his pipe and then opened his newspaper and began to read of people and events in England which now seemed unreal and irrelevant.

'My only living son,' complained Katerina scornfully. 'My eldest child. The head of the Matakis family. For

127

more than a week you have been here. And in that time what have you done? Nothing! You think only of your business in Athens and of how it is perhaps suffering because of your absence.'

Petros Matakis stood in the doorway of the kitchen and watched her as, expertly, she cut off the head of the freshly plucked chicken she was preparing for the pot.

'That is not so, mother,' he said petulantly.

'No?' she demanded, looking up and waving the blade of the knife she was using at him. 'Then tell me, how is it that the Englishman, Haldane, is still in Elounda? Living there in contentment. Building a boat. And each day growing closer to your niece, Elena, and to Annika, your sister. This man who has wronged our family so.'

Matakis frowned. 'You have told me this,' he replied and there was a note of doubt in his voice. 'But only now, when you called me here from Athens last week.'

'You have read the letters. The letters the Englishman wrote to Melina. The letters I showed you.'

'Yes.' Matakis nodded. 'But those are not the letters of a casual, uncaring seducer. They are full of tenderness, of yearning. There is great feeling in them.'

Katerina shook her head despairingly. 'Dear God!' she said. 'Have you lost your spine in Athens, Petros? Where is your anger? Your rage at what he did? It must be plain to you from what he wrote that your sister and this man, who some call Leandros, were lovers.'

'Probably. And in that, perhaps they were wrong,' said Matakis.

'Perhaps! You doubt it? The Englishman took her. And she was only a child.'

Matakis sighed. 'She would have been eighteen years old,' he said patiently. 'A woman. Could it not be that she gave herself to him freely and from her love for him?'

'He dishonoured her,' Katerina insisted grimly, as she slit the skin of the chicken along the underside of the neck and began to loosen it.

Matakis pursued his course of reason. 'And in none of

128

the letters is there one word about a child,' he said. 'Surely it must have been if Melina was carrying his baby she would have told him.'

'She did. She wrote to him in England.'

'How do you know this?'

His mother hesitated but only for a second or two. 'Melina told me,' she said brusquely. 'As she also confessed her sin to me. When she lay dying in the hospital four years ago. She told me these things to purge herself of the guilt which had burdened her soul for so long. The Englishman is Elena's true father. And he knows it. He has always known it. And now he has returned to Crete to make more trouble for our family.'

'Trouble?' queried Matakis. 'What trouble? He has said nothing to Elena, has he?'

Katerina removed the crop and windpipe from the chicken. She shook her head. 'No. But he could,' she postulated. 'If he thought it would be to his advantage.' She paused in her work and looked across at him again. 'And worse. Annika is attracted to him. And he sees much of her. He could destroy her as he destroyed Melina. You have spoken to her since I called you here. You know her feelings for him.'

Matakis shrugged. 'She has said very little to me about him.' And then he went on thoughtfully. 'But yes, it is plain enough. When she does speak of him her eyes tell their own story.'

His mother nodded. 'So she is at risk. And Elena also. While you, brother to one and uncle to the other, do nothing. As for me, I am only an old woman. I can only curse him and this I have done. In the name of God and also in the names of all the old gods. But you must work with the Almighty. Be the instrument of Zeus in seeing that my curses bear fruit.'

'But what can I do, mother?' Matakis sighed. 'You will not permit me to tell both of them the truth.'

'No,' Katerina said adamantly. 'For Elena's sake. For the sake of the family. To protect your dead sister's

129

honour. The truth must remain a secret known only to you and to me.'

'And to the Englishman,' Matakis added quietly.

Katerina shot a look at him. 'Yes. And that is why he must leave Crete. Why you must force him to go.' With a quick flick of the knife she made an incision in the vent end of the bird lying on the table.

Matakis gave a helpless shrug. 'How?'

Katerina regarded him and made little or no effort to conceal her contempt. 'How!' she exclaimed. 'You ask me that. Your blood may have thinned in the air of Athens but it is still Cretan blood. With such a question you shame me, Petros. You shame yourself and you shame the name of Matakis. How! Do you think that your father would have needed to ask such a thing of me? He would have known what he had to do. Besides, you know the answer already. You must go up against this Englishman. In everything he does. In everything he plans to do.'

Matakis looked at her, stunned and disbelieving. 'Vendetta!' he said incredulously.

Katerina nodded. 'What else? It is demanded of you. However little stomach you may have for it.' And then she added quietly and in a matter-of-factly. 'And if all else fails, then you must kill him.'

She reached with her hand into the chicken and with one brisk movement disembowelled it.

'The story of the world does not make happy reading these days.'

Haldane lowered his newspaper. Annika was standing only a little way off from him. She was smiling.

'So I have no regrets for disturbing you,' she added.

'Annika!' Haldane exclaimed, delighted to see her.

This was not their first meeting since Lorna Matthews' departure. Soon after she had left, Annika had come to his house and she had acted as if nothing had happened and she had not mentioned Lorna's visit to her. So all was well again between them but for the past three days she had been in Athens.

Haldane folded the *Times* and put it down on the table. 'When did you get back?'

'Late last night.' She sat down beside him.

'Coffee? A drink?'

Annika shook her head. 'No thank you. I met Babis in Heraklion this morning. He told me how much progress you have made with the boat. I could not wait to see for myself.' She looked at him and smiled again. 'I also came to say hello to you. I could not wait any longer to do that either.'

Her eyes met his and Haldane held her gaze. 'I'm glad,' he said simply. 'Hello.'

'Hello, Leandros.'

It was Haldane who looked away first. 'Well, have you seen it?' he enquired, adopting a light-hearted tone of voice.

'Yes. I have just come from the beach.'

'What do you think?'

'That you should be very proud of yourself. Such a task. So well done. And all alone.'

Haldane shook his head. 'Not alone,' he said. 'Alexis helps me. He is now my apprentice. He hammers well.' Annika laughed. 'It is nearly finished,' he went on. 'Another week. Two at the most.'

'The launching will be a very special occasion. It has to be,' she insisted. 'And it must be done with great style.'

'A bottle of champagne?'

She laughed and nodded. 'Of course. The best.'

'And you shall christen her,' said Haldane.

Annika studied him for a moment, suddenly serious. Then she smiled again gently. 'Thank you. I would like that. What name have you chosen?'

'*The Knot,*' replied Haldane quietly.

Again their eyes met and again they held each other's gaze.

'*The Knot,*' mused Annika. She nodded. 'Yes. That is a good name. The knot which binds you to Crete, eh?'

'Which binds me to many things,' said Haldane, his eyes still on hers.

Once more he looked away from her. He picked up his coffee cup and took a sip from it. 'How was Athens?' He asked conversationally.

Annika pulled a face. 'Tiring. Three days of business, business, business. And very little to show for it I am afraid.'

'I'm sorry.'

'It is not easy for me,' she said. 'Previously Matheos dealt with all the negotiations with the shippers. I merely approved them. But until the new man I have appointed is free to start work...' She shrugged.

'Matheos was a good manager, wasn't he?' Haldane asked.

Annika nodded. 'Excellent.'

'Then why did you get rid of him?'

She frowned and then said gravely. 'He acted foolishly. Out of spite. He tried to hurt someone. Someone I care for. And in doing so he betrayed my friendship for him. He had to go. I had no choice.'

'I'm sorry,' said Haldane.

Annida dismissed Matheos and the memory of his betrayal from her mind and smiled again. 'Did you know that my brother, Petros, is here in Crete again?'

Haldane shook his head. 'No. He's been away then?'

'For many years. In Athens.'

'He has returned for good?'

'No. To visit our mother.' Annika smiled ruefully. 'I think it must be that his conscience troubles him.' Haldane gave her a puzzled, questioning look. 'We have seen little of him since he left,' she explained. 'He has been too busy making money and becoming important.'

'And is he important?'

She nodded. 'To Petros he is.'

'And to you?'

Annika smiled. 'He is my brother. I love him.' Then she added thoughtfully. 'But I am also sorry for him.'

'Oh,' said Haldane. 'Why?'

'He is a man who has forsaken the old horizon but who, I think, has not yet found another,' she said.

'As you have, you mean?'

'Yes.'

'You've seen your brother?'

'Yes,' said Annika. 'He came to my house the day before I went to Athens.' She frowned slightly. 'But it was a strange reunion. He seemed uncomfortable with me. We talked but said nothing.'

'Perhaps I'll meet him,' prompted Haldane.

Annika nodded. 'Yes. That would please me. You shall both come to dinner with me. But not tomorrow. Tomorrow you and I are going up into the mountains.'

'Are we indeed?' exclaimed Haldane in mock affront at her temerity. 'You have decided?'

'That you need a rest from your work on the boat, yes,' she replied firmly. 'That a change of scene would be good for you, yes.' She smiled. 'You agree?'

'What if I said no?' he teased.

Annika shrugged. 'I would insist,' she said stubbornly. And then she switched to pleading. 'Please. A day off. A day away from business for me, from Elounda for you. From everything and everyone that has a claim on us.' She paused and then added, 'And together.'

Haldane hesitated but not for long. The idea appealed to him enormously despite the reservations he still had about their relationship. He smiled and nodded. 'No argument. I agree. And gratefully.'

Annika clapped her hands delightedly. 'Good,' she cried. 'You will enjoy the day I promise you.'

'Where are we going?'

'To the place where I was born. To the village where my mother and father were born and where they were married. You will see. It is beautiful. You will like it.' She smiled. 'And it has a beautiful name. It is called Dhafnai.'

It was later that same morning that Matheos Noukakis

133

brought Katerina the news which his cousin who worked at Heraklion airport had been so eager to tell him on the telephone.

Katerina thought at first that he had come to ask her if she had been successful in persuading Annika to give him back his job. Noukakis had freely confessed to her the reason why Annika had dismissed him and that had pleased her. For she saw in him that she had at least one reliable ally against Haldane and that he hated the Englishman almost as much as she did, even if for a totally different reason. He was to be encouraged, cultivated even, for the time might come when she would need him and could use him. Besides, despite his obsequiousness which sometimes irritated rather than flattered her, she liked the man and she was genuinely sorry to have to tell him that her appeal to Annika on his behalf had been to no avail.

Noukakis thanked her humbly and gratefully for trying but explained that that was not the reason why he had called. Then he passed on to her the information which his cousin had given him on the telephone. 'I felt certain that you would want to know this, *Kyria* Matakis,' he said.

Katerina's reaction was first one of shock which quickly developed through alarm and distraction into furious and calculated venom. 'Dear Lord in heaven,' she lamented, raising her eyes to the ceiling. 'Why have you done this to me? Are my sins such that you must add further weight to the cross I bear?' She took a bunch of keys from one of the drawers in the cabinet and gave them to Noukakis. She told him to open the garage and bring her car round to the front door of the house and wait for her. Noukakis obeyed her eagerly and without question.

'Where are you going?' Petros asked her.

'Where else?' she snapped. 'To see Father Kaphatos.' Matakis offered to go with her but she shook her head. 'This thing must not happen. It cannot happen.' And then she added scathingly, 'And I thank God that in this at least I do not have to rely on you to make sure of that, my son. For this I can do alone.' Her lips tightened determindly. 'And I will.'

Two hours later the old Citroen, with Noukakis at the wheel and Katerina sitting regally in the back, pulled up outside the door of the priest's house.

Noukakis' knock was answered by Father Kaphatos himself, a short man in his middle fifties. His reaction on seeing his visitor was one of surprise then, adopting an attitude of great deference and respect, he ushered her inside.

And the word spread quickly through the small village. And the word was that *Kyria* Katerina was back again in Dhafnai.

CHAPTER FIFTEEN

Haldane was enchanted by Dhafnai from the moment they drove into it. He parked the Fiat in the shade of a pepper tree on one side of the small square in the centre of the village, got out and opened the passenger door for Annika.

It had been an exhilarating journey up into the mountains, driving with the hood down, negotiating the tight bends and all around them the wild countryside of the Cretan uplands saturated in mellow spring sunlight. Often they had had to slow to a crawl to edge past or gently nudge their way through flocks of sheep or goats herded by lean, alert dogs and men in sturdy knee boots and baggy, blue breeches with yellow fringed, black bandannas wound around their heads. On the lower slopes they had passed women in homespun dresses and with dark scarves tied over their hair and draped so as to conceal the lower half of their faces, working patches of rust red soil among gnarled and ancient olive trees while further on from them an old man guided a wooden plough drawn by two oxen. And all of them, shepherds, the women and the ploughman, had waved and called out a greeting.

This was Crete as Haldane remembered it. Here, as in Sfakia, nothing had changed. The coastal strip with its proliferation of hotels and holiday villas seemed a million miles away and in another, far less attractive, age. He was content and at peace with himself. And so was Annika. As they had driven she had sung some of the traditional songs of the island. Whenever he could, Haldane had joined in and she had laughed gaily on the many occasions when he had had difficulty in remembering the words or managing the Cretan dialect. It was a good and happy time on the road and Haldane, as if subconsciously aware that the happiness could not last, had driven slowly so as to linger in it, fearing also that, despite all that Annika had told him about it, Dhafnai might, after the unspoilt beauty alongside the twisting road which led to it, be something of a disappointment.

Looking around the square of the remote, mountain village, though, Haldane could see that his fear had been groundless. Dhafnai, too, had remained largely unchanged by the twentieth century.

There were fewer than fifty white-washed houses nestling in a fertile hollow of orange, lemon and olive groves amid fields bright green after the winter rain and the melting river of snow. The houses, with narrow alleyways between them, were mainly boxed in around the square with only a handful of them straggling out onto the gently rising ground beyond, one slope of which was crowned by a squat, Byzantine chapel, its gold-painted cupola reflecting and refracting the sunlight.

The square itself was dominated by an ancient stone well and drinking fountain from which, as he watched, Haldane saw two women draw water into earthenware *stamnoi*, identical to those depicted in Minoan frescoes, then carry them away on their shoulders through the flock of goats being driven across the square by another, older woman assisted by a beautiful but solemn-faced child who Haldane suspected was probably her grandson. On the opposite side of the square from where he had parked the Fiat was the local taverna, its door open to a dark interior and with half a dozen men sitting at tables outside it playing tavli.

There were other villagers about in the square; women who had been standing talking until the arrival of the car had diverted them from their gossip; three women sitting spinning on the front steps of their houses and a fourth wrapped in a shawl against what was, to the local people at least, the still chill air of early spring, preparing vegetables for the midday meal. Two old men sitting together on the ground, their backs against a wall, were

137

asleep. It was a scene which in minor detail only differed little from any mountain village in Crete over the centuries and Haldane revelled in it. But he too felt the difference in temperature at that altitude and he saw Annika shiver as a breeze fluttered the leaves of the pepper tree, so he reached into the car for his jacket and her woollen cardigan. Then they made their way slowly across the square.

They were the object of much curiosity and interest. Annika had been recognised immediately by the villagers and all acknowledged her with a wave, a smile or a polite greeting. Over polite, over respectful, thought Haldane. Their attitude towards her was uncharacteristically deferential. True she had made good outside the village and she was successful in business but he sensed more than mere admiration in their greetings. He even imagined he detected a trace of awe, if not fear. But if this was so Annika was either clearly accustomed to it or oblivious to it. As she also seemed unaware of the whispering that was going on all around them. Probaby no more than idle chatter and speculation about who she was with, Haldane conjectured. But there was a note of urgency and gravity to the whispers which did not fit in with that theory. He shrugged mentally and decided there was nothing more behind it than exitement at the visit of a stranger which, in a village as isolated as Dhafnai, would be rare event.

However Annika was as surprised as he was when the old woman herding the flock of goats broke away from them, hobbled over to Annika, took her hand, kissed it and then looked up into her face with an expression of sorrow and sympathy. She mumbled something which Haldane did not understand and then, with a nod to the Englishman, moved away again in slow pursuit of the flock which her grandson had, by now, driven across to the far side of the square.

Annika frowned.

'What did she say?' he asked her.

'She said 'Such a sin! And against us all. It shall not

happen', replied Annika, looking puzzled.

'What does she mean?'

'I do not understand.' She shrugged dismissively and smiled. 'Who knows. The people here are very superstitious.' And that explanation seemed to satisfy her.

Taking his arm, she guided Haldane through the village. It was a short tour. There was not much to see. They wandered through the narrow alleyways and in one of them Haldane noticed that a woman, sitting in her open doorway, greeted Annika and then crossed herself as they passed. They visited the chapel, obviously fairly recently and extensively restored, and Annika was pleased by his enthusiasm and knowledgeable admiration of the work that had been done on it and his genuine appreciation of both its interior and exterior beauty. She was clearly very happy about his reaction to Dhafnai in general.

Finally she led him a little way out of the village and up a narrow path to a small, old and ramshackle house which stood alone amid some olive trees. It appeared to be unoccupied but Annika stopped four of five yards away from it and pointed. 'Well you have seen the chapel in which I was christened and now here is the house which my grandfather built. The house in which, for many years, my mother and father lived. The house in which I was born.'

Haldane gave her a look of astonishment. From all that he heard and from what he had seen for himself this simple peasant home in no way fitted into the present lifestyle and wealth of the Matakis family. Annika read his thoughts. 'My father was very poor then,' she explained. 'He had only this house and a little land. But later things changed. He was very clever. And he worked hard.'

Haldane gazed thoughtfully at the house again. 'He must have been quite a man, your father.'

Annika nodded. 'Yes,' she replied quietly. 'He was.'

He turned to her. 'So where now?' He smiled and then added jokingly, 'To the diamond mine he discovered?'

Annika laughed. 'No diamond mine. Just a great deal of

139

sweat. A sharp mind and more than a little cunning I think.' And then, suddenly serious, she frowned as though remembering things and events from the past; times of troubles and difficulties which still haunted her. 'Money, position, respect. For these things my father was hungry,' she added staring into space and Haldane detected a note of bitterness in her voice. And then, conscious that he was looking at her, she shook her head dismissing the ghosts of the past.

'And so am I.' She smiled. 'Hungry. So now we eat, eh?'

They turned from the house and strolled back to the village and into the taverna where the proprietor, a fat, smiling man wearing a vest, trousers, plimsolls and a far from spotless apron, hurried forward to greet them.

'Welcome, *Kyria* Annika. You honour me,' he said with a slight bow.

'Thank you, Christos,' replied Annika graciously and faintly embarrassed. She indicated Haldane. 'This is a friend of mine. He is from England.'

'A friend of *Kyria* Annika,' he said flowerily, 'is a friend of all of us here in Dhafnai.'

Then he led them to a table. Haldane looked around. The taverna was typical of those to be found in any village on Crete as yet undiscovered by tourists; short on comfort and cleanliness, long on atmosphere and hospitaility.

'Do you like *kokoretsi?*' Annika asked him.

Haldane nodded. It was a long time since he'd eaten the dish of offal wrapped around a spit and grilled over a charcoal fire which was a speciality in Crete, particularly during the Easter festivities.

'But should we?' he asked in English. 'It's not very devout. In Lent. We should be fasting.'

Annika frowned, clearly afraid that she'd given offence. 'I had no idea that you had such strong feelings on religious observance,' she replied.

'I don't,' Haldane reassured her.

Annika was relieved. 'Neither do I.' And then she

added, 'I regret to say.

'But if it upsets anyone...' Haldane shrugged.

Annika shook her head. 'As far as Christos is concerned, he'll be only too glad of the business.'

She gave the proprietor their order. He nodded approvingly and scuttled away. He returned almost immediately with an opened bottle of wine and two glasses which he put down on the table in front of them. And then he disappeared once more into the kitchen at the back of the building.

As Haldane filled their glasses, Annika glanced around the taverna. There were not more than a dozen tables, most of them occupied by men from the village and they were all staring unashamedly, not out of any lack of politeness but prompted by their obvious respect for her and by a genuine concern for the well-being and satisfaction of both of them.

Annika picked up her wine and raised it in salute to the assembly. '*Yassou*,' she said.

The men smiled and lifted their glasses in response. '*Yamass*,' they choroused.

The *kokoretsi* was excellent and Haldane savoured it along with a crisp and delicious salad dotted with *feta* cheese which Christos had also prepared for them.

'It is good?' Annika enquired anxiously and looking up from her plate.

'Very good,' Haldane replied and kissed the tips of his fingers in a gesture of appreciation. She was pleased. He sipped his wine. 'Do you come to Dhafnai often?'

'Not as often as I would like to.' She pulled a face. 'Or, as I should perhaps. I have not been here for more than a year.'

'Well, obviously everyone's very pleased to see you. A royal welcome.'

Annika shrugged. 'They are kind to me. Most of them have known me since I was a child. Besides, they are my people.'

They heard the motor scooter roaring across the square and then stop outside the taverna and, together with everyone else, they looked across at the doorway enquiringly as the rider burst in. He was short and thickset and clearly agitated and excited. He paused just inside the doorway and looked around. He frowned when he saw Annika and Haldane and seemed to hesitate. Then he moved quickly through the tables and whispered something urgently to Christos. The eyes of all of the other men in the taverna were fixed on the pair of them.

Alarmed, Christos shot a look across at Haldane and Annika. Then, while his informant hurried out of the taverna again, he moved out quickly from behind the bar and, in a low, inaudible voice, passed on what he had been told to those sitting at the table nearest to him. The news spread from table to table in undertones and as it did so the men's faces took on expressions of anger, concern and resolution. Haldane and Annika exchanged bewildered looks. Annika shrugged.

Christos and a man from one of the tables crossed to the doorway and, standing well back and out of sight from the square but with a good view of it themselves, gazed out into the sunlight.

There was an edgy, expectant silence in the taverna.

From outside came the sound of an approaching car. The car stopped and a door banged. Christos and his companion maintained their watch on the square.

Now Haldane and Annika seemed to have been almost totally forgotten by the other customers; their attention was on the doorway.

The silence was at last broken by Christos. 'He is coming here,' he muttered and he and the man standing beside him turned from the door and moved hastily back down the length of the taverna.

On Christos' announcement, the atmosphere in the place suddenly became charged with menace. Haldane frowned. 'What is it?' he asked Annika. 'What's going on?'

She shook her head and then called across to the proprietor, 'What is it, Christos? What is happening? Who is coming?'

At first Christos seemed reluctant to tell her but then, realising that he had no alternative, he crossed to their table and, after glancing apprehensively at Haldane, cupped his hand to Annika's ear and whispered something to her. As he did so her expression became grave and set hard. She nodded solemnly. Christos moved away from the table and back behind the bar.

Annika gave Haldane an anxious look and bit her lip. She was clearly not sure how to handle the situation. Then she decided. She gathered up her scarf and handbag from the empty chair beside her. 'We should leave,' she said firmly.

'Leave!' exclaimed Haldane, astounded. 'We haven't finished eating.'

'Please, Leandros,' she urged.

'No,' he said stubbornly and beginning to get angry. 'Not without an explanation.'

Annika frowned deeply and desperately searched her mind for one. 'I have to get back,' she said sharply. 'I have a meeting at the factory this afternoon and I must not be late for it.' Then she challenged, 'Is that reason enough?'

She was lying and Haldane knew it. 'Frankly, no.'

She leaned forward across the table and put her hand on his. She was about to say something further and then the stranger entered the taverna and she knew it was too late.

He was tall and athletic looking with a deeply tanned, open, friendly face beneath a shock of blond hair. He was wearing a pair of slacks and a jazzy, open-necked shirt under a light cotton windcheater. Haldane judged him to be in his middle thirties. The man looked around and smiled.

'Good day,' he said and his accent was unmistakably Australian.

Annika stared down at her plate but Haldane saw the looks of unconcealed hostility with which the men in the

143

taverna responded to the stranger's greeting. And their expressions unnerved him almost as much as they did the Australian, who frowned. He was clearly unprepared for such a reception but he did not retreat before it. Instead he moved further into the taverna and looked around again. Christos and the other villagers continued to stare at him sullenly.

Haldane glanced at Annika but she did not look up. Then he caught the Australian's eye, smiled weakly and nodded a greeting to him. But this did little if anything to ease his obviously growing discomfiture. However he stood his ground and forced a grin.

'Anyone here speak English?' he asked. There was no reply. The Australian's grin faded.

Haldane scowled and shot another look at Annika. Surely she, at least, would offer her services as interpreter. But she made no move to do so and did not even raise her head. 'Annika,' he prompted her. Still she did not look up. It was almost as if she had not heard him.

Haldane was now as much angered by her rudeness as he was bewildered. He got to his feet, crossed to the Australian, smiled and put out his hand. 'Hello,' he said pleasantly. 'Alan Haldane.'

The man gave a sigh of relief and shook hands with him. 'Tony Viglis,' he said. And then he added, 'A pom, eh?'

Haldane nodded. 'And you have to be an Australian,' he replied with a smile.

'Right. True blue.' Viglis glanced around the room. 'They're a friendly mob, aren't they?' he said grimly.

Haldane shook his head uncomprehendingly. 'They were,' he said. 'Until you arrived.'

Viglis gave him a look. 'Great,' he said. 'Thanks a bunch. Is it something my best friends should have told me?'

In spite of the atmosphere around them, Haldane managed a laugh. 'In this place? I don't think it would be noticed.'

'What is it then?

Haldane shrugged. 'God knows. Can I help.'

'Do you speak the lingo?' asked Viglis.

'Enough probably.'

'Well, I'm looking for the local priest. Father Kaphatos. I've been to his house. There's someone at home but they're not answering the door. And everyone else out there seems to have taken cover.'

Haldane turned and looked first at Christos and then at the other men at the tables. 'This gentleman,' he announced in Greek, 'is looking for Father Kaphatos. He has been to his house but no one answers. Do you know where the priest is?'

Only Christos looked embarrassed but neither he nor anyone else replied. Haldane surveyed the hostile faces around them. He could feel the tension in the taverna mounting. Then he glanced across at the table where Annika was sitting. She was still sitting, head lowered, staring at her plate and it was clear that she had no intention of intervening.

'Are you deaf?' Haldane shouted angrily in Greek. 'Didn't you hear what I said?'

And this time there was a response. One of the men sitting at the table closest to where Haldane and the Australian were standing cleared his throat noisily and then spat. And his spittle hit the toe of Viglis' right shoe.

The Australian flared, clenched his fists and swung round to the man. The man stood up and as he did so the other villagers around the room also got to their feet, their faces grim, their mood ugly and threatening. The man who had spat at Viglis stood waiting, clearly inviting the Australian to make his move. Viglis took a step towards him ready and willing to throw a punch but Haldane grabbed his arm. 'Don't,' he said. 'Can't you see, that's what they want.'

The villagers edged in a little closer. Haldane crossed quickly to Annika. 'Annika,' he demanded angrily. 'For God's sake what are they doing? What's this all about? He took her by the shoulders and shook her. 'Answer me,' he

145

shouted.

For the first time since Tony Viglis had entered the taverna Annika raised her head and looked at him but her expression was blank. 'Do not interfere, Leandros,' she said quietly and in a dull tone. 'It doesn't concern you.'

'What the hèll do you mean?' fumed Haldane. 'A stranger, a foreigner, walks into a taverna in Crete and is spat at and threatened. One man against so many. Of course it concerns me.'

Annika studied him. 'Then get him away from here,' she said flatly. 'Tell him to leave Dhafnai.'

'Why?'

Annika frowned and an urgent note entered her voice. 'Now Leandros,' she urged. 'Quickly.'

Haldane could see from her expression that there was no point in questioning her further and it was equally clear to him that she meant it when she said he should act without delay. He crossed back to the Australian. 'You drove here?' he asked.

Viglis nodded. 'Yes. In a hired car. It's parked outside.'

'I'll walk with you to it,' said Haldane.

Viglis opened his mouth to protest but Haldane cut in on him quickly and firmly, 'Don't argue.'

Viglis glanced at the faces of the men around them who had now closed in even further and took his point. Together they started to move slowly towards the door. The men were at first reluctant to break ranks and allow them through but, phased by Haldane's unexpected intervention and unsure how to cope with it, after a brief confrontation they made way for them but then, only a few paces behind, followed them to the door.

Outside the taverna there was an even bigger shock awaiting Haldane and the Australian.

A crowd which, with the exception of the very old and the very young, seemed to comprise the entire population of the village had gathered across the square from the spot where Viglis' Volkswagen was parked. The villagers were silent but their expressions were forbidding. Their mood

146

mirrored that of Christos and the customers in the taverna. In the foreground of the crowd some of the young men were carrying stones.

Haldane and Viglis exchanged anxious looks. 'For Christ's sake,' said Viglis quietly, surveying the crowd. 'What's going on here? What have I done?'

'I don't know,' replied Haldane. 'Have you ever been here before?'

'Never in my life. Hell, this is my first trip outside Australia.'

'Come on,' ordered Haldane.

Side by side they walked slowly over towards the Australian's car and as they did so, equally slowly, the crowd moved in beind them like a wave and then stopped when the two men reached the Volkswagen and stood beside it with their backs to them.

'Where are you staying?' asked Haldane trying to keep his voice level and hide the feeling of very real fear which had now gripped him.

'In Heraklion,' replied Viglis. 'The Xenia Hotel.'

The crowd moved in a little closer. Viglis made a movement as if to glance back over his shoulder.

'Don't look round,' said Haldane. 'Just get into that car and drive like hell. I'll try and find out what this is all about. I'll call you at the Xenia.'

Viglis nodded. 'Thanks.'

The first stone struck Haldane in the small of the back and he gasped with pain. The second struck the side of the car and ricocheted off it. Viglis swung round in anger and as he did so the third stone thudded on to his forehead.

With a cry, and already bleeding badly from the gash above his eye and only semi-conscious, the Australian reeled back under the impact of the blow, rolled over and slumped forward over the bonnet of the car and slid to the ground.

Now the opening shots became a barrage. Some of the stones thrown went wide but many of them hit the

147

Volkswagen and Haldane took another glancing blow on his left shoulder.

Enraged, his eyes blazing and his fury overcoming his fear, he quickly bent down, picked up three of the stones lying nearby and then savagely hurled one of them back. One of the young men in the front of the crowd clasped his stomach and then collapsed on the ground, writhing with pain. Turning slightly sideways to the mob and crouching like a boxer, Haldane weighed another stone in his throwing hand.

'Well, come on then, you bastards,' he shouted in his rage. 'Who'd like some more of the same?'

The crowd hesitated. Most of them knew that the Englishman had come to the village with Annika Zeferis but then if he had chosen the wrong side in this dispute he must take the consequences of that choice. And now he stood there taunting them. More stones were gathered up. The villagers began to close in again.

Haldane was now fully aware of the danger he was in and he prepared himself for what he knew would be a fight for his life. At that moment he was suddenly aware of the flaking whitewash on the greyed and decaying walls of the buildings around him, of the meanness of the alleyways which led off from the square and of the stench of urine that hung in the air. Why had he not seen these things and smelt that smell before, he wondered. He drew back his arm to throw the stone he was holding into the still advancing mob, fully intending to maim if not kill.

'Stop it!' shouted Annika in Greek. 'That is enough. Do you hear me? Stop it!'

The villagers paused in their advance and turned to look in her direction. She was standing just outside the doorway to the taverna. 'No more,' she went on. 'The Englishman is Leandros of the Andarte. Would you harm him?'

Some of the people in the crowd looked back at Haldane, still on their guard against him but with expressions of surprise tinged with regret. Worried, questioning glances were exchanged among the crowd.

Annika called out again in Greek. 'I told you. That is enough.' It was no longer an appeal she was making. This was a command. And clearly a command from Annika Zeferis was not to be disobeyed.

The villagers dropped the stones they were carrying, even if some did so sullenly and unenthusiastically. Then the mob slowly began to break up. Once he was satisfied that there was no danger of any further attack, Haldane tossed aside the stones he was holding and then helped Viglis to his feet. The Australian was still half stunned and the nasty wound on his forehead was now bleeding profusely. Haldane opened the nearside door of the Volkswagen and eased him into the front passenger seat. Then he looked up. Annika was standing on the other side of the car. Her face was pale and drawn with worry.

'Are you all right?' she asked anxiously.

Haldane regarded her icily. 'Yes,' he said shortly. 'But he isn't.'

'I did warn you,' she said quietly.

'Me, yes,' he snapped. 'But not him. They might have killed him and you'd have let it happen wouldn't you?'

'I stopped them,' she said weakly.

Haldane nodded. 'Only because I was involved. Not for him.'

'He is not welcome here.'

Haldane gave a short, hollow laugh. 'You surprise me,' he said. He looked across at the villagers who had now dispersed and were standing around the square watching them. 'Bloody savages,' he muttered. And then he shouted to them in Greek, 'Bloody savages!' He looked at Annika. 'Isn't there a policeman in this village?'

'Yes.'

Haldane snorted contemptuously. 'Only he's not around at the moment, eh? How convenient.' He moved around the car and opened the door on the driver's side.

'Where are you taking him?' Annika asked.

'To a doctor,' Haldane replied coldly. 'To my place.'

He pulled the keys of the Fiat out of his pocket and handed them to her. 'You bring my car,' he told her.

Annika nodded. Haldane started to get in behind the wheel but Annika checked him. 'You must not judge them too harshly,' she said. 'They have a reason.'

Haldane studied her incredulously. Then he nodded towards the injured Australian. 'For that!' he exclaimed 'Whatever their reason can you excuse it? Just like that?' Then he added scathingly, 'but then of course I suppose you can. After, all, as you said, they're your people, aren't they?' He got into the car, slammed the door and drove off at speed.

Deeply distressed, Annika watched the car pull away from her.

CHAPTER SIXTEEN

"There is concussion,' said the doctor as Haldane led the way down the stairs from the bedroom. 'And shock of course. But he is a very lucky man. Two inches lower and he would have lost an eye.' They paused at the bottom of the stairs. 'A stone you say?'

'Yes.'

The doctor tut-tutted and shook his head. 'Well, now that the wound is stitched it will heal quickly enough. But he should rest. The sedative I have given him will make him sleep and then I think he will be all right. Perhaps even by this evening he will be on his feet again. But gently, gently, eh? You understand?'

Haldane nodded. 'I'll see he takes things easy,' he said. 'Thank you, doctor.'

He moved over to the front door and opened it. Annika was standing on the doorstep about to ring the bell. The doctor recognised her. '*Herete, Kyria* Zeferis,' he said in a gravely polite voice.

'*Herete, Yatros* Skoulas.' She was clearly very subdued. She shot an embarrassed, ashamed look at Haldane as he stepped to one side to allow her to enter. She crossed to the table and put Haldane's car keys down on it.

'The *Kyrie* will be staying here?' the doctor asked Haldane.

'Yes. I think that's best.'

'Then tell him to come and see me tomorrow at my office. I will change the dressing.'

'Right, I'll do that. And thank you again.'

The doctor shrugged. 'I am happy to be of service.' He nodded his farewells, first to Annika and then to Haldane. '*Kyria, Kyrie.*'

Haldane closed the door behind him and turned to Annika. She could see from his face that his anger had only abated a little.

'How is he?' she asked.

Haldane gave her a hard look. 'Lucky. But badly cut and concussed.' He moved over to her quickly 'And now I want an explanation.'

Annika made a helpless gesture. 'His name is Viglis,' she said.

Haldane frowned. 'Yes I know,' he said irritably. 'He told me.'

Annika turned away from him and moved across to the drawing board by the window. 'Once there were many Vigli in Dhafnai.' She stood gazing towards the windows. 'But they were not good people. They stole sheep, quarrelled, fought and made trouble. Then, one day, two of the villagers were murdered by men of the Viglis family. The people rose up against them. They hanged the murderers.'

Haldane was deeply shocked by this. 'Lynched them!'

'That was often the way of justice in the mountains then.'

'My God!'

'And then,' Annika went on, 'when the murderers were dead, all the others of their name were driven from the village. No Viglis has lived in Dhafnai or dared to return there since.'

Haldane regarded her. 'I see,' he said grimly. 'And when did all this happen?'

Annika gave a little shrug. 'Within the memory of those still living.'

'Well, when?' pursued Haldane. 'Exactly.'

Annika hesitated and then said quietly, almost in a whisper. 'In nineteen sixteen.'

'Nineteen sixteen!' repeated Haldane incredulously. And then he did a hasty mental calculation. 'But that's sixty-one years ago.'

Annika turned to him. 'In the mountains people do not

forget easily.'

Haldane could not, would not, accept this. 'But what quarrel could anyone possibly have with Tony Viglis?' he scoffed. 'This is the first time he has ever been in Crete. He's an Australian. A visitor.'

Annika sighed. 'He bears the name. And he is not just here as a tourist. He has brought with him the body of his grandfather, Kissandros Viglis.'

Haldane still did not understand. 'Well?'

'I understand that it was Kissandros Viglis' wish to be buried in the village where he was born,' explained Annika. 'In Dhafnai. His grandson is here to see that happen. And that is something the villagers will not permit.'

Haldane was staggered by this and it showed clearly in his face. He shook his head in disbelief. 'That's appalling! Keeping a feud alive for so long is senseless enough. But to deny anyone the right to be buried in the place of their choosing. Their birthplace.' He threw up his hand in disgust. 'That's even worse. It's barbaric.'

Annika crossed to him. He had to understand. Somehow she must make him understand. 'These are Cretan mountain people, she said.' 'They are different from those who live here on the coast. They have a special code. They hold their grievances close to them. You know that, Leandros. You fought alongside them during the war.'

Haldane shook his head. 'No,' he said adamantly. 'Not with people like that, I didn't. The men I fought beside had a respect for the dead. They even saw to it that those who sought to destoy them were buried decently.'

'As Kissandros Viglis should be buried,' agreed Annika. 'And in Crete. No one questions that. But not in Dhafnai. Don't you see,' she pleaded. 'To the villagers that would be seen as an act of forgiveness for the past wrongs done to them by his family. And that they do not forgive.'

'Then they must learn to,' retorted Haldane savagely. 'To forgive and to forget. That beautiful chapel you

153

showed me. Doesn't their parish priest preach the Christ-
ion gospel there? 'And the greatest of these is charity.'
Haven't they ever been taught that?'

'Of course.'

'Then why wasn't Father Whatshisname out there in
the square today? Repeating it to them over and over
again instead of hiding himself away,' Haldane continued.

Annika studied him and shook her head sadly. She was
not getting through to him and she knew it. 'Perhaps
because he knows that they would not have taken any
notice of him,' she said quietly. 'And he must live with
them. In this they respond to the voices of older gods. To
other, far more ancient laws.'

Haldane took his pipe out of his pocket and filled it. He
noticed that his hands were still shaking.

'Then someone else must get the message over to
them,' he said. 'Someone who does have the guts and for
whom they have a greater respect than they clearly do for
their priest. And who deserves it more. Someone with
nothing to lose.' He crossed to the fireplace and reached
for the box of matches on the mantlepiece. 'You, for
instance,' he said, turning to her.

'Me!' said Annika, clearly taken aback by the idea.

Haldane nodded. 'Yes,' he said. 'Why not? You have
influence with them. From the way they treated you, from
the way they listened to you, they obviously have a very
high regard for you. And you are one of them. You speak
to them. You make them see what a shameful thing it is
they are doing.'

He struck a match and lit his pipe and then he looked
across at her again. 'Put an end to all this nonsense,' he
said and it was a challenge as much as a plea.

Annika held his gaze but hesitated. She shook her head.
'No, Leandros,' she said levelly. 'I cannot do that.'

'Why?' demanded Haldane, shocked by what she'd
said.

'It is not possible,' she replied simply.

'Because you agree with them!' Haldane exclaimed, all

154

his anger flowing back again. 'Is that it? Agree with what they did? With what they're doing?'

Annika shook her head. 'No. But I understand them. And I cannot interfere.'

'Cannot or will not?' he pressed

She shrugged. 'Between those two words what difference does it make?'

'A hell of a lot,' replied Haldane bitterly. 'To me.'

Annika studied him and again she hesitated. 'Very well then,' she said at last. 'I will not.'

Bitterly disappointed, Haldane regarded her coldly. He shook his head sadly. 'Then you are not only one of them,' he said 'You are no better than they are.'

Deeply hurt by his jibe, Annika frowned. She stiffened proudly. 'No I am not,' she countered icily. 'But then I have never thought myself to be.' She crossed to the front door and opened it and then looked back at him. 'That was my father's curse.'

She closed the door quietly behind her.

At five o'clock, Haldane looked in on Viglis again. He was sleeping peacefully. Satisfied, Haldane withdrew quietly from the bedroom leaving the door ajar.

He was at the head of the stairs and starting down them when the front doorbell rang.

The man standing at the top of the steps up from the street was of medium height with a strong, intelligent face and eyes which, even behind the tinted glasses he was wearing, were both penetrating and compassionate. He was wearing the grey-green uniform of the Greek police.

'Mr Haldane,' he enquired politely and in excellent English. Haldane nodded. 'Major Krasakis. May I come in?'

Haldane opened the door wider and the Major walked into the room and looked around interestedly.

'Is it about what happened this morning?' Haldane asked, closing the front door again. 'Is that why you're here?'

Krasakis turned to him. 'Yes,' he said. 'It is a very serious matter.'

'An attack on a foreigner,' Haldane said sarcastically. 'A tourist. Yes, it must be.'

Krasakis studied him and smiled faintly. 'An attack on anyone,' he said and it was a gentle but firm rebuke.

Haldane had regretted the remark almost as soon as he'd said it. He nodded. 'Yes, of course, Major, I'm sorry. That was stupid of me.'

Krasakis accepted his apology with an inclination of his head. 'How is Mr Viglis?'

'It's a nasty wound. But the doctor says he'll be all right. He's sleeping at the moment.'

The Major nodded and then began to walk slowly round the room taking in every detail of it. 'I have just returned from Dhafnai,' he said. 'It is a beautiful place, don't you agree?'

Haldane watched him as he continued his perambulation. 'Perhaps,' he said. 'But I wouldn't recommend it as somewhere to visit.'

'And the air in the mountains,' Krasakis continued 'So clean, so cool, so fragrant. Some say that it is the breath of God.' He paused and looked across at Haldane. 'Did you know that?'

'No,' replied Haldane before adding bitterly. 'But I can tell you there was little of God in Dhafnai this morning.'

The Major studied him thoughtfully and then said quietly, 'Air is air, Mr. Haldane. It is men who contaminate it.'

He's right of course, thought Haldane. But, for God's sake, what kind of a policeman is he? None of those he'd ever met in England were much given to philosophising. He nodded. 'I take your point, Major,' he said.

Krasakis slowly crossed to him. 'You are aware of the reason for this attack?' he asked.

'Yes. I've been told. Some old feud.'

'More than that,' the Major corrected him. 'A vendetta.'

Haldane nodded. 'I gather that Mr Viglis' ancestors went in for sheep stealing among other things.'

'Yes. But in that I doubt if they were different from most of their neighbours. Sheep stealing was a way of life for many in the mountains in those days.'

'And murder?' said Haldane. 'Was that a way of life too?' Krasakis gave him a quizzical look. 'I understand that the Vigli killed two of the villagers.'

'It was claimed that they did,' replied Krasakis. 'But there was never any real proof of their guilt and, unfortunately, by the time official enquiries were made the accused were not able to defend themselves.'

'So I'm told,' muttered Haldane with disgust. 'Rough justice.'

'If indeed it was any kind of justice,' the Major murmured.

'And now the villagers are determined to stop Viglis burying his grandfather there,' exclaimed Haldane.

Krasakis shook his head. 'No,' he said. 'I do not think so. I do not believe that, left to make the decision themselves, the majority of the people of Dhafnai would be opposed to that.'

'Well they certainly fooled me,' Haldane said scathingly. 'And Tony Viglis will have a scar for the rest of his life to prove it.'

'I said, if left to make the decision themselves,' reiterated the Major. He moved away from Haldane and began to examine the title of the books on the shelves. 'Sadly they have not been allowed that privilege,' he went on, 'by the eldest surviving member of the family who were the rivals of the Vigli. The family who finally declared vendetta on them. The family who saw to it that the alleged murderers were hanged without trial and then drove those others with the name of Viglis from their homes. The family which was powerful then in Dhafnai and which today is even more powerful.'

'Just one family?' Haldane said in amazement.

Krasakis had taken Haldane's copy of the *Essays of*

Montaigne and was leafing through it. He nodded. 'The family which now owns the village and almost all the land around it,' he said. 'The beneficent family which built the new school and restored the old chapel. The family which collects the rents. The family to which almost all the villagers owe their livelihood and, because of that, their loyalty.' He closed the book and put it back on the shelf. 'But only because of that and out of fear of going against them do they collectively oppose the burial.'

'Because they have been told to. Or else,' suggested Haldane.

The major turned to him and nodded. 'Exactly,' he said. 'Even if less bluntly than that.'

'Then it's not so much barbarism but some local Mafia Viglis is up against.'

The major shook his head. 'No,' he said. 'Mafia is too strong a word. Merely a proud and powerful Cretan family. Or one important member of it at least.'

'Who is afraid of a dead man,' Haldane snorted contemptuously.

Krasakis sighed. 'Who is afraid of many things I think.'

Haldane shook his head. 'And knowing this what can you do about it?'

Krasakis moved on to study Haldane's collection of LPs. 'Little if anything,' he replied. 'Although, naturally, I will try. But while the pressure is there the people of Dhafnai will bend to it.' He held up a recording of the Saint Saens *Organ Symphony* and nodded his approval. 'They have been told that Kissandros Viglis is unwelcome in their cemetery. And if for no other reason than to protect themselves, they will go to any lengths to see that he is not buried there.' He put the record back into place. 'You already have proof of that.'

'My God!' Haldane despaired vehemently. 'What kind of people are they?'

Krasakis turned to him. 'The people they have always been,' he said quietly. 'Cretans. Proud, hospitable, independent, brave. My people. Your people from what I've

158

heard of you. People whose good qualities you share. But tell me,' he went on, 'who of us in a lifetime and when tested is not sometimes meek, hostile, dependent.' He paused. 'And afraid? So that is the kind of people they are, Mr Haldane.' He shrugged. 'They are people.'

Haldane regarded him intently. The man interested and intrigued him. 'So what do you recommend?'

'That Mr Viglis buries his grandfather elsewhere on the island,' Krasakis replied. 'That is the simple solution.'

'And if he refuses? What if he insists on Dhafnai?'

The Major shook his head sadly. 'Then he will need a great deal of help and support. And I will give him what protection I can.' He went over to the front door. 'Meanwhile I will try to see to it that those who stoned you this morning are charged and brought before the court.'

'Good,' said Haldane. 'That may help.'

Krasakis opened the door and then turned to him. 'I doubt it,' he said. 'And frankly I do not think that I will be successful. The villagers saw nothing and heard nothing. Certainly no one will identify any of your assailants.'

Haldane frowned and then had an inspiration. 'There was someone with me. Mrs Zeferis. Do you know her?'

The Major nodded. 'Yes, I know her.'

'Well she comes from Dhafnai. She grew up there. She saw it all. She could identify them.'

Krasakis gave him a faint, sardonic smile. 'Undoubtedly. But she will not do so,' he assured him.

'Oh, why?' asked Haldane, surprised.

'Mrs Zeferis was baptised Annika Matakis.'

Haldane shrugged. 'So?'

Krasakis saw from his expression that he would have to spell it out for him. 'It is the Matakis family which owns Dhafnai,' he explained. 'They are the family which claimed they were wronged by the Vigli. It is they who declared the vendetta. And it is Annika's mother, Katerina Matakis, who today keeps it alive. And now fans it into flames once more.' He studied Haldane and frowned. He could see that the Englishman was shocked by what he had just told him and hurt and angered by it. 'You are surprised?' he asked.

Haldane nodded. 'Yes,' he said, tight-lipped. 'Very. Somehow that little detail got left out of the story I was told.'

As the doctor had predicted, Tony Viglis had recovered sufficiently by late evening for him to insist on getting out of bed. He was pale and somewhat unsteady on his feet at first but after a stiff drink claimed that he felt much better, almost himself again.

Haldane had been all for preparing a meal for them at home but the Australian had finally been able to persuade him that he was more than up to going out to eat and that, anyway, he could do with a breath of fresh air. So, together, they had strolled gently along to the Vassilakis' taverna.

Haldane had noticed the look which had passed between Nikos and Elena when they entered the bar. They would both, of course, have heard what had happened at Dhafnai and Haldane realised that having the Australian as a customer could well create something of a quandary for Elena. But Nikos, at least, greeted them warmly enough and neither he nor Elena mentioned the incident.

Nikos showed them to a table in a quiet corner of the patio and Haldane ordered a light dinner for them and a bottle of wine.

As Viglis picked at his food, Haldane told him everything that Major Krasakis had said to him that afternoon. The Australian was as staggered by it as he had been.

'But this is the bloody twentieth century,' he growled angrily.

'Yes,' sighed Haldane, 'And it's barbaric. But even now, in parts of Crete, the vendetta is still a reality. There are some people who still cling to the old ways.' And then he asked. 'Didn't your grandfather ever say anything to you about what happened?'

Viglis shook his head. 'Never a word. He was full of

stories, mind. Some of 'em pretty wild and I've always had a feeling that he left here sort of on the run. But why, he didn't say. Not to me anyway.'

'When did he leave?'

'When he was around eighteen I think,' replied Viglis.

'Which would have been what year?'

The Australian worked it out in his mind. 'Let's see. He was seventy-nine when he died so that would have been . . .' He nodded. 'Nineteen sixteen. It fits.'

'Well, now you know what the situation is what are you going to do about it?' said Haldane.

'Do about it!' exclaimed Viglis. 'What in hell do you think? I'm going to see it through.'

'Major Krasakis advises against that,' Haldane warned him.

'Stuff him!' railed Viglis vehemently. 'And stuff all those bloody abos up in the mountains. No matter what,' he went on defiantly. 'My grand-dad's going to be buried where he bloody well chose to be. In a plot bought with the money he earned with a hell of a lot of sweat. That's what he wanted and that's what I'm going to see happens. Believe me.'

Haldane saw the stubborn determination in his eyes. He nodded. 'Right,' he said quietly. 'I'm with you.'

'Oh, come on now,' protested Viglis. 'Listen, Mr Haldane . . .'

'Alan,' Haldane interrupted.

Viglis grinned. 'Right. Thanks. Well, listen Alan. You've been bloody good to me already. Getting me out of that place, calling in a doctor, letting me rest up in your house and all. But if there's going to be more trouble, and it looks like there is, I don't want to get you involved.'

'I'm already involved. And in a way this is as much my fight as it is yours.'

Viglis looked puzzled. 'Oh! How come?'

'You could say it's a family matter,' Haldane said dismissively. He could see that Viglis was interested but he was not prepared to go into detail. 'The Major is right,'

161

he went on, guiding him back on to the original track. 'You are going to need a lot of help. More than I can give you. We want someone on our side who carries a bit of weight around here.' He picked up his glass of wine. 'And I think I know the very man.'

CHAPTER SEVENTEEN

Haldane stood by the open window. The sounds of the traffic and of people gossiping in 25th August Street intruded into Babis Spiridakis' office along with the warm sunlight. The lawyer was sitting behind his desk with Tony Viglis seated opposite him.

'After you telephoned me, Leandros,' Spiridakis was saying, 'I got in touch with Father Kaphatos. He made many excuses, none of which I would accept. And, finally, he said that it was not possible for the burial to take place in Dhafnai because there is no space in the cemetery. But this is a lie and I know it to be so. However, he clearly considers that to be the end of the matter.'

'So what's our next move?' asked Haldane.

Spiridakis looked across at Viglis. 'To reconsider, I think,' He said quietly.

Viglis shook his head. 'No,' he insisted resolutely.

The lawyer leaned forward, resting his forearms on his desk. 'Leandros brought you to me because I am his friend,' he said patiently. 'He trusts me. And he trusts my judgement. Will you not do the same?'

'Not if you're saying that I should bury my grandfather somewhere else,' replied Viglis with a scowl.

'You are a stubborn man, Mr Viglis.'

'Yes,' acknowledged the Australian proudly.

The lawyer sighed. 'Do you realise what may be the result of such obstinacy?'

'Listen,' protested Viglis angrily. 'I didn't come here to stir things up. Others have done that. And I'm not about to back away from them.'

Spiridakis glanced across at Haldane, clearly seeking his support. 'Leandros?' he appealed.

Haldane turned to him and shook his head. 'No, I'm

with him on this, Babis. I think he's right.'

Spiridakis looked from Haldane to Viglis and then back at Haldane again. He gave a helpless shrug. 'Very well then,' he said. 'If you both insist.'

'But Father Kaphatos says that the cemetery is full,' said Haldane. 'If he sticks to that story what can be done?'

Spiridakis was in no doubt. 'Since I know that to be untrue,' he replied, 'as a lawyer I can only conclude that he is being deliberately obstructive to the rightful claims of the heir and executor of the estate of Kissandros Viglis. And without reasonable cause.' He looked at the Australian. 'In which case, as your representative, it is open to me to appeal to the Archbishop. I take it that your grandfather was not a heretic?'

Viglis was shocked by this. 'Too bloody right,' he exclaimed.

'And that he was in good standing with the Greek church?'

Viglis nodded. 'Right again. He went to services regularly.'

The lawyer shrugged. 'Then there can be no religious grounds on which to refuse him burial,' he went on formally. 'And in the place of his choosing. Once the Archbishop is in possession of all the facts he will have no alternative other than to order Father Kaphatos to proceed with the funeral and officiate at it.' He sighed again and shook his head sadly. 'But that will only be a piece of paper. An instruction. Only another influence can ensure that your grandfather finally rests in peace in Dhafnai.'

'Katerina Matakis,' growled Haldane.

Spiridakis nodded. 'It is she who opposes you,' he said to Viglis.

Haldane moved away from the window and over to the desk. 'Speak to her, Babis,' he pleaded. 'You know her well. I think you're also her friend. Appeal to her.'

Again the lawyer shook his head. 'She would not listen, Leandros. Even to me. I know that. It is a matter of pride to her and her ears would be closed to all entreaties. It would be useless.' He looked across at Viglis again. 'She is much like you,' he said. 'No one will sway her from what she feels deeply to be her duty.'

'You are mistaken, Major,' Katerina Matakis retorted icily. 'The people of my village have acted in this way because of the outrage with which they feel themselves threatened. Not because of any claim which I or my family may have on them.'

With Petros standing on the far side of the dimly lit sitting room, Krasakis and Katerina confronted one another.

'Then if that is so...' Krasakis replied, and he would have gone on but Katerina flushed angrily and broke in on him. 'You doubt my word?' she demanded, challenging him to admit it.

The Major studied her and his expression was answer enough. 'I would say only this, *Kyria* Matakis,' he said. 'Incitement to violence is a criminal offence.'

'You came here to threaten me?' she flared.

Krasakis shook his head. 'No,' he replied almost casually and still refusing to be drawn. 'Merely to acquaint you with that fact.' He smiled. 'It is as well for us all to know how we may place ourselves in jeopardy.'

Katerina scowled. 'There has been no incitement,' she reiterated sharply. 'None was needed.'

'But your interests are close to the hearts of the people of Dhafnai,' Krasakis insisted. 'As their interests are close to your heart.'

Katerina regarded him warily. 'I have no cause to deny that. I am proud of our shared concern in all things.'

'And you would wish to advise them well?' suggested the Major.

'As I have always done,' Katerina replied with a nod, but still on her guard.

'Then warn them. Tell them that if the Australian comes to Dhafnai again, for any reason, and if they go against him, then they will go against me.'

'You would protect him?' Katerina sneered. 'A foreigner. From the anger of people of your own blood.'

Krasakis shook his head. 'No. I do not protect him. The law does.'

The old woman regarded him contemptuously. 'Man's law,' she snarled. 'There is no true justice there.'

Krasakis held her gaze and then said quietly. 'If you call on justice, *Kyria*, then remember this. Justice is blind. She cannot tell a Cretan from a foreigner.' He put on his cap and saluted her. '*Kalimera.*' Then he nodded to Matakis. *Kyrie* Petros.'

'I'll see you to the door,' said Matakis.

The Major followed him out of the room. Katerina sat down in one of the upright armchairs and stared broodingly into space.

Matakis came back into the room and closed the door behind him. Then he crossed to her and stood beside her. 'He means what he says, mother,' he said emphatically. 'He will stand with Viglis. He must.'

'Then let him,' Katerina threatened darkly. 'It changes nothing. Only that in standing with him the Major may also fall with him.'

Matakis made a helpless gesture. 'Why?' he pleaded. 'For what? For a wrong that was avenged years ago? What is there to be gained from what you are doing? For anyone?'

Slowly Katerina lifted her head to look at him. 'There have been times lately, Petros,' she informed him cruelly and in an acid voice, 'when if I did not still remember the agony of your birth, I would doubt that you were my son.' She shook her head despairingly. 'And to think that I have placed the Englishman, Haldane, in your hands.'

Spiridakis got up from his chair and moved around from behind the desk. 'Very well,' he said. 'I will speak to the Archbishop. He will instruct Father Kaphatos. Of that I am certain.'

Viglis got to his feet and shook hands with him. 'Thank you,' he said gratefully.

The lawyer regarded him sadly. 'If it was only as easy as that. If I only believed that you had real cause for gratitude. But in doing that I am merely opening the gate. The path you have chosen is no less stony than before.' He sighed and then continued. 'Now, would you do something for me?'

'Name it,' said Viglis.

'I would like to speak to Leandros for a moment. Alone.'

The Australian shrugged. 'Right.' He looked at Haldane. 'I'll wait for you outside.'

Haldane nodded. When they were alone, Spiridakis took a cigarette from the box on his desk and lit it. Then he turned to his friend. 'You know what I'm going to say, don't you?' he asked.

Haldane was well aware of what was coming. 'This is none of my affair,' he said. 'That I should have stayed out of it.'

'You of all people,' Spiridakis exclaimed. 'You are far too vulnerable, Leandros. When Katerina Matakis learns that you are helping Viglis she will not be pleased. Elena, she is your weakness. The secret only you and I share. In her Matakis blood is mixed with your blood but she does not know that. Offend her grandmother and you risk offending her. And then there is Annika.'

'I already know Annika's position on this,' replied Haldane bitterly. 'She flows with the family current.'

'And you condemn her for that?'

Haldane shrugged. 'Let's say I'm disappointed.'

'She is an educated woman,' said Spiridakis. 'She has travelled. But despite that she is still a Cretan. Of peasant stock. That is a birthright to be proud of. But it is also a heritage which is hard to shake off. Perhaps you expect too much of her?'

'No more than I'd ever settle for,' Haldane countered quietly.

The lawyer tried again. 'And Elena?' he queried. 'Will you risk the relationship you are building with her for this . . .' he shrugged. 'stranger?'

Haldane regarded him closely and frowned. 'You'd have me turn my back on him?' he asked. 'On this whole shameful business?' His expression showed his disappointment. 'If so, Babis', he went on. 'Then as I expect too much of Annika, you expect too little of me.'

The following morning Haldane was working on the caique as usual when he looked up and saw Major Krasakis approaching him from the road where his white, police Land-Rover was parked. He climbed down off the deck to meet him.

'The burial is to take place then,' Krasakis said grimly as he came up alongside the boat.

Haldane nodded. 'This afternoon. Only now there s another problem. The undertakers in Heraklion have backed out from the job. Suddenly they don't want to know.'

'That does not surprise me,' replied Krasakis.

'And no-one's too keen to hire us any transport to get the coffin up to Dhafnai either.'

The Major shook his head. 'Even people who have no stake in this will not wish to offend those of their kind who have,' he said. 'But transport will not be required,' he went on. 'I will provide it. And my men will do all that is necessary.' He sighed. 'They will be needed there anyway.'

Haldane gave him a look of alarm. 'You think there could be a repetition of what happened the other morning?' he exclaimed. 'Despite the order from the Archbishop?'

Krasakis nodded. 'I am certain of it,' he said. 'Perhaps even worse. Unless the police are there in strength.'

'Violence!' Haldane said in an appalled whisper. 'At a funeral!'

'It would require more than an order from the Arch-

·bishop to eliminate that risk.'

'An order from Katerina Matakis, you mean,' said Haldane.

The Major nodded. 'I have spoken to her. I have warned her', he said. 'She knows that if the villagers do make more trouble then I will have to act firmly against them and that people may be hurt.

'And what was her reaction?'

'Scorn. She hardly listened. What I have said to her will make no difference I fear.' He sighed again. 'There will be a confrontation. Perhaps a bloody one. And I regret that.'

'No more than I do,' Haldane assured him. 'No more than Tony Viglis does.'

Krasakis shrugged. 'Only if Katerina Matakis were to relent could that be avoided.'

Haldane studied him. He was right of course. But how? And then he knew that there was only one possible way. 'Then someone else must speak to her,' he said thoughtfully. 'While there's still time. Someone close to her. Someone who perhaps she will listen to.'

'No, Leandros. I told you,' Annika said vehemently. 'I will not interfere.'

She had welcomed Haldane when he had driven up to the house but not without reserve and once he had told her the reason for his visit she had immediately gone on to the defensive. And now Haldane was close to losing his temper.

'But what you neglected to tell me then was that it was your family who is behind all this.'

'I could not,' she replied.

'Why?'

Annika hesitated and looked away from him. 'I was ashamed.'

'Well, that's something in your favour I suppose,' he said scornfully.

Annika met his gaze again. 'I did tell you, though, that I

169

understood why this is being done,' she reminded him.

'But you also said that you didn't agree with it.'

'I do not,' she said. 'What is happening is part of yesterday's Crete. A part I want none of.'

'You say that,' taunted Haldane. 'But do you really mean it?'

'Yes.'

'Then prove it. Speak to your mother.'

Annika shook her head. 'No,' she said adamantly. 'It is none of my concern. No more than it is yours. It is hers alone. That Cretan yesterday is, for her, today. The grievance she feels means nothing to me but it is very real to her. She was there. In Dhafnai. She lived through those tragic times.'

'My God,' scoffed Haldane. 'She can't have been more than a child in nineteen sixteen. And not even a Matakis then.'

'She was eleven years old,' Annika said quietly and with dignity. 'And when she married she willingly took on the burden of the vendetta as part of her wedding vows. To honour my father.' She paused for effect. 'Because, you see, it was his father and his uncle who were murdered by the Vigli.'

Haldane was unimpressed. 'Even that's in doubt.' he snapped.

'Maybe so,' Annika replied, bridling a little. 'But it is a doubt which my mother does not share. For her the injury which she believes was done to her husband's family is still an open wound. One that will never heal. One for which she feels the only balm to be vendetta.' She shook her head and her voice took on a softer tone. 'She is wrong of course. But she is my mother. And close to death. And I am part of the family whose honour she seeks to protect. How can I tell her that she is wrong in what she does without deepening the wound?' Now she was pleading. 'And who am I to judge her anyway?'

'A civilised human being,' retorted Haldane savagely. 'Or so you pretend. Because if you won't do anything to

170

try and end this enmity, to check your mother's craving for vengence, to prevent what may happen this afternoon, well then that's all it is. A pretence. A veneer.' He struggled to control his anger, subdued it a little and tried persuasion once more. 'Speak to her. Try to make her see sense. That's all I ask. That's all anyone asks of you.'

Annika stared into his face for a moment and then turned abruptly away from his. 'No, she said firmly.' 'I will not hurt her.'

'Hurt her!' Haldane exploded. 'A spiteful old woman who uses the respect and fear that others have for her as a weapon so that they fight her battle for her! And run all the risks.'

'Even so,' mumbled Annika.

'Then you are no less of a barbarian than she is,' he derided. He made a sweeping gesture which encompassed the room. 'So why the façade? The books. The records. Oh, yes,' he acknowledged bitterly. 'You've read the words but you haven't learned anything. And you've listened to the music but you haven't heard what it says. So why bother? It's all been a waste of time,' he regarded her scornfully. 'You said you were sorry for your brother, Petros. Because he hasn't found another horizon. But I'm sorry for you, Annika. Because you haven't either. It's only a mirage. It has to be if this vengeance, this spite, even by proxy, even by default, is a part of it.'

He strode across to the side table, snatched up the photograph of Annika's two children and then crossed back to her with it and held it up to her.

'Your children,' he challenged. 'What would they think of your new horizon? Would they be as proud of it as you are? Is it anything like theirs?' He tossed the photograph down on the settee. 'Ask yourself that some time.' Then he swung round from her and stormed out onto the terrace.

Wounded and bleeding but still defiant, Annika watched him go. She picked up the photograph and slowly crossed with it back to the table. She was about to put it down when she hesitated, frowned and stared thoughtfully at the two smiling faces.

The village square was deserted when the convoy drove into Dhafnai and every window and every door was shuttered and barred.

Major Krasakis was in the leading Land-Rover, sitting beside the driver. Haldane and Tony Viglis sat behind them. Following them was a police truck in which lay the coffin of Kissandros Viglis escorted and guarded by six policemen. And there were more policemen in the lorry at the rear of the strange cortege.

Krasakis gazed warily out of his window as the procession moved slowly across the square. There was no movement of any kind; no sign of life. It was just as he had expected it would be. He glanced back at Haldane and the Australian. They, too, were anxiously scanning the square. No, my friends, he thought grimly, it was never here that they would be waiting for us. This is not the place they will have chosen to oppose us. Not in the village. They will be at the cemetery

And he was right.

The small cemetery was situated about a quarter of a mile outside the village; a cedar-shaded grove for the honoured dead of Dhafnai who rested in graves surmounted by stone or marble tombs at the head of which, in a glass-fronted housing topped by a cross, was a photograph of the one for whom the village mourned together with a cup of oil, a candle, a plate of olives, some small and treasured possession and perhaps a few coins; those things which they would need to sustain and comfort them on the long journey on which they had embarked and which was a custom established along before the cross crowning them had any significance in the world.

The villagers were drawn up in ranks four or five deep around three sides of the cemetery, silent, sullen and hostile. Katerina Matakis was there too. She stood beside her car which was parked in a gap in the ranks which had been reserved for her. She was flanked on one side by

172

Matheos Noukakis and on the other by Petros. Katerina's expression was grim, set and determined.

The police convoy drove through the gates of the cemetery and pulled up a few yards from the grave which, reluctantly but on Major Krasakis' orders, the local constable, assisted by another policeman from a neighbouring village, had only recently finished digging. The resting bars and the straps with which the coffin would be lowered were in position. And Father Kaphatos, nervous and agitated, stood waiting at the head of the grave.

There was an angry murmur among the villagers at the appearance of the three vehicles.

As Krasakis, followed by Haldane and Viglis, both carrying wreathes, got out of the leading Land-Rover, the local policeman and his companion moved away from the grave and put on their jackets which were hanging over two spades stuck into the pile of freshly dug soil nearby.

The priest glanced helplessly across at Katerina Matakis. She ignored him.

The policemen in the lorry jumped down from it and, as those men in the truck, at a nod from Krasakis, removed the coffin, they dispersed and took up positions around the grave and facing the crowd. None of the police was armed but each carried a baton.

The burial detail took the weight of the coffin on their shoulders and began the solemn procession to the graveside. Haldane and Viglis fell in behind them. Krasakis and a sergeant followed at a discreet distance.

While Tony Viglis watched as the coffin was lowered onto the resting bars, Haldane stepped back a little and the Major came up alongside him. 'This afternoon will see the old man buried,' Krasakis said quietly, his eyes on the crowd. 'But he will not lie here for long I think.'

Haldane shot him a horrified look. 'They'll desecrate the grave!'

Krasakis shrugged helplessly. 'He is here against the wishes of the Matakis family. These people know what will be expected of them. I shall place two extra men on

173

duty in the village. But I cannot keep them here forever.'

Haldane felt the bile of sickness in his throat.

Krasakis removed his cap and, with Haldane beside him, stepped forward to join Viglis at the graveside. The Major nodded curtly to Father Kaphatos to begin.

Again the priest shot a look across at Katerina but then, very unwillingly, almost surlily, he began to mumble through the words of the Greek Orthodox burial mass.

The villagers were silent throughout the ritual and when it was over Father Kaphatos, with a sigh of relief, made a casual sign of the cross and committed the body of Kissandros Viglis to the grave.

The pall bearers took the strain on the lowering straps. The local constable and his companion removed the resting bars and slowly the bearers began to lower the coffin.

Katerina Matakis shot a look at her son whose eyes were on the grave but he was apparently unmoved by the scene before him. She scowled and then let out an anguished cry. 'Will you let this happen?' she shouted. 'A Viglis buried in Dhafnai.'

As if on cue the villagers responded with a roar of protest and started to move in on the grave. Haldane and Viglis looked up in horror. The bearers hesitated but then, on a signal from the sergeant, continued lowering the coffin.

Krasakis frowned and called out to the crowd. 'Keep back.' But the villagers took no notice and surged in on them. Their arms spread wide, the police escort attempted to hold them back but, outnumbered, steadily lost ground.

'Batons!' ordered Krasakis. The police gripped their batons and prepared to use them. Haldane could see from the look on Krasakis' face that they were only seconds away from the violence which the Major had feared and predicted.

And then, suddenly, the villagers stopped dead in their tracks. Their cries of rage began to die away, first to a murmur, then to excited whispers and finally to silence. The eyes of all of them were on the entrance to the cemetery as were those of Katerina, Petros and Noukakis.

174

Katerina's expression was one of stunned outrage while Petros looked perplexed and confused and Noukakis frowned. Krasakis, Haldane and Tony Viglis turned to look in the direction of the gateway.

Annika Zeferis was standing just inside the entrance. She was carrying a wreath. Very slowly and looking straight ahead, she crossed to the grave and placed the wreath on the ground at the head of it. Then she took a step back and, with her eyes still on the grave, declared loudly and for all to hear, 'Rest here quietly, Kissandros Viglis. You have come home. I, Annika Zeferis, born Annika Matakis, say this.' She stooped, picked up some loose soil and, advancing to the edge of the grave, crumbled it onto the coffin.

Confusion and whispers of bewilderment broke out among the villagers. Viglis surveyed the crowd while Haldane's eyes were on Annika. But she did not look at him. It was Katerina Matakis, however, who was the centre of Krasakis' attention. He waited, anxious to see what her reaction would be to this unexpected development. A great deal still depended on that.

Furious, Katerina seized her son's arm. 'Your sister has lost her mind,' she hissed. 'She shames us. Stop her.'

As if mesmerised, Petros did not move. 'Do you hear me,' Katerina continued vehemently. 'Do something.'

Petros turned his head and looked at her, his expression blank. Then, obediently, he moved forward towards the grave and walked to Annika's side. She turned to him and they confronted one another in silence. The attention of everyone present was on them. Petros held his sister's look for a while and read the message in her eyes. He moved away from her, crossed to a bush of rosemary in flower a yard or so away and broke a branch of blossom from it. Then, returning to the grave, he placed the blossom alongside Annika's wreath and picked up some soil.

'Yes,' he declared in ringing tones. 'Rest here quietly, you Kissandros, who are now with God. I, Petros, head of the Matakis family, say this.

There was a gasp from the crowd. Petros sprinkled the soil into the grave and then glanced at Annika who smiled and nodded to him.

Anguished, Katerina closed her eyes and pressed a clenched fist to her lips to stifle her fury at this betrayal. She was beaten and she knew it.

The villagers exchanged looks and then smiles. The head of the Matakis family had spoken. The vendetta was ended. They were no longer under any obligation. In death Kissandros Viglis had been welcomed back among them. Slowly the crowd began to break up and the villagers drifted towards the gateway of the cemetery.

Two of the men who were among the mob, which only minutes earlier had been close to rioting, moved to the pile of earth close to the grave and took up the shovels embedded in it.

Petros turned from the graveside and walked slowly back towards his mother and Noukakis. Haldane moved to Annika's side. She faced him. They studied one another. 'Thank you,' he said quietly.

'For what?' she asked. 'For seeing the truth? For doing what I should have done at the beginning? Who should be thanked for that?'

Haldane searched her face. If there had previously been any doubt in his mind he knew at that moment that he loved her. 'May I drive you home?' he said.

Annika nodded. 'Yes. I would like that,' she replied. Side by side they moved away from the grave.

Petros rejoined his mother. Noukakis was holding the rear door of the Citroen open for her. In the look which she gave him Katerina no longer made any effort to conceal her total contempt for her son. Petros gazed back at her unflinchingly. 'Annika is right,' he said levelly. 'Kissandros Viglis is dead, and so is the past. I will have no more of any vendetta.'

'Because you have forsaken your heritage,' she spat.

Matakis shook his head. 'No. I am proud of that which is good in it.'

176

'Because you are a coward then,' Katerina jibed.

'If you wish to think that,' Matakis said with a sigh. 'But hear this, mother. From now on I am content to leave retribution, for any sin, in God's hands.'

He offered his mother his arm but she scorned it and got into the car unaided. Petros shrugged and took his seat beside her. Noukakis shut the door and then got in behind the wheel.

Haldane walked with Annika through the gateway of the cemetery and across to her car which was parked on the side of the road just outside it. As he opened the passenger door for her she looked up at him. He smiled and kissed her lightly on the cheek.

The Citroen, moving slowly through the villagers now silently spilling out of the cemetery, came through the gateway, accelerated and swept past them. Katerina grim faced, stared straight ahead but Petros saluted his sister with a wave.

Annika waved back. Sadly she watched the Citroen pull away from them then, with a sigh, she got into her car. Haldane closed the door, moved around the bonnet, settled himself into the driving seat and started the engine.

In the cemetery the policemen assembled alongside their vehicles and, on the orders of the sergeant, began boarding them. The two men from the village were filling in the grave and Tony Viglis watched each spadeful of earth as it fell. Krasakis stood a little way off from him, waiting patiently.

Viglis looked down, then stooped and picked up the branch of rosemary which was Petros' tribute to his grandfather. He gazed for a moment at the blossom and then, reaching out, dropped the branch into the grave.

Katerina did not speak to her son on the drive back to Neapolis. Her thoughts were elsewhere. She gazed at Noukakis. Such foresight, she congratulated herself. I was right. I will have need of him.

CHAPTER EIGHTEEN

Noukakis opened the front door of Haldane's house and cautiously peered out. He had seen Haldane leave and he had waited until the Englishman had set sail in the caique with Annika and Nikos. Looking across the lagoon he could see the boat way out to sea and approaching the island of Spinalonga. But he still had to make sure that he was not seen by anyone.

He edged out of the doorway a little. The street and square were deserted. The only people about were some fishermen down by the moorings and they were too busily occupied preparing their nets and too far off to trouble him. He stepped out of the house, closed the front door quietly and ran quickly down the steps. Still unobserved, he reached his car which was parked unobtrusively in a side street fifty yards up the road. He got into the car and drove immediately to Neapolis.

Katerina Matakis received him cordially and then listened in silence as he made his report. When he had finished she crossed to the wooden cabinet and poured him a glass of raki.

'It is my shame that, because my son lacks the stomach for it,' she said gravely, as she handed him the glass, 'I have had to place this burden on your shoulders, Matheous. The burden of vendetta. And for a wrong done to my family which I cannot reveal to you.'

Noukakis made a dismissive gesture. It mattered little to him that she had not explained her reason for hating Haldane. The mere fact that she did was enough and it suited his purpose admirably. Besides, who was he to question anything in the face of the inducement which she had offered in return for his co-operation. However, Katerina was not to be deflected from her declaration.

'But you are performing a sacred duty,' she went on in the same solemn tone. 'On my behalf and with my support. The Englishman must be driven from Crete. And if he will not go. . .' She shrugged. 'Well, then you know what must be done. What I expect of you. And you will not find me ungrateful. You know that. You have much to gain. The inheritance which my son has forfeited.'

Noukakis gave her what he hoped was a suitably grateful but, at the same time, humble smile and then threw back his head and emptied the glass.

The caique was a joy to sail. The modifications which Haldane had made to her hull and by stepping the mast slightly further aft had greatly improved her balance and had, he felt certain, given her a much improved response and performance, particularly when close hauled, over those sailing caiques built to the traditional Cretan design. And, he congratulated himself, without sacrificing any of the beauty of those old craft.

The restoration had been completed almost exactly to the schedule Haldane had set himself. The caique had been launched just three days before Easter. And now, twenty-four hours later, on the boat's second sea trial and running before the wind on a starboard tack towards Spinalonga, his hand on the tiller and with Annika beside him, he felt happy and exhilarated. And both Annika and Nikos, who had eagerly volunteered to crew for him, shared his excitement and satisfaction.

Nikos, standing in the bow, turned and, smiling broadly, gave Haldane a thumbs-up sign. Haldane smiled back at him, waved and nodded. And Annika saw the look of pride and almost child-like excitement on his face.

'You are pleased with her, eh Leandros?' she said, delighted by his expression.

'Very,' replied Haldane, his eyes on the set of the sails and hauling the mainsheet in a little tighter. 'She handles beautifully. Even better than I expected.'

Annika clapped her hands. 'Good,' she exclaimed. 'So

now she may be christened.'

Haldane glanced at her. 'Now? Today?'

'Why not?' she demanded, smiling. 'I have brought the champagne with me. And you promised me the honour, remember?'

Haldane smiled gently and nodded. 'I remember.'

Then, looking past him, suddenly Annika frowned and almost at the same time Haldane saw Nikos, who was also gazing out over the port side, cross himself.

Puzzled, he turned his head to follow the direction of their gaze. The caique was now entering the channel between the peninsula of Spinalonga and the small island on which stood the ancient Venetian fortress, now deserted and crumbling with decay. As they drew abreast of it the castle loomed over them, mournful and desolate, not more than a few yards off their port side. And above the roof of the ruined chapel on the upper ramparts Haldane could see two hawks slowly circling, their wings motionless, riding the air currents.

Annika gave an involuntary shudder.

'Spinalonga disturbs you?' Haldane asked.

She nodded. 'Everyone, I think,' she replied quietly with her eyes still on the island.

Haldane shrugged. 'It's just an old leper colony.'

Annika, her attention now fixed on the circling birds of prey, shook her head. 'It is a place of the dead,' she said. And again she shivered.

Then they were through the channel and Haldane altered course to take the caique round the island and then back down the lagoon to Elounda.

Xenophon Hasapis watched the craft manoeuvring with great interest. He was standing on the cliffs opposite the island fortress, alongside his sons and a few yards from where a dilapidated and rusty Mazda pick-up truck was parked.

Hasapis, a well-built man in his middle sixties but upright and muscular, with sun and wind-leathered skin, lazy, crafty eyes and greying hair and moustache, lowered the old pair of British Army binoculars through which he had been observing the caique and smiled. He looked at his sons and nodded.

Manolis, the eldest, took the binoculars from him and trained them on the boat while Costas impatiently waited his turn.

Manolis was forty-one and his brother three years younger, and both had inherited not only their good looks from their father but also his appetite for roguery.

When Manolis, with a smile reflecting and confirming Hasapis' thoughts, passed the binoculars on to his brother and after he had observed the caique first come about and then begin to tack back down the lagoon, Costas handed the glasses back to his father, grinned and nodded in agreement.

The three men turned from the cliff edge and strolled over to the pick-up truck.

'For Leandros who gave new life to you,' proclaimed Annika. 'I christen you *The Knot.*' She swung the bottle of champagne and it exploded against the stem of the caique. 'May you and those you carry sail in the palm of God.'

The boat was now tied up at the moorings in Elounda and the christening ceremony had been witnessed by a small group of gravely interested villagers and as Haldane and Nikos, both lightheartedly enjoying the occasion, applauded, the faces of the spectators broke into smiles and they clapped too.

Haldane took the neck of the broken bottle from Annika's hand. 'Thank you,' he said quietly. Their eyes met.

'You chose well,' she said. 'That is a fine name. *The Knot.* May it always hold fast and keep you bound to Crete and to all those here who love you, Leandros.'

Haldane smiled and then, with a fleeting expression of consternation, looked away from her and tossed the jagged glass into a waste bin.

At the sound of the approaching vehicle everyone

gathered around the boat turned to look across the open ground behind the moorings. Xenophon Hasapis' pick-up truck had pulled off the road and was pitching and rolling its way towards them. The truck stopped and Hasapis and his sons got out of it and approached the group gathered around the bow of the caique. They were immediately recogised by the villagers who nodded and smiled in greeting to them. Xenophon responded with a broad grin and a cheery wave.

The trio were also known to Annika and Nikos, both of whom frowned at the sight of them and were instantly on their guard. Haldane regarded the strangers with interest.

With Manolis on one side of him and Costas on the other, Hasapis stopped two or three yards off from the Englishman and gave him an even broader grin. '*Kalimera*,' he said. Then he nodded to Annika and Nikos in turn. '*Kyria* Zeferis, *Kyrie* Niko.' Annika inclined her head in acknowledgement. Nikos, while in no way showing any hostility towards the newcomers, was clearly very wary of them. '*Kalimera*' he replied guardedly.

'How are you?'

Nikos considered him suspiciously but his reply was polite enough. 'I am well. And you?'

'Good,' said Hasapis expansively. 'Very, very good.' He fixed his eyes on Haldane and his grin changed to a warm but wicked smile. 'So you are the one, uh?' He put out his right hand and advanced on him. 'You are the Englishman. The one who they call Leandros. The one who was with the Andarte in the war.'

Haldane shook hands with him. 'Yes,' he said, faintly puzzled.

Hasapis held on to his hand tightly and gazed into his face. His smile changed to a look of wonderment. 'Such stories are told of you,' he exclaimed soulfully. 'Of the man you were then.' He shook his head and Haldane could have sworn that there were tears in his eyes. 'This is a great honour for me.' And then, to Haldane's surprise and embarrassment, he released the Englishman's hand,

182

took him in his arms and kissed him on both cheeks.

Annika and Nikos exchanged looks and from the other's expression each could see that they both found this warmth of welcome equally suspect.

Hasapis released Haldane and took a step back from him. 'I am Xenophon Hasapis of Sitia,' he announced. 'These are my sons, Manolis and Costas.' Haldane smiled and nodded to the two men. 'You have heard of me?' demanded Xenophon.

It was quite clear from Haldane's expression that he had not but this did nothing to deter Hasapis.

'But then of course you have,' he affirmed grandly. 'Who has not? Am I not the best fisherman in all Crete? And is it not known for the truth that in my life and my way I have been the equal to Heracles. He to whom Eurystheus gave the twelve great labours.'

Now it was Haldane's turn to grin. 'Heracles indeed,' he said and he looked impressed. 'Then it is I who am honoured.' His face took on a puzzled expression. 'But Heracles? Not Odysseus?', he enquired.

Hasapis was flummoxed by this. His smile faded and he frowned. 'No' he reiterated. 'Heracles.'

'Oh!' said Haldane innocently. And then he added with a faint smile. 'But surely it was Odysseus who was given to boasting, wasn't it?'

The jibe hit home. Hasapis' frown deepened, his eyes narrowed and he studied Haldane warily.

Fully aware that their father had just been insulted, however politely, Manolis and Costas scowled and stepped in closer to him. Annika shot Nikos an anxious look. Haldane smiled at Xenophon and unflinchingly stood his ground and slowly Hasapis' expression softened from anger to admiration. He has spirit this Englishman, he thought. He grinned and then laughed, now genuinely enjoying the joke against him. His sons relaxed.

'Odysseus! Heracles!' laughed Hasapis, playfully punching Haldane on the shoulder. 'It makes no difference. I am a match for either of them. I like you

Englishman.'

'Thank you, *Kyrie* Hasapis,' said Haldane.

Xenophon looked deeply hurt. 'Oh no,' he begged. 'Not *Kyrie* Hasapis! Xenophon! And I shall call you Leandros, eh?'

Haldane nodded. 'Please do,' he said, but all the while turning over in his mind just exactly what it was his new found friend was up to.

Hasapis moved to the edge of the quay and studied Haldane's caique with a critical eye. 'So this is what you have done with the wreck which Andreas Hagieleftheris gave you? And with your own hands I hear.' He nodded approvingly. 'You have done well. That is a beautiful caique.'

'Thank you.'

Xenophon turned to him. 'You are proud of her, uh?'

'I am pleased,' replied Haldane.

'Pleased!' roared Hasapis. 'That is too modest. A man must be proud of the work he does otherwise what joy will he find in it?' He wagged a finger at Haldane. 'And I see your joy, Leandros. It is in your eyes.' He turned to study the boat again. 'Mind you,' he went on casually. 'In your work there will be mistakes. Many.' Again he turned to Haldane and smiled but this time condescendingly. 'But then you are a foreigner, uh? Not that I am against foreigners you understand,' he hastened to assure him. 'I am often in Athens. The people there are good people.' He shook his head sadly. 'But it is known as the truth. Only a Cretan can build a caique for our waters. Now I have one. Much like yours.' He made a deprecating gesture. 'Not so fine looking perhaps, and older.' He nodded thoughtfully. 'Much older. But with a sail.' He spat contemptuously. 'I despise engines,' he confided and then held up his right hand, his thumb and forefinger held two inches apart. 'So I have only a little one.' He grinned and then winked and went on. 'For those days when there is no wind, you understand.' He shrugged. 'I am a fisherman. And a man must make a living.'

'True,' said Haldane.

Hasapis put an arm around the Englishman's shoulders. 'But what I am saying is this, Leandros,' he said earnestly. 'I built my caique. As my father built his and his father before him also. And they were Cretans as I am a Cretan. So, old as it is, between your caique and mine it must be that mine is the better of the two.' He smiled. 'You agree. That has to be so, uh?'

Realising that Hasapis was about to show his hand, and more and more intrigued, Haldane was only too willing to play along with him. He frowned thoughtfully. 'No,' he said uncertainly. 'Not necessarily.'

Hasapis adopted an expression of surprise and shock. He took a step back from Haldane and looked at him in astonishment. 'You doubt it?' he said.

Haldane shrugged. 'Without proof, yes.'

Xenophon regarding him sorrowfully but then, as if seeing the reasonableness of his argument, nodded sagely. 'You are right, Leandros,' he said. 'A man should accept nothing without proof.' He made a helpless gesture. 'But how can one prove such a thing? That my caique is better than yours. How?'

Now Haldane knew what was coming and he smiled quietly to himself. He nodded. 'Yes, that's difficult,' he agreed.

The two men studied one another and Hasapis's inspiration came as no surprise to Haldane. 'Unless of course . . .' Hasapis said eagerly. But then he broke off and shook his head. 'But no. That would not be fair,' he sighed.

'What wouldn't be fair, Xenophon?' enquired Haldane, a lamb led to slaughter.

'I was thinking,' explained Hasapis in a manner which suggested that he had already dismissed the idea. 'That perhaps there is a way in which we could settle this matter. To prove that mine is the better boat.'

'Oh! How?'

Xenophon shrugged. 'A test.'

The trap was sprung. Haldane willingly stepped into it.

'A race?' he asked doubtfully.

Hasapis had the Englishman hooked and he was delighted. 'How better?' he asked and then shot a look at his sons and winked.

The villagers gathered around them had been listening to their conversation with great interest and now there was a buzz of excited conversation at the prospect of a race. Annika and Nikos did not share their enthusiasm. They were both deeply concerned and it showed in their faces.

Haldane studied Hasapis as though turning the idea over in his mind. Then he nodded. 'When?' he asked.

'The sooner the better,' exclaimed Xenophon. 'At any other time I would say now. Today. But it is Easter. Tonight Christ will once more be in agony on Calvary.' He crossed himself. 'And tomorrow we must bury him.' He shook his head. 'There can be no race while we are in mourning,' he said respectfully. 'That would not be fitting. But on Sunday Christ will rise again,' he went on, smiling craftily. 'Is that not so?'

Haldane nodded. 'That is so.'

'And that is a time for celebration.'

'Yes it is,' agreed Haldane. 'Sunday then?' he enquired.

Hasapis nodded. 'In the afternoon.'

'Over what distance?'

Xenophon shrugged dismissively. 'That is unimportant,' he said. 'Whatever the distance, whatever the course we follow, the result will be the same.'

'You are that certain you will win then?' Haldane said with a smile.

Xenophon gave him a serious look and shook his head. 'No, Leandros. I am certain of nothing. Except death.' Then he smiled craftily again. 'But I am confident. As you must be. Come,' he prompted. 'Admit it. Only a fool enters a race he does not think he can win.' He paused to study the Englishman once more. And then he added, almost as an afterthought. 'As only a fool enters a race for which there is no prize.'

This was the crunch that Haldane had been waiting for. 'You're right, Xenophon,' he agreed thoughtfully. 'A prize. There has to be a prize.' He shrugged. 'But what?'

Hasapis, apparently equally at a loss to think of one, shook his head. But then he had another, sudden inspiration. 'I have it,' he cried. 'Your boat or my boat. That shall be the prize. Whoever wins will have not one caique but two. We will race to hold that which is ours and to gain from the other.'

Annika and Nikos, who had shared an uneasy feeling from the moment of Hasapis's arrival, were deeply alarmed by this development while the villagers, born Cretans and thus born gamblers, were a joy to see if the Englishman would accept the bet.

Haldane, his eyes on Hasapis and weighing him up further, hesitated. Nikos moved to his side. 'Leandros,' he murmured as a quiet warning. Haldane ignored him. Still he hesitated.

Manolis and Costas, just as anxious as their father that Haldane should not wriggle off the hook now, decided the moment had come for them to step in and administer the coup de grace.

'Such a stake, father,' said Manolis with mock concern. 'Such a risk.' He paused and then added. 'For the *Kyrie*.' He looked at Haldane sympathetically. 'Remember,' he said. 'It was a long time ago he was with the Andarte.'

Costas nodded. 'True,' he agreed quietly and with a faint and insolent smile. 'And it is well known that with some men the years rust the iron of their nerve.'

Hasapis snapped a look at his son. 'Costas!' he exclaimed in a gentle rebuke. Haldane smiled quietly, greatly enjoying the charade. Xenophon turned to his sons, seemingly on the defensive. 'It was only a thought,' he said. 'It seemed to me a fair wager. One worth the winning.' He sighed and nodded. 'But you are right. Between Cretans perhaps. And with the odds so much against Leandros.' He shrugged. 'And who will think any the less of him.' He turned back to the Englishman and his smile was warm but provocative. He clapped his hands. 'So, my friend. Some other prize then. What shall it be?' He looked into his eyes. 'Something you can afford to lose, eh? Choose.'

Haldane smiled back at him. 'No,' he said. 'I am content, Xenophon.'

There were renewed murmurs of excitement among the villagers. Nikos frowned and shook his head in despair. He looked across at Annika. She shrugged helplessly. Hasapis could hardly believe his good fortune and it showed in his expression. But then it suddenly occurrred to him that the Englishman really did believe that he had a chance of winning. He frowned briefly but then quickly dismissed the thought as nonsense. 'You agree,' he said. 'The winner takes the other's boat.'

Haldane nodded. 'Yes. I agree.' Then he added casually 'I only hesitated because I don't need two caiques.' He grinned. 'But that's no problem,' he went on. 'I see that now. I shall sell yours.'

Greatly taken by Haldane's audacity and relishing the joke, Hasapis roared with laughter. Then he put out his hand to Haldane. The Englishman took it. The race was on and the prize agreed.

'Till Sunday then,' said Haldane. He turned and, together with Annika and Nikos, walked slowly away from the moorings in the direction of the taverna.

Smiling, Xenophon looked at his sons and winked.

It was Nikos who told Elena about Hasapis's challenge and about the wager.

'Leandros!' she exclaimed aghast. 'Tell me that this is not so, that you have not done such a foolish thing, that Niko is joking.'

Nikos added ice to the two glasses of ouzo he had just poured and placed them on the counter in front of Haldane and Annika, together with a flask of water. 'But I am not joking,' he said. 'It's the truth.'

Elena frowned angrily. 'Then what you have done is an

act of madness,' she told him. She gave Nikos a look of rebuke. 'You were there. Why did you not stop him?' she asked.

'I tried to warn him,' sighed Nikos. 'But he would not listen.'

'That's right,' Haldane confirmed. 'He did try, Elena.'

'And you, Aunt,' challenged Elena. 'Did you not say anything?'

Annika poured some water into her glass. 'I know better than to interfere when men gamble,' she said disapprovingly. 'Particularly when it is a question of honour, of pride, with them.' She shot a look at Haldane. 'Besides, I do not have the right to say anything.'

Haldane took out his tobacco pouch and his pipe and began to fill it. 'I take it that you are against the idea?' he said.

Annika nodded. 'Yes. I think it is a great pity and foolish of you to put at risk something on which you have worked so hard. Something which means so much to you.'

'Just so,' agreed Elena. 'Annika is right.'

Haldane laughed. 'It's only a boat,' he argued.

Annika picked up her glass. 'Is it?' she asked quietly.

'Xenophon Hasapis has raced before,' Elena went on. 'Against others.' she sighed. 'And always he has won.'

Nikos nodded. 'He is a fine sailor.'

'I'm sure he is,' said Haldane calmly.

'But as some comfort, I will tell you this,' added Nikos. 'He has not got a caique which is as good as yours.'

Elena shook her head. 'Maybe,' she said ruefully. 'But after the race I think that perhaps he will have.'

'We'll see,' said Haldane. He gave Nikos an enquiring look. 'I can't handle the boat alone. Will you crew for me?'

Nikos nodded. 'Of course.' He smiled. 'And if nothing else, we will make Hasapis sweat a little,' he assured him. Then, picking up two crates of empty beer bottles, he moved away behind the counter with them and disappeared through the archway. Haldane struck a match and lit his pipe.

A noisy group of tourists entered the taverna and drifted through to the patio. Elena sighed. 'We are short of staff,' she muttered. 'Georgios and Pelopidas are both away today. They sent word that they are sick.' She snorted. 'But I think the truth is they wish to spend Easter with their families.' She left the bar and went out onto the patio to take the party's order.

Haldane glanced at Annika. She was staring at her glass. 'This race,' he said gently. 'I didn't have much choice, did I?'

'Anyone can walk away from a challenge,' she said.

Haldane frowned. 'Would you?' he asked. 'Do you?' Annika shrugged. Haldane shook his head. 'No, you don't. I'm sure you never have. And as for the risk involved, well there's risk in almost everything we do. It's just a question of weighing it.'

Annika slowly turned her head to look at him. She studied him intently. 'You are a strange man, Leandros,' she said. 'You say that. And it is true. And yet even when the scales are in your favour and you know it, it seems that there is still one risk that you will not take. And I wonder why.'

Haldane was well aware of the question in her mind but it was one to which he could not give an answer. He reached for his drink. 'There doesn't have to be a race. I could always back out.'

Annika shook her head. 'No, you cannot do that. Not now.'

'Of course I can. I'll just send word to Hasapis that I've changed my mind.'

'He would spread the word across the island. The story would be told as a joke in every taverna. A joke against Leandros, hero of the Andarte.'

Haldane nodded. 'Yes.'

Annika looked at him again. 'And while you remain on Crete you would have to live with that.'

He shrugged. 'I'd survive.'

Annika frowned. 'And you would do that for no other reason than because you know that what you have done distresses me?'

'Yes,' said Haldane, turning his face to her once more. 'If that's what you really want.'

She searched his face thoughtfully and then shook her head. 'There are many things that I want from you, Leandros,' she said. 'And in some perhaps I ask too much of you. But in this I want only one thing.' She smiled. 'That you win.' She glanced at her watch. 'And now I am sorry to say that I must go. There is much I have to do at the factory before we close for Easter.'

Haldane nodded understandingly. 'Yes, I'm sure there is,' he said. 'And I've been away too long from my drawing board. The design is coming on well but I've still got some way to go and I must get it finished.'

Annika smiled. 'Well just as long as you do not work too hard over the holiday. I am looking forward to our spending at least some time together.'

Haldane gave her a surprised look. 'Us? Are you going to be in Elounda for Easter then?' he asked.

Annika nodded. 'Here. I am staying in the taverna. I shall be back later tonight. Are you surprised?'

'Yes. I'd thought you'd probably spend it with your family. With your mother.'

Annika frowned at the memory of the last time she saw her mother at the cemetery in Dhafnai. 'Elena is part of my family, isn't she? And I want to be here.'

'Good,' he said. 'I'm glad.'

She smiled wryly. 'Glad! That is a word like *nice*. Polite but without heart.'

Haldane smiled, reached out and took her hand. 'Yes, you're right,' he agreed. 'Happy then. Very happy.'

Annika needed to know this, to believe it; this and much more. 'Are you, Leandros? Are you?'

'More than I can say,' he replied.

Haldane opened the front door of his house and pulled

up abruptly in the doorway with a look or horror on his face. The room was a shambles and in chaos. His records, his books, all his personal possessions had been swept from the shelves and the furniture flung in all directions. Many of the books had been savagely torn and some of the LPs were twisted or bent double. His radio and his camera lay trampled and wrecked on the floor. His worktable had been overturned, its drawer pulled out and its contents strewn wildly. The designs for the new dinghy on which he had been working for the past two and a half weeks had first been daubed with indian ink then wrenched from the drawing board and ripped apart. More ink had been poured over the letters and papers spilled from the drawer.

Stunned and with an expression of disbelief, Haldane moved further into the room. His foot touched something lying on the floor. He looked down, stooped and picked it up. It was the framed photograph of his wife, the glass smashed, the frame buckled and the photograph, lying alongside the wreckage, torn in half. Haldane stared at the ruined picture and then looked up from it and gazed around the room, sickened and deeply wounded.

CHAPTER NINETEEN

'How long were you away from the house?' asked Krasakis, surveying the havoc around them. A policeman stood just inside the open front door.

'Four hours,' muttered Haldane. 'A bit longer perhaps.'

'And the front door was unlocked?'

'As always. Who locks doors in Elounda?' Haldane asked. 'In the daytime anyway.'

Krasakis nodded in understanding and agreement. 'Or in any village in Crete,' he said. 'What need is there for keys where there is trust and respect. But, sadly, times are changing, my friend. It is becoming the age of the locksmith. Even here.' He moved further into the room. 'And nothing has been stolen you say?'

'As far as I can tell. So why? Who'd do a thing like this?'

The Major sighed. 'Regrettably it is not only money the tourists bring with them.'

'You mean that this was just senseless, bloody vandalism!' exclaimed Haldane.

Krasakis turned to him. 'One of the sicknesses of Europe. And the carriers of that sickness arrive here every day by air or by sea. Even we Cretans are not immune to infection.'

'No. I don't believe it,' said Haldane adamantly. 'No Cretan would do this.'

'No. I agree,' concurred Krasakis. 'That would be out of character. Destruction merely for the joy of it. So it has to be the work of a foreigner. Or foreigners. We will, of course, need to make tests for fingerprints.'

Haldane nodded. 'If you really think that will help.'

'Probably not. But who knows. It might. And it is, in

any case, a matter of routine.' Krasakis looked across at the policeman standing by the front door. 'Get on the radio,' he told him. 'And tell headquarters that I want a scientific and fingerprint team here as soon as possible.'

The policeman saluted. 'Yes, sir.' Then he turned and hurried away down the steps.

Haldane picked up the pieces of the ruined drawing and looked at them sadly. 'Why? Why?' he questioned savagely.

'That was important to you?' asked Krasakis.

'Very,' replied Haldane bitterly. 'A hell of a lot of work went into that.' The Major gave him a questioning look. 'They're the drawings of a new type of sailing dinghy I've designed,' he explained. He tossed them down onto the table. 'Now it's just waste paper.'

Annika heard the news of the outrage when she returned to Elounda at nine o'clock that night and she went straight to Haldane's house. By then he had disposed of those things which were clearly beyond repair and had restored some semblance of order to the room. His torn and ink-smeared drawings still lay in pieces on the table. Annika crossed to them and picked up one of the fragments.

'I am so sorry, Leandros,' she said, close to tears. 'So very sorry.'

'So am I,' sighed Haldane. 'It means I'll have to start again from scratch. And just about when I was ready to show Nikos the drawings. He still hasn't given me an answer about the sailing centre and I wanted to keep him interested and keen. I'd hoped this would do it.'

'Who could have done such a terrible thing?'

Haldane gave a weary, dispirited shrug. 'God knows.'

'But it has to have been the act of a sick mind, the act of a savage,' she declared. And then suddenly practical she asked with an anxious frown. 'Have you eaten?'

Haldane shook his head. Somehow he had not felt like it. He protested when she said she would prepare some thing for him but she would not listen and hurried away into the kitchen.

They ate together and afterwards took their wine out on to the balcony. It was a warm night. The village was quiet and still. Earlier the church had been filled to capacity for the Maundy Thursday services symbolising the crucifixion and women had hung wreathes of fragrant lemon blossom on the cross in the centre of the church and then, while the other villagers had pushed forward to kiss the feet of the Saviour, they had tossed flower petals into the air to form a multi-coloured, candlelit, sweet-smelling cloud which had slowly drifted down again like snow to settle on the heads and shoulders of the congregation. And then the people had walked home in silence. Christ was in agony and dying and Elounda mourned. Tomorrow they would bury Him and He would be given a resplendent funeral.

Far out to sea were the lights of a ship and Haldane stared at them pensively. He and Annika stood side by side, Annika's left hand resting on the balcony rail. There had been little conversation during the meal. Haldane had huddled in his depression and Annika had only occasionally attempted to coax him out of it but with little success and they had both been grateful for the music from the record player in which they could each take refuge. Now, gazing out into the night, their thoughts were set to the melancholic strains of Faure's *Elegie* filtering softly from the room behind them.

'It's difficult to believe,' Haldane reflected, remembering the scene which had greeted him when he had returned to the house earlier that day. 'That such a thing should have happened. In a place so beautiful and peaceful as this.' He shrugged.

Annika nodded. 'And yet without ugliness and violence there would be no beauty or peace, would there?' she said quietly. 'As without evil there would be no goodness and without hate no love. The mountain and the valley – neither would exist without the other.'

Absently Haldane put his right hand onto the rail and it

195

touched Annika's. She made no attempt to move her hand away and they looked at one another and there was a mutual longing, a mutual need in their eyes.

Without taking her eyes from him, Annika moved her hand from the rail and turned to Haldane, willing him to take her into his arms. And for a moment he considered doing just that. But it was not possible, not with the shadow that lay between them. And yet, and yet, he argued inwardly, perhaps it is better to lose something precious which one has held, however briefly, than never to have possessed it at all. But then the thought of her hurt if, after giving herself to him, she ever found out the truth, again scored his conscience. If that happened she would have lost nothing, it would have been stolen from her with forethought and by him. And what kind of a crime would that be? He turned from her, took a sip from his wine glass and then looked at his watch. 'It's very late,' he said. 'Nearly a quarter to one. I'll walk you back to the taverna, shall I?'

Annika studied him. Why? Why? she questioned. For God's sake, why? Why does he still hold back from me, from the love I have for him, the comfort I am offering? Why does he still deny the love I see there in his eyes? She nodded. 'Very well, Leandros,' she said. 'If that is what you want.'

Haldane hesitated. He did not look at her 'Yes. I'd like to walk with you,' he said.

Still Annika studied him. Still not understanding. But she could only go so far. Even for him her pride had set boundaries beyond which she would not, could not step. The next move must come from him. But he made no move.

Annika frowned and then, impulsively, she leant forward and kissed him on the cheek. 'Shall we go then,' she said. She moved away from him and back into the room.

Haldane, sad, troubled and silently cursing his resolve, watched her go, Then he drained his glass and followed her.

The following morning Haldane got up early. He made himself a mug of coffee and then, with the mug in his hand, stood in the kitchen doorway and surveyed the living room thoughtfully. He crossed to the table and picked up the pieces of his design and stared at them. With a sigh he moved slowly over to his worktable and, putting the mug of coffee down on one side of it, pinned a fresh sheet of cartridge paper to the drawing board. He filled his pipe and lit it. When it was burning well he settled himself on his stool, picked up a T square and a pencil and, with a look of resolve, began again.

He was still working when, that afternoon, Annika quietly pushed open the front door. He had not drunk his breakfast coffee and his pipe, still in his mouth, was unlit and filled only with cold, wet tobacco ash. And so intent was he on what he was doing that he was completely unaware of her presence and that he was being watched.

Annika smiled to herself and stepped back through the doorway.

He was equally engrossed when she returned in the evening and he had achieved a great deal. But this time she interrupted him.

'That is enough for one day.'

As though coming out of a trance, Haldane focused his eyes on her, smiled and then stretched and examined the work he had done. He was pleased with it.

'Yes, you're right,' he agreed gratefully.

'Have you finished?'

He nodded. 'Almost.'

'So now you can relax a little,' she insisted. 'First we shall eat and then we shall watch the procession together.'

Nikos and Elena were delighted to see Haldane and Elena fussed over him, refusing to give them a menu.

'Barbounia,' she told Haldane. 'Your favourite. Freshly caught today. And I will grill them myself for you.'

And while she was preparing the fish, Nikos presented him with a bottle of wine. 'This is very special, Leandros,' he said. 'And you will please me if you will accept it as a gift.' The Englishman protested but Nikos waved his protests aside. 'We are all ashamed of what has happened to you here in Elounda. This bottle cannot compensate you in any way for that evil act but the good wine will, I hope, help to wash the bitter taste from your mouth.'

The wine was excellent and so were the tender, red mullet served with a salad and preceded by dishes of *taramosalata, fasolya, kalamarakia* and half a dozen other appetisers.

And when Haldane and Annika had finished eating and Alexis had been scrubbed and then, with his parents, put on his best clothes, they all went out to choose a good position from which to watch the procession that marked Christ's funeral.

All of Elounda was on the streets that night and many dozens of tourists as well. Despite the solemnity of the occasion, the villagers were clearly all set to enjoy themselves. There was a great deal of horseplay and excited chatter which did not even die away as Haldane heard the procession approaching the spot where he was standing with Alexis on his shoulders and Annika, Nikos and Elena beside him.

Heralded by small boys banging hammers on iron bars and ringing bells, the procession finally came into view. It was led by the bearded priest, resplendent in rose-gold robes and swinging a silver censer, its chains clanging and rattling. The air was filled with incense.

The priest was attended by cantors and choirboys carrying the cross and banners. Behind them young men carried the flower, ribbon and streamer bedecked coffin which the girls of the village had spent hours decorating that morning. They were followed by the large crowd of worshippers who had been in the church for the service which led up to the funeral ceremony. And, as the procession passed, many of the onlookers also fell in behind, swelling its number, while others ran out from the pavement to kiss the priest's hand or to perform the good luck gesture of bending double and almost crawling under the upraised coffin as it was carried past them. It was a festive scene and almost as though the villagers were not only paying homage to Christ who had died on the cross for them but, in joyous spirit and in an almost pagan manner, were celebrating, as their ancestors had celebrated thousands of years before at this time of the year, the Earth Mother's return among them.

The procession made slow progress, the priest stopping frequently to pose proudly and with great dignity for the ever-clicking cameras of the tourists.

Matheos Noukakis was among the spectators in Elounda that night but his eyes were not on the procession. From where he was standing he could see Haldane and Annika and the Vassilakis family and his full attention throughout was on the Englishman.

And from his vantage point on a balcony overlooking the street, Major Krasakis caught sight of Noukakis and saw the look on his face and the object of his attention. And what he saw made Krasakis wonder.

Saturday was also a day of mourning but, at the same time, one of great activity and hushed excitement in anticipation of the miracle and the renewal to come. Very shortly after dawn women carried the large Easter cakes which they had made to the bakers who would bake them for them in their ovens. And, throughout the day, while children sat quietly in corners dyeing and stencilling eggs in bright colours, the local butchers, their hands, forearms and aprons stained with blood, were kept busy slaughtering lambs for the feasting which would begin on Easter Sunday morning and continue for some days.

That night the church was again packed to capacity; the men standing at the front, the women at the rear, according to custom. And everyone clutched a long, unlit candle.

On their arrival the priest had personally conducted Haldane and Annika to the place of honour in the stalls to one side and at the front of the church.

'Can you see all right?' asked Annika in a whisper as she handed Haldane his candle.

Haldane nodded. 'Yes. Fine. But I can't help feeling that we ought to be in among the others. With Nikos and Elena.'

'No,' whispered Annika. 'In Crete a stranger, someone from another place, is thought to be from God. You are not a stranger here, Leandros, but the people of Elounda wish to show you the same respect. Even more so after the shameful thing that was done to you.'

Haldane looked around. The church was decorated with boughs of rosemary, laurel and myrtle and filled with their heady scent. The electric lights illuminated the frescoes on the walls and the painted ceiling which together depicted, in the Byzantine convention, biblical scenes, including the Last Supper and the grieving Virgin and the other Mary at the foot of the cross and the faces of saints and prophets.

The service began and it went on and on, seemingly interminable; the priest intoning, the congregation responding, their voices a dirgeful drone and their faces solemn and sorrowful.

'*Kyrie Eleison,*' chanted the worshippers.

'*Kyrie Eleison,*' confirmed the priest.

The chant and the response were repeated endlessly until Haldane began to feel that he could stand it no longer.

But then towards midnight the voices and the expressions changed, expectation grew, melancholy gave way to hope. As the great moment approached a feeling of excitement filled the church and the worshippers murmured and shifted restlessly, scarcely able to contain themselves.

'*Kyrie Eleison,*' they chanted.

'*Kyrie Eleison,*' boomed the priest.

And then it was twelve o'clock. As though at the turn of a switch, the chanting suddenly ceased. And then a switch was turned and the church was plunged into total darkness

200

and the darkness seemed to Haldane to last a long time and it was made even more eerie by the complete silence and stillness which was part of it. Then a single flickering light appeared from behind the iconostasis, the flame of the consecrated candle held by the priest.

'Come and receive the light,' the priest proclaimed. Those in the front of the church pressed forward to light their candles from the flame. Then the first lighted tapers were passed from hand to hand and into the darkness at the back of the church until, in less than a minute, the whole building was filled with hundreds of bobbing candles, illuminating excited faces and casting dancing shadows on the walls.

Annika lit her candle from a man standing close to her and then turned to Haldane. 'Come,' she said quietly. 'Receive the light.' And she lit Haldane's candle with the flame of hers.

Followed by the cantors and his other attendants, the priest moved through the throng towards the door of the church. The door was thrown open and the priest, followed now by everyone holding their candles, processed out into the night.

Three times the priest led the procession around the church before mounting a small platform and reading the Gospel passage describing the Resurrection. Coming to the end of the verses, he closed the bible and looked down at the throng of expectant, candlelit faces, around him and made the proclamation they had all been waiting for.

'Christos anesti,' he cried.

'Christos anesti,' came the answering cry from the crowd. And in a corner of the churchyard a bonfire burst into flames, fireworks exploded and rockets and Roman candles flared up into the night sky.

The villagers, still holding their candles, milled around the church, joyously repeating the cry of 'Christ is risen' and greeting friends, relatives and tourists alike with the salutation, 'Chronia polla,' to receive the answer from those who understood it as 'Many years' of 'Episis – 'And

201

you.'

Haldane and Annika stood facing one another. Annika's face was radiant in the light from their candles and the flames from the bonfire. High above them the rockets exploded noisily and cascaded coloured stars.

'Christ is risen,' Annika said lovingly and looking into his face.

'Christ is risen,' responded Haldane quietly.

'*Chronia polla.*'

Haldane studied her. '*Episis,*' he replied with great feeling.

Nikos and Elena came up to them. '*Christos anesti,*' they cried in unison. '*Christos anesti,*' answered Annika. Nikos put out his hand to Haldane. '*Chronia polla,*' he said with a smile. '*Episis,*' said Haldane, gripping his hand. And then they embraced.

Elena kissed her aunt. '*Chronia polla.*'

'*Episis,*' smiled Annika. She turned to Haldane. 'And now we must each return home with our candles still alight. If we do, it is said that is a sign that we shall have good luck in the coming year.' She paused and then added. 'And all that we desire.'

The bonfire was fed with more wood and flared even higher. More rockets exploded and cascaded in the darkness against a background of stars.

Side by side Haldane and Annika, with others around them, walked slowly away from the church guarding the flame of their candles with cupped hands. The darkness around them was punctured by dozens of other tiny points of zealously protected flame.

On a street corner they passed a group of young men who were singing a soft and romantic *mantinade* to the accompaniment of *lyra* and *luia.* They paused to listen to them and then moved on again, Annika picking up the song and singing it quietly as they walked. Above them rockets and Roman candles continued to flare and arc across the sky.

They reached Haldane's house and together started to

climb the steps to the front door and as they did so the flame of Haldane's candle, caught unguarded in a sudden light breeze, flickered and went out. Outside the front door they turned to one another.

'I didn't quite make it,' Haldane said quietly, holding up his candle. 'Nearly but not quite.'

'My light is your light,' she replied, her eyes on his. 'My good fortune is your good fortune. Share it with me. Receive the light, Leandros.' She lit his candle from the flame of hers once more and then again looked up into his face. 'And all that you desire,' she added.

Haldane studied her and suddenly he knew that he no longer cared, that nothing was more important than she was, than they were.

'Stay with me,' he said simply.

Annika smiled.

He took her into the house and to his bed.

They made love beautifully with passionate tenderness and later, lying side by side to the accompaniment of songs drifting into the room from the street below, Haldane gazed up at the ceiling lost in thought.

Annika put a hand on his bare chest and caressed it. 'What are you thinking?' she asked.

He looked at her and smiled gently. 'I was just wondering what it was that I have done to ever deserve this moment.'

'Love is a prize we are given for doing nothing,' she answered. 'Only after we have it do we have to earn it.'

Haldane turned to her, took her in his arms again and kissed her.

CHAPTER TWENTY

'Are you ready then, Leandros?' shouted Hasapis with a grin.

His caique was moored a few yards away from *The Knot* and he was standing alongside the mast with his sons on either side of him. Both boats had their bows pointed seaward.

The Easter celebrations were in full swing and, judging by the size of the crowd which had gathered in the open space before the moorings, in Elounda at least one of the high spots of the day was to be the eagerly awaited race between the Englishman and Xenophon Hasapis.

People had gathered there in their hundreds, men, women and children, villagers and tourists. Babis Spiridakis was among them. So was his wife, Sia, a very attractive woman in her mid-forties. They had left their own family celebration and had driven down from Heraklion to be present. It was something Babis had assured his wife that they could not possibly miss.

Also in the foreground of the crowd was Andreas Hagieleftheris, inwardly confident, despite the odds being given around him in Hasapis' favour, that Leandros, with what he had done to the boat he had given him and being the man he was, would surely win. And he had placed 200 drachmas which he could ill afford to lose on him at one hundred to one as a mark of his confidence.

As the seconds before the race ticked away so the air of anticipation and excitement grew among the crowd where, in the warm afternoon sunlight, the *souvlakia*, bread and pastry vendors and balloon sellers were doing a brisk trade.

Minds finally made up, last minute bets were made

between friends and worry beads were very much in evidence among the men and being well used as an antidote for nervousness against the prospect that their owners might just have put their money on the wrong man.

Haldane checked his boat. Nikos was in position and so was Annika who, despite his trying to argue her out of it, had insisted on making up his crew. He looked across at Hasapis and nodded.

'Yes, I'm ready, Heracles,' he called out.

Hasapis roared with laughter. 'Very well then,' he shouted and pointed out to sea where, some way off from the moorings, a rowing boat was riding at anchor with an old fisherman sitting in the bow. 'The rowing boat there marks the starting line. And old Georgillis is the starter. The race begins on his signal and the course is as we agreed. Yes?'

'Yes,' called Haldane. 'From here to Spinalonga, through the channel, up the east side of the island, round the headland and back.'

Hasapis nodded in agreement. 'And the first past Georgillis again is the winner,' he shouted. He looked up at the sail of his caique flapping gently in the north westerly breeze and then back at Haldane again. 'We have a fair wind. Good fortune, Englishman. May Poseidon be kind to us both.' He grinned broadly and teasingly. 'But take good care of my caique, uh?' At this Manolis and Costas laughed and then, on a sign from their father, prepared to put to sea.

Stern lines were cast off, the sails of both boats were trimmed to catch the wind and the two caiques moved slowly away from the moorings and towards the starting line. Georgillis raised a handkerchief, held it high for a few seconds until the boats were both level and then dropped his arm. The race was on.

For some distance the caiques sailed practically bow to bow. Haldane, Hasapis and their crews were alert and on their mettle to gain every possible advantage from the following wind. But then, slowly at first but with a steadily increasing lead, Hasapis pulled ahead.

Nikos and Annika exchanged anxious looks but Haldane, his face expressionless, was intent on the helm and the set of the sails.

Hasapis and his sons jubilated over their widening lead. And as Xenophon steered his caique into the channel between the Spinalonga peninsula and the island fortress, *The Knot* was lagging badly and fell even further behind as they raced up the easern side of the island.

On the turn for home Hasapis and his sons were confident of victory but now they were sailing into the wind and having to tack. And Manolis, glancing astern, reacted with a look of dismay and shouted to his father. With each tack Haldane's caique, with its ability to sail closer to the wind and its quicker response, was narrowing the gap between them.

It was Annika's and Nikos's turn to be excited and encouraged now. Concentrating furiously and shouting orders which were instantly and expertly obeyed, Haldane steered the boat from one tack to another.

Xenophon swore and his sons grew more alarmed when they saw exactly how fast *The Knot* was catching up with them.

Half a mile off the finishing line the two boats were almost level on each tack but with Haldane still gaining. Helplessly, Hasapis watched as finally *The Knot* overtook his caique and, despite his efforts and those of his sons, their vessel was soon trailing well behind.

To the cheers of the spectators as *The Knot* passed the bow of the rowing boat, Georgillis dropped his hand to signal the end of the race. It was a convincing win.

Overjoyed, Annika and Nikos hugged one another and, for the first time since they set sail, Haldane smiled. To continuing cheers he brought *The Knot* bow on to the moorings and Nikos jumped ashore with a line and secured it. Then Haldane and Annika lowered the sail.

Hasapis caique crossed the finishing line and also

headed for the moorings. Xenophon and his sons were looking very subdued.

Spiridakis was the first to congratulate Haldane and Annika as they stepped ashore. 'Well done, Leandros,' he exclaimed with a broad, happy smile. 'Such a win.' Then he looked across at the losing caique and his smile faded. He shook his head sadly. 'And for Xenophon Hasapis, such a loss,' he went on. 'For he has lost everything. Without his boat he has nothing. He is a rogue and as cunning as a fox but he is not a rich man.'

Haldane laughed. 'You don't think I'll hold him to the bet, do you?'

The lawyer looked at him gravely and with a hint of alarm in his expression. 'But you have to,' he said. 'Not to do so would be to dishonour him. And in public.' He appealed to Annika. 'Is that not so?'

Annika, nodded. 'Yes. You have won, Leandros. You must take his boat as he would have taken yours.'

As those in the forefront of the crowd surged in around them, cheering and shouting congratulations, Haldane frowned. Then the crowd parted to allow Hasapis and his sons to approach the victor. Xenophon was holding an unopened bottle of Metaxa brandy. He came face to face with the Englishman. The people around them were suddenly silent. It was the moment of settlement and a solemn one for every one of the Cretans among the spectators was aware of the true extent of Hasapis' loss.

Xenophon had shed little of his jauntiness and none of his dignity and pride but Manolis and Costas, while showing no resentment, were clearly very worried.

'This Metaxa was to console you, Englishman,' said Hasapis, holding up the bottle. 'But you have no need for it. So I shall drink it myself, with my sons.' He nodded. 'You did well. I am proud to have been beaten by such a fine boat. By such a fine sailor.'

'Thank you,' said Haldane quietly.

'And now my caique is yours,' declared Hasapis. 'Take it. But you said that if you won it you would sell it.

Without a boat I am nothing and I have nothing. So what do you ask for it, Leandros?'

Now there was an almost unbearable silence around the two men. Everyone in Elounda was well aware of what Hasapis' caique was worth and there were few who did not know that he could not afford to meet such a price. Suddenly the air was charged with tension. Haldane, his eyes on Hasapis, hesitated.

'Well? How much? What is your price?' demanded Xenophon.

Still Haldane hesitated. He realised now that Hasapis must not lose face and somehow he had to find a way to ensure this. But how? Seeing the Englishman's hesitation, Hasapis frowned. Then Haldane decided. 'A bottle of Metaxa,' he declared loudly.

There was a gasp from those around them. Annika and Spiridakis exchanged looks and then quiet, comprehending smiles. Hasapis' face was expressionless. His eyes were on the Englishman. He knew full well what Haldane was doing and he appreciated it. But his honour and his pride would not allow him to accept a deal in which there was even a hint of charity. With even such a generous price as had been demanded, *philotimo* and Cretan business custom called for him to haggle. He shook his head and made a counter proposal.

'A glass,' he offered.

Haldane, fully aware of Hasapis' position and feelings, entered willingly and solemnly into the charade. He shook his head 'A bottle,' he insisted.

Hasapis smiled and made a conciliatory gesture. 'Two glasses,' he suggested.

Again Haldane shook his head, resolute and immovable. 'A bottle,' he said adamantly. And then added warningly. 'My last offer.'

Hasapis made a show as if to argue further but then, shaking his head ruefully, capitulated with a shrug. "You drive a hard bargain, Englishman," he sighed. He handed Haldane the bottle of brandy and then, his face breaking into a broad smile, he swept him into his arms and embraced him as, in their turn, did Manolis and Costas, both of them much relieved, both very grateful.

As the story of the settlement was relayed through the crowd a resounding cheer went up. Leandros had won but no one had truly lost anything other than a race. And honour had been satisfied. Hasapis put his hands on Haldane's shoulder's and held him at arms' length.

"And now we celebrate," he ordered. "Your victory; friendship; and the Resurrection."

The celebrations were enthusiastic and noisy and seemed to centre on the Vassilakis' taverna. There was eating on a gargantuan scale, singing and dancing of unparalleled joy and verve and drinking such as Haldane had never seen before. The festivities went on long into the night.

The moorings were deserted so it was easy for Matheos Noukakis to reach them unobserved carrying two cans of petrol. He boarded *The Knot,* opened one of the cans and emptied it over the deck and superstructure. Then he tossed it aside and opened the second. He was smiling.

The taverna and the patio were packed with people and everyone still on their feet seemed to be having a wonderful time. The musicians, their faces wet with sweat, played seemingly without ever tiring, bolstered by copious draughts of wine.

Haldane sat with Annika at a table on the patio watching a group of young men expressing their feelings in the way that Cretans know best, by dancing. Their sentiments and the raki they had consumed dictated that they dance the *pentozali* and they vied with one another in feats of athletic bravado when each one's turn came to lead the line; with high leaps and pirouettes and deep knee bends. And the revellers applauded and encouraged them with cries of "*Opah!*" and threw plates which shattered on the floor around the dancers' feet.

Babis Spiridakis and Sia had stayed for longer than they intended but finally, firmly dismissing all further entreaties to see the night out in Elounda, they had, with Haldane's help and a little reluctantly, managed to slip away to join their children and their relatives in Heraklion for the remainder of the Easter Sunday festivities.

Now Haldane wanted more than anything else to be alone again with Annika. And he knew from the looks which she gave him that this was her dearest wish too. He took her hand and looked at her questioningly. She smiled and nodded.

Haldane was just getting to his feet when Xenophon Hasapis pushed his way through the crowd and over to their table. He was holding a bottle, smiling happily and a little unsteady on his feet. He peered into Haldane's face, nodded and then said solemnly. 'It is true. What you said. I have to be Heracles. For you are Odysseus. And I salute you. One hero to another.' He raised the bottle and drank from it. Then he pointed to Annika. 'And guard that woman well, my friend,' he went on. 'For she is your Penelope I think. And good for you.'

'And that is the truth,' smiled Haldane. He slapped Hasapis on the shoulder. 'You are a wise man, Heracles.'

'Fire!' someone shouted in the distance. And then again. 'Fire!'

Haldane and Hasapis frowned. They had both detected the note of real alarm in the voice.

Nikos burst out onto the patio from the taverna in a state of great agitation. 'Leandros!' he shouted as he bulldozed his way through the throng. 'Your boat! It is on fire!'

Haldane and Nikos, with Annika and Hasapis only just behind them, were the first of those on the patio to reach the street and join those already gathered on the pavement and staring across at the moorings, their faces lit by the conflagration down by the edge of the sea.

The Knot was a mass of flames.

Elena thrust her way through to Annika's side. Horrified and stunned, they gazed at the blazing caique hypnotised by the sight and unable to say or do anything.

Nikos turned and shouted orders to those around him. 'Buckets! We will need buckets. Many buckets. And men to use them. Come on! All of you!'

There was a general movement to obey.

But Haldane did not move. He knew that there was nothing to be done to save the boat. The flames had too strong a hold on it. He could only watch it burn; disbelieving, sickened and in a state of almost total shock.

The next morning the streets of the village were deserted and an air of melancholy hung over Elounda.

The Knot, hauled out of the water once the fire had been extinguished, lay on her side on the open ground above the moorings. She was almost a total wreck. The mast, sails and rigging had been devoured by the flames and those timbers not completely destroyed were scorched and charred. Only the frame, beams and the keel appeared to have escaped the fire largely unscathed.

Haldane and Major Krasakis stood alongside the burnt-out boat while, a little way off from them and out of earshot, Annika and Spiridakis watched. The lawyer had hurried to Elounda the moment he had heard the news.

Haldane was devastated. He stared at the wreck like a beaten man. All those hours, weeks of hard work gone for nothing in only a few minutes. Another loss. Another defeat.

Annika felt wretched. She wanted so desperately to comfort Haldane. She had already tried but without any success. Now she felt utterly helpless and, having seen his reaction to the disaster, a dreadful fear had begun to nag her.

'This has been a terrible blow to him, Babis,' she said.

Spiridakis nodded. 'I know,' he replied quietly. 'That boat meant so much to him.'

"*The Knot,*' Annika remembered, almost in a whisper.

211

'The knot that bound him to Crete.'

Spiridakis looked at her. 'To more than just Crete I think,' he said. 'He will need us, Annika. Need you. Desperately. For at a time like this, with so much of what he has built with such love destroyed, a man could be tempted to give up everything.'

Annika frowned deeply. This was the fear which nagged her so.

Krasakis looked at Haldane. 'You have to know, Leandros,' he said gravely. 'That this was not an accident.'

Haldane did not take his eyes off what was left of the caique.

'And you must also know,' the Major went on, 'that I am now certain that what happened at your house was not just a thoughtless, uncaring act. It was a deliberate one. As was this. My men found an empty petrol can on the deck when they searched the boat after the fire. And much of the timber stills smells of petrol. You have an enemy. An enemy who wishes to drive you from Crete.'

Haldane shrugged. He had almost given up. There was no anger and little inquisitiveness left in him. 'Why?' he asked in a flat, unemotional voice. 'Who?'

'There is someone I think who may be involved,' replied Krasakis. 'I have already spoken to him this morning. He claims that he was elsewhere last night when the fire started. And there are those who support his story. So there is little I can do. For now.'

'What's his name?' enquired Haldane dully and apparently without any real interest.

The Major shook his head. 'No. Not until I am certain. Not until I have the evidence I need. And then I will act, and you will know.'

Haldane sighed deeply. 'I'm not sure it matters much any more.'

The Major studied him and frowned. 'To me it does,' he said quietly. 'For the law has been broken. But to you?' He shook his head sadly. 'Perhaps not. For I think that your enemy may already have succeeded in that which he desires.' He saluted. "*Kalimera*, Leandros.' He turned and walked away in the direction of his Land-Rover which was parked on the road.

Haldane, his eyes on the boat and his thoughts elsewhere, hardly noticed him go. Annika, seeing the Major leave, moved away from Spiridakis and the lawyer watched her as she crossed to his friend. He made no move to join them.

Haldane seemed unaware of Annika when she came up beside him. She touched his arm. 'Leandros,' she said gently. Slowly he turned his head to look at her and, from his expression and the look in his eyes, at that moment she felt certain that her worst fears were confirmed.

Then Annika heard the sound of the vehicles approaching. She looked in their direction and reacted first with surprise and then delight and joy. 'Leandros!' she cried excitedly. 'Look!'

Xenophon Hasapis' Mazda pick-up, with Hasapis driving and Manolis beside him and with Costas sitting in the back astride a load of timber, was leading two other trucks along the road, in the back of one of which, precariously balanced and not very securely tied, was a mast.

As the three vehicles turned off the road and were driven across the open ground towards them, with Xenophon, Manolis and Costas shouting, waving and smiling at them; so from every house on the main road and from all the narrow streets and alleyways leading off it appeared the men of Elounda, young and old. They carried tools, lengths of timber, coils of rope and wire, buckets of nails, caulking material; everything needed to rebuild a boat.

The villagers swarmed over the open ground in the wake of the pick-up trucks which pulled up close to the wreck. Hasapis, his sons and the two other drivers, grinning broadly and encouragingly, got down from their vehicles and walked across to Haldane and Annika. And as they did so the villagers fell in behind them and then spread out to form a half circle around the wreck.

Haldane frowned, puzzled. He did not understand.

Hasapis, his arms folded across his chest and a beaming smile on his face, stood a pace or two from the Englishman and regarded him. 'Well, Odysseus,' he demanded. 'How then shall we begin? You are the man who best knows how to build boats.'

Mystified, Haldane glanced questioningly at Annika. 'Did you arrange this?'

Annika shook her head. 'No,' she said quietly. 'What they are doing they are doing for you.'

Xenophon frowned in astonishment. 'Did we not celebrate friendship yesterday?' he asked, shocked. 'And are we not your friends?' He nodded. 'We are your friends. And so what you rebuilt and was destroyed we will rebuild again. Together.' He frowned again. 'Is that not how you would have it? To work alongside friends. Alongside your own people.'

Suddenly Haldane's helplessness and despair were lifted from his shoulders. He looked to Annika for final reassurance. She smiled at him. 'Receive the light, Leandros,' she whispered. 'Love, friendship.' With a movement of her head she indicated those around them. 'And belonging.'

Haldane, his mood of despair completely dispelled, smiled back at her and nodded. Quickly he crossed to Hasapis and embraced him. Then, taking a step back from the delighted Xenophon, he grinned and stripped off his jacket. He was ready to go to work again.

Spiridakis came up alongside Annika. 'He is home,' he told her. 'He is ours again.'

She nodded. 'And we shall hold on to him, Babis.' There was determination in her voice.

'So what are we waiting for?' Hasapis shouted to the assembled villagers. 'There is work to be done. Let us start.'

Some of the villagers swarmed in on the wreck while others unloaded the three pick-up trucks. Enthusiastically, Haldane and Hasapis began to strip away the timbers from the frame of the caique. Haldane paused in his work, looked across at Annika and smiled. She smiled back at him. Then, with tears of happiness in her eyes, she turned from the scene and absently gazed out to sea. As she did so her smile faded and she frowned. Way out across the lagoon the two hawks were slowly circling over the roof of the ruined chapel on the upper ramparts of the old fortress. Circling, wheeling, sharp-eyed and merciless.

And Annika sensed in them a menace stronger than she had ever felt before.

CHAPTER TWENTY-ONE

'But to kill the Englishman!' Noukakis exclaimed. 'In that you are asking much of me, *Kyria* Matakis.'

Katerina stood with her back to him staring grimly at the plaque depicting the three Fates which hung on the wall beside the sitting-room door.

'The last resort. We agreed that,' she said without turning to him. And then she added scornfully, 'But now, like my son, you do not have the stomach for it, Matheos Noukakis. Is that it?'

Noukakis hesitated. He was more than willing to kill Haldane. He would even enjoy killing him. But he was not going to do it for nothing. There must be more in the Englishman's death for him than mere satisfaction. And he knew that he must bargain. 'I will be risking much,' he said defensively. 'I told you that after the burning of the caique I was questioned by Major Krasakis.'

'But he could prove nothing.' Katerina dismissed his fears with a shrug.

'No. But he still suspects me.'

'Then you will just have to be very careful in choosing how and where it is done. It is as simple as that,' she countered in a flat, unemotional voice. Noukakis frowned and shook his head dubiously. Katerina swung round to face him. 'Did Haldane not rob you of any chance of marrying my daughter, Annika?' she spurred him angrily. 'And you have told me that he is now her lover. Do you not hate him enough?'

'Perhaps not as much as you do, *Kyria*,' Noukakis replied adroitly. 'And for a reason which you will not tell me.'

Katerina regarded him coldly. 'Nurse your own hatred, Matheos Noukakis,' she said. 'And I will nurse mine. We both wish to be rid of him. That is enough.'

Noukakis wilted slightly under her gaze. 'I have already done much to hurt him,' he said sullenly. 'To try to drive him from Crete.'

'For me? Only as part of my vendetta? For us both I think,' the old woman challenged.

Noukakis nodded. 'For us both,' he admitted.

'And without success,' she snapped bitterly.

'But what you are asking now . . .' protested Noukakis.

'Has to be,' she cried vehemently. 'And whatever the risks you have much to gain from it. My son's inheritance. Have I not promised you that?'

'Yes, you have,' replied Noukakis hesitantly. 'But . . .' He broke off as if not wishing to press the matter.

Katerina studied him. 'But?' she demanded quietly.

Noukakis shrugged and then gave her an ingratiating smile. 'That is in the future, *Kyria* Matakis,' he said. 'And, forgive me, who knows what the future may truly hold for any of us?'

'You doubt my word?' Katerina scowled.

Noukakis hastened to reassure her. 'No. Believe me,' he said. 'But we both know that what is said today can be lost in the shadows of tomorrow.' He smiled again and there was a hint of craftiness in it. 'Without intent. I do not suggest that of course. But through forgetfulness? Chance? Other events?'

Katerina regarded him intently and then she asked. 'What is it that you want?'

'Some protection. Some guarantee,' he replied in a guileless, almost casual, tone. And then he added. 'And perhaps some more immediate advantage.'

The old woman's eyes narrowed warily. 'And this guarantee,' she enquired coldly. 'What form would you have it in?'

Noukakis shrugged. 'A letter perhaps,' he suggested. 'A letter in which you acknowledged that what you ask and what I will do, I do for both of us.'

Katerina hesitated, only too well aware of the dangers

which lay in his demand. 'A letter for you to hold against me for as long as I live,' she said.

Noukakis put on a show of being greatly shocked by this. 'Never, Kyria!' he protested in a hurt tone. 'What need would there be for that? As you said, I have your word. Insurance against the unknown. Nothing more. A pact. A statement of mutual interest and in writing. That is all I ask. Is it too much?'

Katerina continued to study him searchingly. 'And the more immediate advantage you spoke of?'

Noukakis smiled. 'Well, it is my belief, *Kyria,*' he said, 'That the Matakis brickworks are not being managed as well as they should be.'

'And that you could serve me better as manager than the man I now employ?'

'I am confident of that,' replied Noukakis proudly. 'To your advantage and greater profit. And if you should also feel that to be so . . .' Again he shrugged.

Still Katerina studied him, despising him but admiring his ruthless self-advancement. And she knew that for her to be able to rejoice in Haldane's death she had no alternative but to agree to his demands. She nodded. 'Very well,' she said. 'I will arrange that.' Noukakis smile broadened and Katerina quickly added a rider. 'Once the Englishman is dead.'

Noukakis made an understanding gesture. 'Of course,' he said generously. 'That is understood.'

Katerina crossed to the wooden cabinet, took out an old-fashioned pen, a bottle of ink and some writing paper from it and then moved back to the table and sat down.

Noukakis watched as she opened the ink, dipped the pen in it and began to write in a laborious hand.

In a little over two weeks, more had been done to restore and refit *The Knot* again than Haldane had previously achieved in six. But then, the first time, he had been working alone but now he had help; a great deal of help and from every able-bodied man in the village. Each morning when he walked across to the caique he would find at least four or five villagers, who were either giving up their leisure time or had been let off from their regular employment for the day, waiting to start work under his supervision. and at least twice a week Xenophon Hasapis and his sons would drive over from Sitia to give a hand.

This morning Haldane had been working alongside three local fishmen and Spiros Tsitsanis who proudly boasted, and not without some justification either, that he was the best baker in Elounda.

They had made an early start as usual and at one o'clock they broke off for their mid-day meal which would be followed by a siesta until five when, Haldane's companions assured him, they would put in another two or three hours. He thanked them and then, as they headed for their homes, he strolled over to the taverna.

He was surprised to find Annika's car parked just along from the entrance. He was expecting her but not until that evening.

She was sitting on a stool at the bar counter talking in a low, conspiratorial voice to Elena and Nikos. All three of them looked expectantly towards the doorway as Haldane entered. There were no other customers at any of the tables.

Haldane smiled cheerily and waved. "*Yassou*," he called, then moved down towards the counter.

It was then that he saw their expressions; all three looked grave, over grave even and they did not acknowledge his greeting. He felt a sudden sickness in the pit of his stomach. Something was wrong, he was certain of it.

'What is it?' he asked anxiously as he came up to the counter and searched their faces questioningly. Even Annika did not smile instead she looked away from him, avoiding his eyes. 'What is it?' he repeated.

Elena and Nikos glanced at one another. Elena nodded. 'Tell him,' she said flatly.

'Tell me what?' enquired Haldane, frowning and now very concerned.

Nikos shrugged helplessly. 'It is about the taverna, Leandros', he said. 'Last night you asked me if I had come to a decision about your offer, about the sailing centre.'

'Yes,' said Haldane.

'And I said nothing.'

Haldane nodded. 'You changed the subject.'

Again Nikos shrugged. 'Well, now is the time for me to give you an answer.' He sighed. 'A final answer. One which nothing can change.'

Haldane had, by now, anticipated what Nikos was going to say to him and he was bitterly disappointed. And it showed. 'I see,' he said quietly. He looked at Elena. 'And how do you feel about Niko's decision?'

Elena picked up a clean glass and busied herself needlessly polishing it. Still Annika did not look at Haldane. 'Oh, now I am in complete agreement with Niko,' Elena said. And for a moment Haldane thought he saw the beginnings of a smile in the corners of her mouth. But if it was ever there, she suppressed it. 'There is symphony between us,' she added.

'Have you any idea of how much money the people who wish to build a hotel where this taverna now stands are willing to pay for it?' asked Nikos.

'A lot I'm sure,' replied Haldane.

'A lot!' exclaimed Nikos. He made a gesture as if to show there was no way in which the sum could be expressed. 'More than we could make in profits in ten, twenty years with your idea.' He pulled a face. 'If we made a profit that is.'

'All right Niko,' sighed Haldane. 'I understand. You've said enough.'

'More than enough,' reprimanded Spiridakis and his voice came from behind Haldane who swung round sharply.

The lawyer was standing in the doorway to the patio. He shook his head chidingly and, crossing to the bar, wagged a finger at Annika, Nikos and Elena. 'This is a cruel game you are playing with Leandros,' he told them.

'So now the joke is over, eh?'

Totally bewildered, Haldane shot a look first at Annika and then at Elena and Nikos. Despite Spiridakis' admonition, their expressions remained grim and serious and then, realising that they could no longer keep up the charade, their faces broke into smiles and all three of them burst into laughter.

'Oh Leandros!' exclaimed Elena, almost doubled up with mirth. 'If only you could have seen your face. So solemn. So sad.'

Still laughing, Annika nodded in agreement but then shook her head and gave Haldane a wryly apologetic look. 'Babis is right. It was perhaps too cruel. Forgive us.'

Only slowly did Haldane begin to realise the truth. 'You mean . . .?' he stammered. He looked at Spiridakis. The lawyer nodded.

'Why else do you think I am here?' he said. 'Only for rich clients or for my brother, Leandros, would I leave my office on a matter of business.' He gave the trio of conspirators a stern look and then smiled. 'So, let us now eat together and discuss the terms of the partnership.'

Overjoyed, Haldane impulsively kissed Annika on the cheek. She gazed into his face, delighted by his happiness and sharing in it.

They had lunch on the patio and during the meal went over every point that would have to be written into the contract in detail. Spiridakis made notes. Haldane was even happier when he found there was nothing on which he and Nikos disagreed. When every point had been covered, Spiridakis closed his notebook and sighed contentedly. 'Good,' he said. 'Full accord then. Between both parties. And since I represent both parties, and with equal concern, not only does that prove that I am a brilliant lawyer but it also makes my job much easier.'

This was greeted with laughter by his companions.

'And your fee?' teased Annika.

'Will be none the less for that,' replied the lawyer with mock haughtiness. 'I was, after all, quite prepared to haggle for either party.'

Haldane smiled. 'Against yourself?'

'On your behalf, Leandros,' Spiridakis assured him.

'And on ours,' exclaimed Elena indignantly.

'Of course,' acknowledged the lawyer gravely. 'And am I not a fair man? Had there been a dispute I would have listened to reason. And what better reason than my own? So the result would have been the same. Only the business would have taken much longer.'

This prompted more laughter. Haldane shook his head admiringly. 'You should go back into politics, Babis,' he said jokingly. 'Government and Opposition. All in one. Everything would be so much simpler.'

Spiridakis' expression changed. Now he was no longer playing a game. 'No, Leandros,' he said sadly. 'Reason has little part to play in politics. I know. In that world self interest rules with expediency as her consort'. He smiled. 'But I get serious,' he apologised. 'Forgive me.' His eyes on Haldane, he raised his glass of wine. 'To the new partnership, Haldane and Vassilakis.'

Haldane smiled at him, anxious to dispel any of the doubts which might still be troubling him. Spiridakis looked away from him and across at Elena and Nikos. 'Or as your lawyer,' he mediated. 'Vassilakis and Haldane.' The others laughed again. Spiridakis shrugged. 'Either way, the partnership.'

His companions lifted their glasses. 'The partnership,' they chorused. Then they all sipped their wine.

'And when will it be official, Babis?' Haldane asked eagerly. 'How long will it take you to draw up the agreement?'

'There are certain formalities. But a few days only,' said Spiridakis.

'And then we sign?' said Nikos. The lawyer nodded.

'That must be a very special occasion,' declared Annika. She turned to Spiridakis. 'Can you have the documents completed by next Sunday?'

'Certainly. That I can guarantee.'

'Excellent,' she exclaimed. 'Then next Sunday you will all come to my house. The agreement can be signed there. I would like that. And we can eat a little, drink a little and enjoy each other's company. And, Babis, you must bring Sia.'

'Are you sure, Annika?' Haldane asked her doubtfully. 'It'll be putting you to a lot of trouble.'

'What trouble?' she demanded with a smile. 'And I insist. Nikos, you and Elena can get away for a while, can't you? With Alexi?'

Nikos glanced at his wife. She nodded, her expression pleading. He conceded. 'For a while,' he said. 'For such an event. In such a gathering. And to visit your beautiful house. Of course.'

Annika triumphantly brushed her hands together, Greek style, showing that the question was decided and all further argument fruitless. 'Bravo,' she cried. She looked at Haldane. 'You see. It is settled.'

Haldane smiled gratefully. 'Thank you.'

'One thing,' said Spiridakis. 'What name will you give to this new business of yours? Have you thought about that?'

Nikos and Elena exchanged shy, hesitant looks. Haldane shrugged. 'I haven't,' he admitted. 'It never occurred to me.'

'Nikos and I have,' Elena quietly.

'Doesn't this place have a name already?' asked Haldane.

Elena shook her head. 'No. It is just known as the Taverna Vassilakis. But now it should have a name. A real one written up outside. And if you are not against it, Leandros, we would like to name it after my mother.' She paused. 'The Taverna Melina.'

Spiridakis frowned slightly. Haldane looked down at the table.

'You object, Leandros?' asked Nilos anxiously.

Haldane raised his head again and smiled. 'No,' he said. 'I don't object.' He looked at Elena. 'It's a beautiful name,' he assured her. 'So let's drink to that.' He picked up his glass. 'The Taverna Melina,' he murmured softly.

Annika, sitting up in the bed beside him, her arms around her knees, gazed thoughtfully into the shadows on the other side of the room. 'Elena's happiness is important to you, is it not?' she said in a low voice.

'Yes,' said Haldane.

Annika nodded. 'I am glad.'

Haldane put out a hand and stroked her arm. 'As your happiness is important to me. Even more important. You and I. That's important to me. Us. That's the ost important thing of all.'

Annika looked at him and smiled. 'And now I am very glad,' she said. And then she went on, studying his face closely. 'And you have a great affection for Alexi.'

Haldane nodded. 'He's a good lad.'

Annika shook her head. 'No,' she said. 'It goes deeper than that, your feeling for him.'

'You think so?' he said casually to cover his unease.

'Yes. I think so. I have seen the look you give him some times. It is as if he were your own flesh. Yours are perhaps the feelings of a man who has had no children of his own.'

Haldane stared up at the ceiling. 'But I have,' he said quietly. 'There was a child. A boy. Only he died when he was two months old. And I'm not sure that really counts, does it?'

Annika frowned. 'That is something I did not know,' she said. 'Something you have never talked about.'

Haldane kept his eyes on the ceiling. 'No,' he admitted. 'Well, not much to say about it, is there? Two months. Nine weeks. Sixty-one days. Hardly an eventful life. Not many memories. And my wife couldn't have any more.' He turned his head to look at her and smiled gently. 'But you do have children. Two. And we've never talked about them either.'

'They are hardly children,' said Annika. 'Andreas is twenty-two and Katerina is twenty.'

'And they are studying in France?'

She nodded. 'At the Sorbonne. Both quite clever and both very sophisticated.'

'That's good. They might even approve or at least understand.' She gave him a questioning look. 'About our relationship,' he went on. 'About how we feel towards each other.'

'About how we love one another,' sighed Annika. 'Is that what you mean? Love. Use the word, Leandros. It is not one of which to be afraid. Or to be ashamed of.' She nodded. 'Yes. They would understand.'

'And approve?'

'Of you? Yes, I am sure of that.'

'Of us?'

'Probably. Although they could be a little concerned.'

'About what?' asked Haldane.

'That I might be hurt by it,' replied Annika. She studied him. 'It is strange. We have become so very close and yet we are still strangers. There must be much that we still do not know about each other. Things of the past.'

Haldane frowned. 'Yes,' he said. He held her gaze for a while and then he reached out for her and took her in his arms. And when they had made love, she fell asleep in his embrace.

An hour later when she suddenly woke again Annika found that he was no longer beside her. Puzzled, she got out of bed, put on her robe and went downstairs.

Haldane was sitting at his worktable poring over detailed drawings of the designs and extensions to the taverna using as a reference the meticulous, pen-and-ink sketch which he first showed to Elena. He'd put on a dressing gown and slippers and, smoking his pipe, he was fully absorbed in what he was doing.

Half-way down the stairs Annika paused and called quietly. 'Leandros?'

Startled, Haldane swung round on the stool. Annika continued on down the stairs and crossed to him. He put his pipe down into an ashtray on the table and smiled at

225

her apologetically. 'I couldn't sleep,' he said. 'Had a lot on my mind.'

She nodded. 'Ever since lunch I think.'

'Well, now that's all settled there's so much to do,' he pleaded.

'That will not wait until later?' she enquired gently.

Haldane shrugged. 'Lying there. Just thinking. It seemed such a waste. I'm sorry. I didn't mean to disturb you.'

'You did not disturb me. Only just now did I wake.'

Haldane smiled. 'Were you worried?' he asked. 'Did you think I'd gone out on the town. To celebrate. On my own.'

Annika smiled back at him. 'No. I was not worried about that,' she said. And then she added teasingly. 'But, of course, if that is what you want . . .'

'I don't,' he said and he drew her close to him. 'It never even entered my head.' He kissed her. 'I love you.'

She looked at him approvingly. 'Bravo, Leandros. And I love you. And every second of the time we spend together is like a jewel to me because I am not with you often enough. I woke and you were not beside me. I felt robbed. The hours are slipping by. Soon it will be dawn and in a little while I must return to my home.'

Haldane frowned. 'Do you really have to?' he asked.

'It is a working day. I must be at the factory. I have a business to run.'

'When will I see you again?'

'I am not sure, my dearest,' she sighed. 'Tomorrow I must go to Chania. For meetings. I will have to be there for two or three days.' She pointed to the drawing board. 'And you, too, have many things to do.'

Haldane nodded. 'Yes.'

'So perhaps, sadly, we will not be together again until next Sunday.' She smiled reassuringly. 'But then for certain.'

Haldane looked into her eyes. 'I'll miss you,' he said simply.

'And I will miss you. Even more I think.' She put her arms around him. 'So, come back to bed,' she whispered.

When Haldane stirred out of a deep, dreamless slumber the next morning Annika had gone. There was a note lying on the bedside table. Haldane picked it up and, rubbing the night out of his eyes, crossed to the window and pushed open the shutters. He read the note.

My darling,
It is time for me to go and you are sleeping and there is nothing to say except andio. Know that your joy in what there is now between you, Elena and Nikos is also my joy. May the future treat you well, as you deserve. And may it also be a future in which there is a place, however small and however fleetingly, for someone who loves you as much as I do.

Annika.

Haldane looked up from the letter, troubled and frowning. Then he read it again, twice. And after the third reading his expression was no longer distressed or uneasy. He had about him the air of a man who has made a decision against which doubt no longer had any appeal.

In a mood of resolve and purpose he turned from the window and crossed to the bathroom.

An hour later, showered, shaved, dressed and breakfasted, Alan Haldane drove to Neapolis. He had visited Melina's grave once before and not long after he had moved into the house in Elounda. And then, as now, he had brought flowers with him.

He placed the fresh blooms on the marble tomb and then scrutinised the face in the ornately framed photograph attached to the headstone.

He gazed at the picture for a long time; the face of the woman he had loved and who had carried and given birth to his child; the woman from whom he once again silently begged forgiveness; the woman he now called upon for understanding and release; the woman to whom he had come to say farewell.

And when that was done, he put out a hand, touched the photograph lingeringly, smiled gently and then turned and walked away from the grave.

Back in his house once more, Haldane opened the drawer of his worktable and, from under a pile of papers, took out the snapshot of Melina taken so many years ago. He studied it intently. The face of the forty-nine-year-old woman buried in Neapolis was that of a half-remembered stranger. This was the Melina he had known. This was the image which he wished to retain in his memory forever.

With his eyes still on the snapshot, he crossed to the fireplace, took a match from the box on the mantelpiece and struck it. Then he set fire to the photograph, placed it carefully in the grate and, straightening up again, watched it burn.

Spiridakis gathered up the contract and the other documents on the table. 'So,' he said. 'You now own the property you wanted in Anoyia and Stelios Prevelakis is content.'

Katerina Matakis grunted. 'As he should be,' she muttered. 'At such a price.'

The lawyer smiled. 'A fair one. And almost half that which he first asked.'

'True,' Katerina acknowledged grudgingly. 'You will take another glass of raki?'

'Thank you, no,' replied Spiridakis with a look of regret. 'I must return to Heraklion. I have a great deal of work waiting for me there.'

Katerina nodded understandingly. 'I am grateful to you for coming,' she said. 'For humouring an old woman who does not like travelling.'

Spiridakis gave her another smile and put a hand on her arm. 'No,' he corrected her gently. 'To see a friend. A valued friend.'

He put the papers into his briefcase and closed it Katerina turned from him and crossed to the window. 'And my daughter?' she enquired. 'Have you seen her recently?'

Spiridakis nodded. 'Yesterday.'

'How is she?'

'In good health,' the lawyer assured her.

Katerina gazed out of the window. 'I have not seen her you know. And we have not spoken. Not since that day at Dhafnai when she betrayed me,' she said bitterly.

Spiridakis sighed. 'She did not betray you, Katerina. What she did, she did because she thought it was right and just. Not to hurt you. She acted out of conscience,' he argued quietly. And then he added. 'And conscience is everyone's cross, Katerina. As guilt is our crown of thorns.'

She swung round to look at him, frowning slightly.

'And it grieves me that there is this rift between you,' continued Spiridakis. 'If there is anything I can do to . . .'

Katerina's mouth hardened into a tight, unyielding grimace. 'No,' she interrupted him and her tone was adamant. 'There is nothing you can do. It was her choice.' She studied the lawyer. 'Tell me,' she said. 'Is it true what I have heard? That Elena and Nikos have taken the Englishman you call brother as a partner?'

'Yes.'

'Against your advice?'

Spiridakis shook his head. 'No. Leandros is a good man.'

'The bargain has been made?' she probed. 'The terms settled?'

'Yes. I am preparing the agreement. It will be signed on Sunday. At Annika's house.' Spiridakis suddenly had an idea and it seemed like a good one to him. 'Be there, Katerina,' he pleaded. 'I will come and drive you there myself if you wish it. Meet Leandros. Heal the wound between you and Annika. Nothing would please her more. That I know. She loves you.'

The old woman shook her head. 'Perhaps,' she replied icily. 'But not enough. It would be a wasted journey. And, as I said, I do not like travelling.'

The lawyer could see from her expression that any further argument or entreaty would be to no avail. He sighed once more.

'*Andio*, Babis', she said.

Spiridakis took the hand she was holding out to him and kissed it. '*Andio*'.

Katerina went to the window again. He was dismissed. He picked up his briefcase and walked over to the sitting room door.

'Oh, one more thing', Katerina said as he was about to step into the hallway. Spiridakis paused and looked across at her. She kept her back to him.

'I am going to make Matheos Noukakis manager of my brickworks'. It was a casual statement. 'Do you approve?'

The lawyer shrugged. 'If you believe that a change is necessary I would say that you have chosen well', he replied. 'He is a good businessman'. Katerina nodded. 'When will he be taking up the position?'

'Very soon I think', the old woman said softly.

CHAPTER TWENTY-TWO

The following day Major Krasakis was sitting at his desk studying a report when there was a knock on the door of his office.

'Come,' he called.

The door opened and the duty Sergeant entered and crossed to the desk. Krasakis looked up at him enquiringly.

'An Englishman,' the Sergeant informed him. 'A *Kyrie* Haldane is asking to see you, Major.'

Krasakis' eyes narrowed slightly behind his tinted glasses. Then he nodded. 'Show him in.'

Krasakis initialled the report and tossed it into the out-tray on his desk. Then he took out a cigarette and lit it.

The Sergeant ushered Haldane into the room and hovered. Krasakis stood up. 'Thank you, Sergeant,' he said. The man retreated, closing the door behind him.

The Major stepped out from behind his desk, put out a hand to Haldane and smiled. 'Leandros! This is an unexpected pleasure.'

'Major,' Haldane greeted him as they shook hands.

'Are you well?' asked Krasakis.

'Yes, thank you. I am well,' replied the Englishman. And then he gave a faint smile and added. 'And richer.'

The Major regarded him with a puzzled look. From out of his pocket Haldane took the envelope which he had found lying on the floor by the front door when he had come down to breakfast that morning. He handed it to Krasakis.

'I thought you ought to see this,' he said.

The Major examined the envelope. It was unaddressed. Inside it was a single sheet of cheap notepaper. Krasakis unfolded it and read what was written on it. There were just two words in block capitals; *For Charon.*

'And these came with it,' said Haldane holding out his hand again.

The Major took the two twenty-drachma coins from him, glanced at them and then re-read the note aloud. 'For Charon.' Frowning deeply, and with his eyes still on the note, he moved back behind his desk. Then he looked up at Haldane with a grave expression on his face. 'Do you know who Charon is?' he asked quietly.

'Was', replied Haldane, correcting him.

Krasakis shook his head. 'Remains. For some. For many even here on Crete.'

'The Ferryman,' said Haldane.

The Major nodded. 'On the river which all souls must cross to enter the Underworld and the Elysian Fields beyond. And for that service Charon demands a fee. The Ferryman must be paid.'

He studied Haldane and he was clearly very disturbed. 'Someone wishes you dead, Leandros,' he said.

Haldane did not mention the warning letter to anyone other than Krasakis. He had absolutely no wish to alarm his friends and certainly not Annika. So, over the next few days, he had kept to his usual routine; working on *The Knot,* eating in the taverna and putting some time in each day at his drawing board.

But, as the Major had advised, when he had laughingly but firmly declined Krasakis' offer of a round-the-clock protection, he had kept on the alert and had taken what precautions he could, including locking and bolting all the doors and windows of the house at night. He had also avoided, as much as he could, straying too far from the village or, except in the relative safety of his own home and within reach of a telephone, of being alone too often.

Not that he felt really threatened. He never had. His first reaction on reading the note had been that it was either some sick joke or yet another attempt to intimidate him and that whoever had written it had no intention

232

whatever of following through on it. And when, by Sunday morning, nothing had happened he was convinced that this was the case. Just the same he opened the doors of the garage with care and, remembering the booby traps which he and the Andarte had often used during the war, checked his car inside and out before climbing into the Fiat and setting off, with the hood down, on the drive to Annika's house.

As he approached the taverna he saw Nikos' car parked outside with the bonnet raised and Nikos peering in at the engine.

Haldane pulled the Fiat into the kerb, got out and walked back to him. Elena was sitting in the front passenger seat with Alexis, standing in the back, leaning forward over her shoulder and gazing anxiously at his father. Haldane noticed that all three members of the Vassilakis family had dressed for the occasion in their Saint's Day, weddings and christening best and for a moment thought of returning home and changing out of the short-sleeved shirt and slacks he was wearing into something more formal. But that would probably embarrass them he decided, so he dismissed the idea.

"Yassou,' he said as he came up to the car.

Elena smiled at him. *"Kalimera,* Leandros,' she said.

'Kalimera," echoed Alexis.

Nikos nodded. *"Yassou."*

'What's the problem?' asked Haldane.

Nikos shrugged. 'The engine turns but it does not start.'

Moving to his side and joining him in his renewed inspection of the engine, Haldane checked the sparking plug leads and found one of them to be loose. He pressed the cap home. 'Try it now,' he said.

Nikos got into the car and turned the ignition key. Still the engine would not fire. Cursing silently, Nikos came back alongside Haldane. Elena and Alexis hung out of the windows and watched them.

'Could be that the plugs are dirty,' suggested Haldane. 'Look, leave it', he said. 'We'll all go in my car.'

Nikos looked down the road at the Fiat and shook his head. 'There is not room for four in that, Leandros,' he said. 'No. You go on. You will see. I will get this started. It is temperamental.' He winked. 'Like a woman. And, like a woman, you have to know how to handle it. To coax it.' He grinned. 'And I am an expert with women.'

'Po! Po! Po!,' mocked Elena. 'Omar Sharif, eh?'

Haldane looked doubtful. 'Are you sure you can get it going?'

Nikos laughed. 'Am I not a genius,' he exclaimed.

Elena shook her head in mock despair. 'Listen to the man,' she cried. 'Now he is Einstein.'

'Take no notice, Leandros,' retorted Nikos, giving his wife a look of playful disdain. 'I will fix it. You go on ahead. We will follow. Tell Annika we are coming'.

'Well, all right', agreed Haldane reluctantly. 'But I still think it would be a lot easier . . .'

Elena interrupted him. 'Do as he says, Leandros.' She sighed. 'That he is a genius I doubt. But that he is stubborn I know for sure.'

Haldane laughed. 'See you there, then,' he said. And then added. 'Hopefully.'

'Papa,' called Alexis. 'May I go with Leandros?' Nikos and Elena exchanged glances. 'Please,' pleaded the boy.

Nikos looked questioningly at Haldane. The Englishman was delighted by the prospect. 'Of course he can come with me,' he said. 'Elena too, if she wants to.'

Elena shook her head and laughed. 'No. I will stay with Einstein,' she said. 'This magic way he has with women. That I want to see.' She turned to Alexis. 'Go with Leandros then.'

Excitedly the boy jumped down out of the car and ran to the Fiat. Haldane picked him up and swung him into the passenger seat and then he moved round to the other side.

'If you are not there soon after we are,' he called to Elena and Nikos. 'I'll come back for you.'

'And meet us on the way,' shouted Nikos. 'I guarantee

it.'

Laughing, Haldane got in behind the steering wheel, put the car into gear and drove off. Alexis turned to wave to his parents. In the rearview mirror Haldane saw Elena and Nikos wave back and then Nikos plunge under the bonnet once more to tinker with the engine.

By the time they reached the outskirts of the village and turned on to the main road, Alexis was standing up alongside Haldane holding on to the windscreen and enjoying the sensation of the warm wind on his face. Haldane glanced at him, saw the look of pleasure on the boy's face and accelerated a little.

And soon they were climbing up into the mountains and as they did so, so the bends in the road became tighter and the many curves more dangerous. Haldane maintained a good speed but drove carefully and kept alert. Around any of the bends, they could suddenly come upon a bus bearing down on them or one of the many minor landslides which so often occurred in the mountains after the spring thaw. In which case he would have to brake hard and edge gingerly past. Very gingerly, for there was no guardrail along the edge of the road and as they corkscrewed and wound higher and higher so there was always, on one side or other of them, a steep, almost sheer drop.

Haldane took the Fiat into a particularly sharp hairpin bend. Alexis looked down over the side of the car and at the precipitous drop only a few feet from the nearside wheels of the car and, confident in the Englishman's skill as a driver, he was thrilled by the sight.

Noukakis sat in his car. I will wait just a little longer, he thought. Let them all get settled.

In the half hour since he had seen first Spiridakis and his wife and, finally, Nikos and Elena drive past him down the track he had smoked five cigarettes.

Although Haldane had been totally unaware of the fact, Noukakis had never been more than a few hundred yards behind him from the moment when the Englishman had turned the Fiat on to the main road outside Elounda. And Noukakis had stayed with him, always keeping enough distance between them to remain undetected, throughout the climb into the mountains. And when Haldane had turned off the road and driven down the track through the olive grove, Noukakis had parked his car out of sight among the trees but in a spot where he had a good view of the entrance to the track.

He looked at his watch. Now, he decided. And he smiled. He stubbed out his cigarette and got out of the car. Reaching under the passenger seat he pulled out a canvas wrapped tool kit, laid it on the seat and unrolled it. From the tools inside he selected a wrench which he slipped into his pocket. Then, closing the car door quietly and keeping in the cover of the olive trees, he started to move cautiously in the direction of the house.

'Tackle him,' shouted Nikos. 'Get the ball away from him! Oh, foul! Foul! Bravo! Bravo!'

Nikos and Elena, laughing, their arms around one another, stood on the edge of the clearing in the olive grove and watched Haldane and Alexis playing football.

Encouraged by his father's support, Alexis got possession of the ball and dribbled it across the open ground with Haldane in pursuit. The boy stumbled and Haldane got the ball back from him, turned with it and ran towards Nikos and Elena. But Alexis caught up with him and neatly regained control of the game. And as he got close to his parents, keeping the football just ahead of him, Nikos, no longer able to resist the temptation, broke away from his wife and, with a wild cry, tackled Alexis, got possession and raced across the clearing with his son only just behind him.

Out of breath, Haldane gave up and, breathing heavily, joined Elena. 'I'm getting too old for football I think,' he gasped.

Elena smiled. 'That is not so, Leandros,' she said

236

consolingly. 'You are still a young man. How do you say, in your prime.'

Haldane smiled and bowed to her still panting. 'You are too kind,' he said before adding ruefully, 'I only wish that were true.' He took out a handkerchief and wiped the sweat from his face.

Elena studied him thoughtfully. 'Watching you playing with Alexis, I was thinking,' she said, 'if my father had lived he would have been about your age now.'

Haldane gave a slight start and shot a look at her. He nodded. 'A year or two younger, I think,' he said almost casually.

'Of course. I forgot,' she said. 'You knew him. In the Andarte.'

'Yes. I knew him.'

Elena shook her head. 'It is strange,' she mused. 'But he has been in my thoughts a great deal during the past few weeks. I do not know why. I do not even remember him. But I wish he were here today. With us. With you. His comrade of the war.' She looked at Haldane and smiled. 'He would be pleased do you not think? About our partnership.'

Haldane held her gaze and then he said quietly. 'Yes, Elena. Your father would be very pleased.'

While Annika gave a final basting to the suckling pig which was spit roasting over the barbecue pit and Sia laid the table for the lunch which they had decided they would eat out on the terrace, Spiridakis helped himself to another drink from the bar trolley and then settled in one of the wicker armchairs facing another, smaller, marbled-topped table on which he had previously and ceremoniously placed the two copies of the partnership agreement.

The boisterous sounds from the clearing just a little way off from the house invaded the quiet of the terrace.

It had been a wonderful day. The agreements had been signed and witnessed and the new partnership toasted in champagne. Then they had eaten well, sitting under the shade of the large carob tree which grew in the middle of the terrace. They had lingered over the meal. And then they had moved to more comfortable seats out of the heat of the sun and sat and talked and lazed.

Now it was late afternoon and cooler and, at the far end of the terrace, Haldane was giving Alexis a lesson in how to the fly kite which he had given him. Elena and Sia, sitting side by side on a canopied hammock seat, and Annika, Nikos and Spiridakis, relaxing in three of the cushioned wicker armchairs, watched them, amused and interested as the kite soared high and far out over the olive grove.

'Alexis loves his present, eh?' said Sia.

Nikos nodded, then shook his head and smiled. 'Leandros spoils the boy,' he sighed.

'And only Alexis?' demanded Elena, raising her arm and jiggling the silver bracelet around her wrist.

Nikos gazed at the new wristwatch he was wearing. 'No,' he admitted thoughtfully. Again he shook his head. 'Such handsome gifts.'

'As Leandros said,' smiled Annika. 'To mark the occasion.'

Nikos gave her an embarrassed look. 'But we gave him nothing,' he protested.

'You have given him happiness,' Annika assured him.

'More than you know,' confirmed Spiridakis quietly.

Elena stretched contentedly. 'This has been a beautiful day,' she murmured dreamily. 'One I shall never forget.' She looked at Annika and smiled gratefully. 'Thank you, Aunt.'

Annika shrugged. 'I have also enjoyed it', she said. 'But it is not over yet.'

Nikos checked the time on his new watch. 'Sadly, for us it is,' he said. 'We must go.'

Elena gave a deep sigh and then nodded. 'Yes, I am afraid Nikos is right.'

'But it is early,' Annika exclaimed, disappointed. She

238

glanced at her wristwatch. 'Only a quarter to five.'

Elena pulled a face and shrugged helplessly.

'We shall be busy tonight in the taverna I think,' said Nikos. 'Elena and I must be there. And Alexis has to go to school tomorrow. He has studying to do before he goes to bed.' He stood up. 'Alexi, come,' he called out. 'We must leave.'

Annika, Elena and Spiridakis also got to their feet. Alexis made no move to obey.

Nikos called again. 'Now, Alexi. We are going. You have studying to do.'

Bitterly disappointed, Alexis looked appealing at Haldane.

'Alexi!' Nikos called for the third time and with a firm note to his voice.

Haldane gave the boy a regretful, resigned shrug. Together they began to haul the kite in. 'We'll fly it again tomorrow, eh?' whispered Haldane. 'After school.'

Alexis smiled broadly and nodded. Spiridakis strolled across the terrace and joined them. As soon as the last few feet of string had been wound in Alexis took the kite and its reel from Haldane and ran off with them towards his parents calling out loudly and excitedly. 'Leandros says that we can fly the kite again tomorrow.'

'It seems that you are now one of the family,' said Spiridakis quietly.

Haldane nodded. 'Perhaps. By adoption anyway.'

'And you are content with that?'

Haldane looked at him. 'I've made my decision, Babis,' he said. 'I paid my respects to the past.'

The lawyer regarded him sadly. 'Nothing has changed,' he reminded him.

'No,' agreed Haldane. 'I still owe it a debt. But I have a debt to the future as well. To happiness. And not just mine.'

'The shadows are still there.'

'Yes. And I know the risks,' his friend assured him. 'But they are worth taking.' He paused. 'All of them.'

239

Spiridakis studied him, then nodded and gripped his arm affectionately. Together they moved forward to rejoin the others and as they came up them Elena was kissing her aunt goodbye.

'Do you really have to go?' Haldane asked Nikos.'

Nikos pulled a face. 'Unfortunately.' Then he grinned. 'But really only to impress you. So that you shall know that you do not have idle partners.'

Haldane laughed. 'Now you make me feel guilty.'

'Oh, do not worry, Leandros,' Elena teased him with a smile. 'You will be kept busy enough I think. But from tomorrow, uh? Tonight, enjoy yourself.' She turned to Sia and kissed her. '*Andio*,' she said.

'*Andio*,' said Nikos. He kissed Annika and shook hands with Spiridakis and Sia.

'I'll walk to your car with you,' said Haldane. He looked at Annika. 'I won't be a minute.'

Slowly Haldane, Elena and Nikos, with Alexis running ahead of them, walked towards the head of the steps which led down to the parked cars.

Annika, Spiridakis and Sia watched them go and then they settled down again; Spiridakis and Sia on the hammock seat; Annika in one of the wicker armchairs. Spiridakis took out a cigarette and lit it. Annika looked up at the sky. She smiled. 'Elena was right,' she said quietly. 'It has been a beautiful day.'

Standing alongside the Vassilakis' car, Nikos shook hands with Haldane. '*Andio*, Leandros,' he said. 'Until tomorrow, eh? Or later tonight perhaps.'

'Tomorrow, I think,' replied Haldane. '*Andio*.' He smiled at the boy. '*Andio*, Alexi.'

Alexis smiled back at him. '*Andio*, Leandros. And you won't forget what we are going to do tomorrow, will you?'

Haldane shook his head. 'I won't forget,' he assured him.

Nikos and Alexis got into the car. Haldane turned to Elena. '*Andio*, Elena.'

Elena nodded and then studied his face, her expression

suddenly serious and thoughtful. 'What has happened today has pleased me so much, Leandros', she said. 'And I thank you for it. We have gained a partner, Niko and I. But you are much more than that to us. To all of us. You must know that.' She paused and then went on, her eyes on his. 'And in my heart you have a very special place. I spoke earlier of my father. A man I did not know. And I regret that.' She smiled gently. 'Well, now I feel that, at last, I have one. A father.'

She kissed him on the cheek and then smiled at him again. 'God bless you and keep you safe, Leandros', she said. She turned away from him and went to get into the car.

Haldane frowned. Sooner or later she would have to know the truth. Sooner or later it had to come out. There was no way of avoiding it and he knew it. Perhaps this was the moment. 'Elena,' he called.

Elena paused by the side of the car and looked back at him. 'Yes.'

Haldane gazed at her. Should he? Dare he? He decided against it. For now anyway. The time would come when it would be right to tell her. But this was not it. He smiled and shook his head. 'It's not important,' he said. She looked at him questioningly. 'Well, anyway, some other time perhaps,' he added.

Elena smiled and got into the car.

Spiridakis and Sia heard the car pull away but Annika was lost in thought. Happy and contented, she began to sing quietly to herself, oblivious of everyone and everything around her. Spiridakis looked across at her and smiled.

Haldane, filling his pipe, came up the steps and onto the terrace. As he crossed to them, Annika came out of her reverie and drawing one of the armchairs closer to hers, patted the cushion. Haldane sank down into it.

'Niko is going to send someone up for his car in the morning,' he said.

Annika gave him a look of surprise. 'Oh! Is there

something wrong with it?'

Haldane nodded. 'Starter motor's gone I think.' He struck a match. 'Finally.'

'How are they getting home then?' asked Spiridakis.

'I've lent them mine,' replied Haldane, drawing on his pipe.

Nikos, with Elena sitting beside him and Alexis perched on the hood, swung the Fiat off the track and on to the road. The little Fiat had a good feel to it and Nikos was enjoying the sensation of driving it. And Alexis was delighted to be riding in the sports car once again.

Annika stood by the table and poured wine into four glasses. She handed one glass to Sia and another to Spiridakis. Picking up the third glass, she crossed to Haldane with it.

Sia looked thoughtful. 'If you do not have a car how will you get back to Elounda, Leandros?' she asked.

Haldane reached out to take the glass of wine from Annika. Their eyes met and she gave him a quiet, secret smile. 'Yes,' she said softly. 'That is a problem.'

Spiridakis had seen this exchange of looks. He sipped his wine.

'We will take him, eh, Babis?' suggested Sia.

Spiridakis sighed. 'Drink your wine, my darling,' he said with a faint smile. 'This is not a time to be helpful, I think.'

Sia looked at him blankly and then across at Haldane and Annika who were still gazing at one another. She got the message and shook her head ruefully at her foolishness.

Annika crossed back to the table, picked up her own glass of wine and then sat down again beside Haldane. The atmosphere was one of sleepy contentment, four people at peace with one another and with the world.

Spiridakis regarded Annika and Haldane over the rim

of his glass. Then he said quietly. 'Every day, as a lawyer, I am asked for my opinion. On matters of great importance.' The couple looked at him with interest. 'And believe me,' the lawyer went on, 'often my opinion is costly. So listen well, Leandros and Annika, when I offer you one for nothing.'

Annika laughed. 'Oh! And what is this opinion which you give so freely, Babis?'

Spiridakis hesitated but only for a second. 'I believe,' he said, 'that you should get married.'

Sia smiled. 'Bravo,' she approved quietly.

Haldane regarded Spiridakis thoughtfully. He nodded. 'That's an opinion worth any price,' he said. And then he looked at Annika. 'Don't you think?'

Annika put out a hand to him and he took it and kissed it. 'More than beautiful,' she murmured happily. 'A perfect day.'

Each time he had braked to take a corner the Fiat had left a trail of brake fluid on the road behind it. And there had been many bends to negotiate. But Nikos had not noticed the leak and, exhilarated by the surprising turn of speed of which the small car was capable, had, to Elena's consternation and Alexis' encouragement, taken full advantage of it on the homeward run down the mountain road.

Now the Fiat was approaching a very tight bend with a steep drop on the left hand side of the road. The car was travelling fast, too fast for Elena. She shot an anxious look at her husband. Nikos grinned and braked. There was no response. Alarmed, Nikos pumped the brake pedal. Nothing. With a look of horror on his face, he swung the wheel, grabbing for the handbrake. The car skidded across the road, slammed into the wall of rock on the right, ricocheted off it, spun round and catherine-wheeled back across the road. Alexis, dumb with terror, gripped the hood hard with both hands.

Elena screamed as the Fiat shot out into space, seemed

to hang for a second and then fell. And as it fell Nikos heard his son cry out as the boy was catapulted over his head.

CHAPTER TWENTY-THREE

As Annika and Sia cleared the table under the carob tree of the last of the debris of lunch, Haldane uncorked another bottle of wine. Annika had put on a record of Dvorak's *Romance for Violin* and the music lilted out from the house.

Spiridakis was standing by the wall of the terrace looking out across the olive grove, the trees darkening and softening in the evening sunlight. He took out a cigarette and lit it and, as he did so, he saw the police Land-Rover approaching.

It pulled up two or three yards from the house and Major Krasakis got out and stood staring up at the terrace for a few seconds. His expression was grim and it was plain to Spiridakis that he was steeling himself against something. Then, wearily and reluctantly, the Major moved towards the steps.

Spiridakis frowned. 'We have a visitor,' he said quietly and without turning.

Haldane, struggling with the cork of the wine bottle, glanced across at him.

The first thing Haldane was really conscious of, as they jolted over the rough ground more than 300 feet below the point where the Fiat had come off the road, was Alexis' kite. It was caught up in the branches of a thorn bush; its frame shattered, its torn fabric fluttering in the gentle breeze.

An ambulance was parked on the narrow goat path together with a police motorcycle, a second white Land-Rover, its blue light still flashing, and a pick-up truck.

Alexis' body, covered by a blanket, lay beside the track, a policeman and one of the ambulancemen standing alongside it. They looked up as Krasakis' vehicle, followed by Spiridakis' car, bumped and rolled towards them and then stopped within a few feet of where they were standing.

The Major got out of his Land-Rover with Haldane and Annika while, just behind them, Babis and Sia got out of their car.

The wrecked Fiat, after leaving the road, had hit the ground about twenty yards above the path and had then rolled down across it to fall a further thirty feet or more into a gully where it now lay, overturned and firmly wedged between some large boulders, with the bodies of Nikos and Elena trapped beneath it.

More policemen, the motorcycle patrolman among them, another ambulance attendant and a handful of men from a nearby village, using ropes and the trunks of freshly felled young trees, were trying to dislodge the car and roll it over to enable them to pull the two bodies clear.

Spiridakis and Sia moved up alongside the Major, while Haldane and Annika, distraught and anguished, ran to the blanketed mound lying beside the track. The ambulanceman stooped and lifted a corner to expose the dead boy's face.

Haldane winced and, with a cry of despair, Annika fell to her knees beside the body and cradled Alexis' head and shoulders in her arms.

'Who reported the accident?' Spiridakis asked the Major quietly.

'Two men who were working in the fields over there,' replied Krasakis. 'They saw it happen. They say that the car seemed to be out of control.'

Haldane stared disbelievingly at Alexis' bloodstained face for some time and then he looked down at the wrecked car. 'Elena! Niko! Elena!' he cried out wildly. And, distracted with shock and grief, he began to scramble recklessly down the steep slope of the gully and towards the Fiat.

He reached the car and saw Elena's arm with her new

bracelet on it protruding from under it. Pushing his way in among the men around the Fiat, he tried desperately to help raise it; first with a thin tree trunk lying discarded nearby and then, when that snapped, even more desperately with his bare hands. And all the while he continued to cry out and it was the piteous cry of a wounded animal. 'Elena! Elena! Elena!'

Despite her own grief, Annika, still cradling Alexis in her arms, looked down from the path at Haldane scrabbling at the wreckage, faintly surprised at the extent of his agony.

Both Spiridakis and Sia were deeply moved by Haldane's emotion. Babis even more than his wife, for he alone knew the reason and was very concerned for his friend.

While Sia moved to comfort Annika, Krasakis, slipping on the loose stones and soil, half clambered, half slid down into the gully and crossed to the Englishman who, straining every muscle, was still trying fruitlessly to lift the wreckage.

The Major took him gently by the shoulders and turned him to face him. Krasakis shook his head.

"It is no use, Leandros," he said quietly but firmly.

Haldane stared at him blankly and then struggled to free himself but Krasakis held on to him.

"It is no use,' he repeated. 'Do you not see that? They are dead. They are all dead.'

Haldane stared at him again, then, overwhelmed by the realisation that what Krasakis had said had to be true and with all hope gone, he sank on to his knees beside Elena's outstretched arm and, his head lowered, took her hand in his. And he began to cry.

Katerina opened the front door of her house to Matheos Noukakis and scowled at him.

Noukakis smiled, unconcerned. He was in a jaunty mood and clearly very pleased with himself. He had had a few drinks to celebrate but he was a long way off being drunk. The raki had, however, induced in him an air of cockiness and self-assurance.

Katerina led him into the sitting room. 'Since this morning I have been expecting you,' she said sullenly as she closed the door. 'Where have you been?'

'With my brother,' smirked Noukakis. 'And if he is asked he will say that I was with him all day.'

Katerina looked at him sharply. 'That might be necessary?'

Noukakis shrugged. 'A precaution. So that if I am questioned I will again have an alibi.'

A gleam came into the old woman's eyes. 'It is done then?' she whispered.

Noukakis nodded. 'The Englishman will not return to Elounda alive,' he said casually. 'That you can be sure of, *Kryia* Matakis.'

Katerina studied him approvingly. 'Good.'

'So now will you offer me a little raki, eh?' prompted Noukakis with a boldness he had not dared to display in her presence before.

Katerina did not hear him. Her thoughts were elsewhere. Turning from him, she crossed the room and stood gazing at the plaque of the three Fates hanging on the wall. Noukakis frowned and then shrugged insolently. Moving to the wooden cabinet, he opened the top cupboard and reached for the decanter of raki.

'Oh, you daughters of Themis!' invoked Katerina quietly but vehemently. 'Children of the goddess of justice! You, The Fates, hear me! It is done. And in this, as were the Keres, the dogs of Hades in ancient times, I, Katerina Matakis, was the instrument of your will'.

Noukakis, pouring himself a raki, glanced across at her and frowned. Then he shrugged and grinned. 'What!' he exclaimed, mocking her. 'You do not mention my part in this to your friends, the gods. Now is that fair?'

Katerina, her eyes still on the bas relief figures, ignored him.

Noukakis downed the raki in one swallow and then

poured himself another. Glass in hand, he crossed to her. 'But then,' he said slyly. 'It is not the gods I must look to for recognition, is it?' Katerina turned to him and regarded him coldly. 'Your son's inheritance,' he went on. 'And the Matakis brickwords have a new manager. Is that not so?'

'You have my word,' Katerina said stiffly.

Noukakis nodded. 'And a letter,' he reminded her. 'We must not forget the letter, must we? So when do I take up my new job?'

'As soon as what you say you have done is confirmed,' she snappped.

A car stopped outside the house. The old woman looked questioningly at Noukakis who shrugged and then moved to the window and peered out through the slates of the shutters into the twilight, fast fading into night.

'It is Annika,' he said. 'And Babis Spiridakis and his wife are with her.' Katerina frowned. Noukakis turned to her and smiled. 'Your confirmation, perhaps,' he said.

He emptied his glass and put it down on the table. The front doorbell rang.

'I will let them in.' He moved over to the door and opened it. And then he paused and looked at Katerina. 'I am here to discuss my duties with you. As your new manager,' he hissed. 'Remember that.' Then he went out into the hallway, leaving the door ajar.

Katerina positioned herself to greet her unexpected visitors. Annika, Spiridakis and Sia came into the room with Noukakis just behind them. Annika regarded her mother sadly, dreading having to break the news to her. Spiridakis and Sia looked very solemn.

Katerina studied all three of them dispassionately. Then she nodded to Spiridakis. '*Herete*, Babis,' she said formally.

'*Herete*,' replied Spiridakis quietly.

Katerina looked at Sia. '*Kyria* Spiridakis.'

'*Herete*,' acknowledged Sia, her eyes lowered.

And then, lastly, Katerina looked at Annika stonily.

'I am pleased to see you, my daughter,' she said but without any obvious enthusiasm. 'It is a long time since you have visited me.'

'Yes,' acknowledged Annika. She hesitated and her eyes filled with tears. 'And now I come to you bringing terrible news.'

Katerina appeared unmoved and unconcerned. 'Oh,' she said calmly. 'And what is this news?'

Spiridakis crossed quickly to her side. 'Katerina,' he suggested solicitously. 'I think it would be better if you were to sit down.'

The old woman gave him a gracious nod. 'I thank you for your concern, Babis. But I am sure that will not be necessary.' She looked at her daughter again. 'Well, Annika. Tell me.'

Annika took a deep breath and closed her eyes. 'There has been an accident.'

'An accident? Where?' Katerina asked but without urgency.

'In the mountains. Not far from my house. Leandros' car came off the road and fell more than a hundred metres.'

Her face expressionless, Katerina studied her daughter and then nodded. 'And the Englishman is dead,' she said. 'Is that what you have to tell me?'

'No, Katerina,' replied Spiridakis gently. 'Leandros was not driving. Nikos was.'

The old woman reacted with a start. Her eyes widened and she shot a look at Noukakis whose expression reflected surprise and then, suddenly, fear.

'Nikos!' gasped Katerina in a whisper.

Annika opened her eyes again, looked at her and nodded. 'He had borrowed the car because his would not start,' she explained. 'And Elena and Alexis were with him. It is they who are dead, mother. They were killed instantly. All three of them '

Katerina visibly recoiled under the blow. She could not believe it, did not want to believe it.

'Elena! Nikos! Alexi!' she cried on a rising note of anguish. 'Dead!' She shook her head. 'No, No. That is not so. That cannot be.'

Alarmed, Annika took a step towards her. 'Mother,' she said, putting out a hand to her. Katerina waved it away.

'No!' she keened wildly. 'That cannot be.' She turned to Spiridakis. 'How? How?' she demanded.

'The two men who saw it happen say that the car appeared to be out of control,' replied the lawyer.

Katerina swayed on her feet and pressed the palms of her hands to her forehead. 'Elena, my grandchild,' she wailed. 'Dead! Nikos, her husband, dead! And little Alexi, also dead. In the Englishman's car.' Demented, she staggered across to the wall plaque and stared at it in horror. 'What trick is this?' she screamed. 'What have you done to me?'

Annika, Spiridakis and Sia exchanged troubled, anxious looks. Now, very unsteady on her feet and breathing badly, Katerina swung round from the plaque, staggered over to the table and, head down, gripped the edge of it for support.

'Noukakis . . .' she croaked and she had difficulty in speaking. 'Matheous Noukakis . . . hear me . . . I . . . I curse . . . I curse . . .'

Noukakis paled. Oh my God, he thought, now she's lost her mind. The old fool's about to bring us both down. Panicking, he turned and ran from the room and out of the house.

Annika, Spiridakis and Sia had no time at that moment to give even a second thought to Noukakis' strange behaviour for, even before the front door slammed behind him and before Annika could cross to her, Katerina Matakis' knees buckled and she collapsed onto the floor.

While Spiridakis bent over them, Annika and Sia knelt beside her. Annika turned her mother over on to her back. She was unconscious and her skin had taken on a strange pallor.

251

I will get the doctor,' said Spiridakis and he hurried across to the door.

Matheos Noukakis ran out of his house carrying a rifle and a heavy rucksack. He threw the rucksack and the gun into the back of his carelessly parked car and then got in behind the steering wheel and drove off at speed.

Spiridakis and Sia were alone in the sitting room awaiting the doctor's diagnosis. Sia gazed at the plaque of the Moerae. 'What do you think *Kyria* Matakis meant when she spoke in that way to Noukakis?' she asked pensively. 'Was she cursing these, the Fates?' She turned to her husband. 'Or was she cursing him?'

Spiridakis shook his head. 'I do not know,' he said thoughtfully.

'And why did he run from the house?' Sia pressed him.

'That is another question I cannot answer,' Spiridakis replied. 'But there are many things in my mind. Things which trouble me greatly.'

The sitting-room door opened and Annika and the doctor, a grey-haired, stoop-shouldered man in his sixties, came into the room.

'She has had a stroke,' Annika informed them quietly.

The doctor nodded. 'And a very severe one I fear,' he confirmed. He looked at Annika. 'But, as I said, just how severe and how much damage has been done...' He shrugged. 'Well, that I cannot tell until she regains consciousness.'

'And when will that be?' asked Spiridakis.

The doctor gave another shrug. 'In minutes from now or not for several hours. A day. Longer perhaps. It is not possible to say. That is if she does regain consciousness. She may not. Again he looked at 'Annika. 'You must be prepared for that,' he warned her. Annika nodded. 'I will send a nurse to you,' the doctor went on, 'tonight. And if there is any change see to it that I am informed at once. I will, in any case, return in the morning.'

Annika thanked him. The doctor nodded to Spiridakis and Sia. *'Kalinicta.'*

'Kalinicta,' they replied.

He turned to Annika. *'Kalinicta,'* he repeated quietly. 'And please accept my deepest sympathy. For both the tragedies which have struck your family today.' He took her hand and pressed it. 'Have courage.'

Annika gave him a faint smile and then went with him to the front door.

'Annika cannot carry this burden alone, Babis,' said Sia urgently in a low voice. 'She needs her brother here at a time like this. He is head of the family.' She gave a helpless shrug. 'And where is he? Not even in Athens. On his way to San Francisco on business. When will he get the cable.'

'As soon as he arrives at his hotel,' her husband assured her.

Sia frowned. 'Is there no way of contacting him sooner than that? Cannot the airline send a radio message to the aircraft?'

Spiridakis nodded. 'Yes, I imagine so,' he said patiently. 'But what purpose would that serve? The plane will be half way there by now. The pilot cannot turn round and come back.'

Sia shook her head. 'San Francisco is such a long way away.'

Spiridakis put his arm around her shoulders. 'Yes, it is,' he agreed. 'But Petros will return as quickly as he can. Be sure of that.'

Annika came back into the room. Sia broke away from her husband and crossed to her.

'You will stay here tonight?' she asked.

Annika nodded. 'Yes, of course.'

'Then I will stay with you.'

'No,' said Annika. 'It is very kind of you, Sia, but you have a family of your own to look after. Go home. Cherish them. And give thanks.'

'But I do not wish you to be alone,' protested Sia. 'Not

253

tonight.'

'I shall not be alone. You heard what the doctor said. He is sending a nurse.'

Sia made an impatient gesture. 'A stranger,' she said. 'It is not the same.'

'No,' replied Annika. And then she smiled kindly. 'But it is sometimes better.'

Sia searched her face and then nodded. 'Yes,' she said. 'I understand.'

'Is there anything we can do?' asked Spiridakis, crossing to them.

Annika nodded. 'Yes, there is. On your way home go to Elounda for me,' she said. 'See Leandros. I am worried about him. This terrible thing that happened on the mountains. It has hurt him badly. Even more than it has hurt me I think. And God knows I am wounded badly enough by it. But you saw his reaction. It was as if Niko and Elena and Alexi were more than just dear friends to him. Much more.' She shook her head. 'I do not understand it.' Spiridakis frowned and then Annika went on, 'But I do know that his agony has cut into him and that he is bleeding.' She took the lawyer's hand. 'Go to him,' she asked. 'As I would if I could. And comfort him a little if you can. Will you do that for me?'

'Of course,' replied Spiridakis gripping her hand tightly and then releasing it.

'And give him my love,' added Annika.

Sia took her into her arms and held her close. 'Anything,' she whispered. 'Anything you need. You have only to speak. You know that.'

Annika nodded. And, in an attempt to conceal the fact that she was crying, Sia turned away from her and crossed to the sitting-room door.

Spiridakis kissed Annika. 'And at any time,' he assured her. 'And do not worry. Those things which have to be done. I will attend to them.'

He crossed to his wife and they moved away down the hallway and out of the house.

Watching them go, Annika's eyes fell on the plaque hanging on the wall beside the door. She walked slowly over to it and stood gazing at it. She frowned.

The lights were on in the living room of Haldane's house when Spiridakis parked his car outside it. Motioning to Sia to stay where she was, the lawyer got out of the car.

The music blaring out through the open windows was Stravinsky's *Rite of Spring*, strident with anguished savagery. Spiridakis hurried up the steps to the front door. It was ajar. He pushed it open.

Haldane was sitting at his worktable, slumped forward over his drawing board, his head resting on his arms, a glass held limply in his right hand and an empty brandy bottle lying on the table beside him. The raging music filled the room.

Spiridakis closed the front door, crossed to the record player and switched it off. Then he moved to the worktable and looked at Haldane and shook his head sadly but decided against disturbing his drunken sleep. Gently he eased the glass from his hand and set it down on the table. Then he studied his friend thoughtfully and sighed.

Crossing back to the front door, he switched off the lights and stepped out into the night again, closing the door quietly behind him.

Later that night Major Krasakis was sitting at his desk, speaking on the telephone and making notes. 'Yes...' he said urgently. 'Yes... How?...'

There was a knock on the door and Krasakis looked up briefly from the telephone as a sergeant ushered Spiridakis into the office.

'You are absolutely positive of that?...' the Major said into the telephone. He nodded to the sergeant and beckoned Spiridakis across to his desk. The sergeant withdrew.

'There can be no doubt, eh?... Right. Thank you.'

Krasakis replaced the telephone and stood up.

'I am glad that you are here, *Kyrie* Spiridakis,' he said. 'I have just received some very disturbing news.' He nodded towards the telephone. 'That call was from our Vehicle Section. Their experts have examined Leandros' car and they are in no doubt that what happened was not an accident. Apparently the car's brakes had been tampered with. Clumsily but very effectively.'

Spiridakis was deeply shocked by this. 'My God!'

The Major nodded. 'So now we are faced with a case of murder.'

'Multiple murder,' Spiridakis corrected him quietly.

'Yes. But in error I believe.' Spiridakis frowned. Krasakis went on, 'Because of a twist of fate which the murderer could not possibly have foreseen, because his intended victim was not driving the Fiat as he expected him to be. As he normally would have been had not Nikos Vassilakis' car broken down.'

'Leandros!' exclaimed the lawyer. 'Someone meant to kill Leandros!'

The Major nodded. 'There can be no doubt about that.' He studied Spiridakis. 'You are surprised?'

'Of course.'

Krasakis frowned. 'Leandros did not tell you about the letter he received?'

'What letter?'

Krasakis crossed to a filing cabinet, took a file from it and opened it. On top of the other reports and statements which it contained was the anonymous note which Haldane had received and the coins which accompanied it were in a small plastic envelope clipped to one corner of it. The Major handed the file to Spiridakis who read the note and frowned. He looked up at Krasakis. 'When did he receive this?'

'Less than a week ago. He did not mention it to you?'

The lawyer shook his head and returned the file to him. 'And you did nothing about it?' he scowled.

Krasakis shrugged. 'There was little I could do. The

paper is of a type which has a very wide sale. The only fingerprints we found on the note were those of Leandros and myself. And it was the same with the coins. I offered him protection but he refused it.' He made a helpless gesture. 'I could not force it on him. And he did promise me that he would be careful.'

'But who?' enquired Spiridakis incredulously. 'Who on Crete would want Leandros dead? And why?'

'Why?' Again the Major shrugged. 'Jealousy perhaps.' He moved back behind his desk. 'Although that may not be the only motive. As to who. Well, I think I know the answer to that question.' He sighed. 'But I do not believe it will be easy for me to prove it.'

'And are you willing to tell me who it is you suspect?' asked Spiridakis.

The Major studied him for a moment and then nodded. 'In the strictest confidence, yes,' he said. 'It is the same man I have always thought was responsible for the damage done to Leandros' possessions in your house. The man who I also believe set fire to his caique.' He picked up the cigarette box on his desk. 'Matheos Noukakis.'

Spiridakis frowned. 'Matheos!'

The Major nodded, opened the cigarette box and held it out to Spiridakis who shook his head.

'But if you thought him responsible for those acts why did you not arrest him?' he demanded angrily.

Krasakis gave him a patient look. 'Oh, come now, *Kyrie* Spiridakis,' he said. 'You are a lawyer. You know that it is one thing for a policeman to believe someone to be guilty of a criminal act and quite another for him to prove it.' He took a cigarette from the box and lit it. 'For that,' he went on, 'he needs evidence. The evidence I had against Noukakis was not sufficient to bring him before the courts. And when I questioned him about his whereabouts when Leandros' boat was destroyed I could not break his alibi. From time to time since then I have had him under surveillance. But with the limited number of men at my disposal it has not been possible twenty-four hours of every day. But I shall, of course, bring him in for questioning now,' he assured the lawyer.

Spiridakis nodded. 'Yes, Major,' he said grimly. 'And I would do that now if I were you. For you must know that when I went with *Kyria* Zeferis to break the news of the tragedy to her mother, Matheos Noukakis was there with her. And that when he heard what had happened he seemed greatly affected by the news and ran from the house.'

Krasakis reacted with an expression of alarm. Stubbing his cigarette into the ashtray, he snatched up the internal telephone on his desk and pressed one of the buttons on it.

'Major Krasakis,' he barked into the telephone. 'I want three men and a car. Immediately'.

CHAPTER TWENTY-FOUR

'Noukakis killed them!' breathed Haldane, stunned and bewildered.

He had not been to bed all night. His eyes were bloodshot, his clothes rumpled, his hair unkempt and his face unshaven. He had been awake for only a short time but he had already opened another bottle of brandy and poured himself a stiff drink from it when Spiridakis and the Major called on him early the following morning.

Now he sat on the settee in a lingering haze of alcohol which he had so recently freshened and in the grip of an emotion which was beginning to overwhelm his feeling of loss and feed off it.

Krasakis nodded. 'But by mistake,' he said. 'You were the one he planned to kill, Leandros.'

'You are certain of this?' Haldane asked flatly.

'Yes', confirmed the Major. 'I am certain of it.' He paused and then went on. 'Now. Just as I am sure that it was he who was responsible for the outrages committed against you previously.'

'And he has gone into hiding you say?'

'When we went to his house last night he was not there,' said Spiridakis. 'And his brother, Ioannis, has also disappeared. They are together it seems.'

Haldane looked at the Major. 'So what are you doing to find them?' he challenged. 'They could have left Crete by now.'

Krasakis shook his head. 'No. They are still on the island. A police patrol found Matheos Noukakis' car abandoned just outside Karto Asites. Like all Cretans in time of trouble they have gone into the mountains. And they are armed. But they will be taken. Be sure of that.'

Haldane scowled and gave him a scornful look.

'Perhaps,' he muttered. 'But when?' He got to his feet and crossed to the table. 'Up there around Oros Idi,' he went on bitterly. 'Anyone who knows the mountains, who knows how to survive, can hide for years from an army of men. I know.' He turned to Spiridakis. 'We did it, didn't we Babis? You and I. And others.'

'Yes,' agreed the lawyer. 'But the people who live there were on our side. We had friends, Leandros.'

'And the Noukakis brothers don't?' retorted Haldane.

Krasakis hesitated. He shrugged. 'A few perhaps,' he said. 'But the two men will be found. However long it may take. I will keep you informed.' He gave Haldane a salute. *'Kalimera, Leandros.'* He moved over to the front door and opened it.

'Why, Major?' asked Haldane quietly. Krasakis turned in the doorway to look back at him. 'Why should Matheos Noukakis want to kill me?'

Krasakis regarded him thoughtfully, then he said, 'He was jealous of you. That you know surely? But the real answer has to lie in the past I think.'

The Englishman frowned. 'There's nothing in my past that's in any way connected with Noukakis.'

'Perhaps not,' replied Krasakis, 'directly.' Again he studied Haldane. 'But in a lifetime, in every act, among the seeds we sow is the seed of tragedy. We would all do well to remember that. And tragedy is a plant which can take many years to grow, and even longer to blossom and bear its bitter fruit. It is possible that Matheos Noukakis may only have brought that fruit to market.' He paused just long enough to let his words sink in and then he turned and walked out through the front door.

Haldane reached for the bottle of brandy and poured some into his glass. Spiridakis moved to his side.

'How is Annika?' asked Haldane, staring at the drink in his hand.

'Holding on,' said the lawyer quietly. 'Her mother is very ill.' Haldane glanced at him. 'A stroke. Brought on by what has happened, I think.'

Haldane nodded. 'I'm sorry to hear that,' he said. And then he sighed. 'Poor Annika. So much to bear.' Again he looked down at his glass. 'You have not told her anything?' he asked.

'No. But she is worried about you.'

'I wish I could go to her,' Haldane sighed. 'But I can't. Not yet.'

He raised his glass to eye level and gazed at the brandy in it. Spiridakis frowned. 'You do not need that, Leandros, do you?' he asked gently.

Haldane turned his head to him and met his gaze. 'No.' His voice was cold. 'I don't need this. Not any more.' Swinging round, he savagely hurled the glass across the room and it shattered into the fireplace. 'There is only one thing I need now, Babis,' he continued almost in a whisper. 'And you know what that is.'

He looked at the lawyer and saw the troubled expression on his face. Spiridakis knew only too well what it was he was asking for. But he hesitated.

'It was my daughter,' said Haldane, pleading his cause, 'and my grandson who Noukakis killed. And Nikos is also dead. There is no one else. And I have the right.'

When Spiridakis left the house he was surprised to find Major Krasakis waiting for him at the bottom of the steps.

'Tell me,' he asked when the lawyer came level with him. 'Do you know of any reason why Katerina Matakis should hate Leandros? Enough to want him dead.'

'No,' exclaimed Spiridakis, genuinely taken aback. 'Why?'

The Major took a sheet of notepaper out of his pocket. 'When Matheos Noukakis' house was searched last night this was found,' he said. 'I did not wish to raise the question with you earlier when we were with Leandros because I know of his relationship with her daughter.'

He handed the letter to Spiridakis who unfolded it and read it.

'It is a pact,' went on Krasakis. 'An agreement. And it

clearly implicates *Kyria* Matakis in at least conspiring to kill the Englishman, of initiating the attempt.'

Stunned, the lawyer looked up from the letter. 'But from what motive? I know of none. That I swear to you.'

The Major held his look. 'And it also makes her an accomplice,' he continued, 'to the murder of her own granddaughter, and her great grandson.'

Spiridakis nodded. He was appalled. 'Dear God! No wonder she was struck down by the news. And with Noukakis there.' And then it became clear to him. 'It was him then that she cursed,' he added reflectively. He sighed, shook his head despairingly and then indicated the letter. 'What will you do about this?' he asked. 'Katerina Matakis is desperately ill. She is probably dying.'

The Major took the letter from him. 'In that case,' he said gravely, 'she will answer elsewhere for her part in this. And whatever God or gods she believes in perhaps there she will find some mercy.'

Katerina's eyes were open but it was obvious that she had no control over any of her limbs. Not once throughout the examination did she speak. When the doctor had finished he nodded to the nurse who pulled the bedclothes back over the old woman. The doctor smiled and nodded encouragingly at Katerina and then, picking up his bag from the bedside table, he left the room.

Annika was waiting for him in the sitting room, strained and exhausted.

'The damage is very bad I am afraid, *Kyria* Zeferis,' the doctor said with a sigh. 'Your mother is completely paralysed. She cannot move at all. She can hear and she can see. But she cannot speak. And that is how it will be with her until the end.'

Annika nodded. 'I understand,' she said. 'And how long will she live?'

The doctor shrugged. 'A day. A week. A month. Months even. A year perhaps. There is no way one can tell.' He shook his head. 'I am sorry.' There is nothing I can do. Nothing anyone can do. Except to make her as comfortable as possible. She will need constant attention. You would like the nurse to remain here?' he asked.

'Yes.'

'I will arrange it. And I will call every day.'

'Thank you,' said Annika.

The doctor shook his head once more and again he sighed. 'I only wish I could do more,' he replied wearily. 'To help her, and to comfort you.'

Once the doctor had left, Annika climbed the stairs to Katerina's bedroom. The nurse was sitting beside the bed intent on some embroidery. As Annika entered she made a move as if to stand up but Annika motioned her to stay where she was and then crossed to the bed and looked down at her mother, lying with her paralysed arms stretched out by her sides above the cover. Katerina Matakis stared up at her daughter desperately. There was so much that she wanted to say, to explain but she could not.

Annika smiled at her, lifted Katerina's right hand and kissed it. Then, gently, she put the useless and lifeless hand back on the bed again.

Lying on the bedside table was the key to the wooden box in the cabinet in the sitting room. Casually Annika picked it up and then turned and moved towards the door. Katerina was aware that she had picked up the key and frantically she tried to cry out, to speak but her lips would not move and she could not make a sound.

Annika slowly descended the stairs and went back into the sitting room. She crossed to the carved cabinet, opened the drawer and took out the wooden box. She carried it over to the table and set it down. Then, pulling up a chair, she settled herself on it and, with a sigh, unlocked the box and lifted the lid. Reaching inside, she pulled out the documents and the papers which it contained and which, with her mother no longer able to manage her own affairs, she knew she must now examine so as to be ready to discuss them with Petros when he arrived.

She was sorting through the papers when she found the letters addressed to Melina. Interested, she picked up the top envelope and studied it. She frowned slightly. The letters were written long ago and to her sister but somehow the handwriting seemed vaguely familiar. Curious, she pulled the letter out of the envelope, unfolded it and began to read.

Spiridakis drove along the rough, narrow, unpaved road to the point where it petered out entirely and they could go no further by car. He stopped the old Mercedes and he and Haldane got out. To the left a barely discernible goat track led the way up into the mountains and to the peaks of Oros Idi.

Both men were suitably dressed to make a long journey on foot across difficult terrain. Haldane had a knapsack slung over one shoulder and a pair of field glasses hanging from a strap around his neck. Together they went to the back of the car and Spiridakis opened the boot. Reaching into it, he pulled out a hunting rifle and a box of ammunition which he handed to Haldane.

The Englishman took the bullets from the box and slipped them into his pocket. Then, expertly, he checked the action of the rifle and fed some of the ammunition into the magazine.

Spiridakis pointed to the goat track. 'They were last seen above the village of Visagi, heading west.'

'Do the police know this?' asked Haldane.

Spiridakis shook his head. 'Not from me. And not from any man who was with the Andarte. They will report any sightings.' He took a second rifle and some ammunition from the boot. 'But only to us,' he added.

Haldane looked at him and then at the gun he was holding and shook his head. 'To me,' he said firmly.

Spiridakis frowned. 'Noukakis is not alone,' he protested. 'His brother, Ioannis, is with him. He is a wild one, and they are very close.'

'On my own, Babis,' insisted Haldane flatly. 'This is my affair. My vengeance.' He clipped the magazine into the rifle and, snapping home the bolt, drove a cartridge into the breech. He put on the safety catch. 'And I want no one else at risk,' he said adamantly.

Spiridakis searched his face and saw from his expression that there was no point in arguing. He put the second rifle and the ammunition he was holding back into the boot of the car and closed it. Then he turned to Haldane and embraced him. 'Take care, Leandros,' he said. 'And God be with you.'

Haldane nodded, slung the rifle on to his shoulder and then, moving away from the car, started to make his way up the track.

For some time Spiridakis stood watching him climb, sure-footed and with purpose, higher and higher up into the mountains.

As Spiridakis entered his office he pulled up sharply with a look of surprise. His secretary had not been at her desk as he had strode past it so he was unaware that Annika was waiting for him.

'Annika!' he exclaimed.

She was standing looking out of the window. She turned to him. Spiridakis closed the door.

Annika, her eyes on his face, opened her handbag and took from it the three letters which Haldane had written to Melina. She held them out to the lawyer.

'I found these,' she said tonelessly, 'locked away in a box in my mother's house.'

The letters meant nothing to Spiridakis. He had never seen them before. He walked over to her, took them from her and examined them. He frowned and then, after shooting a worried glance at her, pulled one of the letters from its envelope and scanned it. His frown deepened.

'You knew of this?' she asked.

Spiridakis looked at her again and he could see that there was nothing to be gained from lies. He nodded.

'Yes,' he said quietly and with a sigh. 'And I also knew that Leandros had written such letters because when he first returned to Crete he told me that he had. But Melina never received them. Of that I was certain and I said this to him. But I could not explain why.' He shook his head sadly. 'Now I know. Katerina intercepted them.'

'Melina was very much in love with him?' she asked. And from her expression the lawyer could tell that the answer was very important to her. 'Deeply,' he said.

'And he with her?'

'Yes.' This was the moment. The moment he had dreaded. For her and for Leandros. But there was no evading it. 'And there are other things that you must know, Annika.'

CHAPTER TWENTY-FIVE

Matheos Noukakis and his brother, a short, thickset, ill-tempered looking man in his mid-thirties, slithered down the tree and rock-covered slope and on to the road. They each had a rucksack on his back and each carried a rifle.

They hesitated, crouching behind the cover of a bush. Noukakis glanced up the road. Apart from two men sitting at a table under the shade of a tree outside the local taverna intent on their game of tavli, the village street appeared to be deserted. Matheos signalled to his brother and, keeping low, they dodged quickly across the road.

Out of the corner of his eye, the younger of the two tavli players was aware of the sudden movement down the street from where he was sitting. He glanced up and saw the Noukakis brothers take shelter behind the drinking fountain. He frowned and then turned his attention back to the tavli board.

Matheos and Ioannis waited for a few seconds, crouching beside the water trough, then they climbed up into the sanctuary of the trees on the rising ground behind them.

The sun was beginning to set when Haldane, following almost exactly the same path taken by his quarry, came down the slope and stepped onto the road. He looked around cautiously and then crossed to the fountain and, leaning his rifle against the trough, drank from the cool, sweet water gently spouting from the pipe above it.

Very much on the alert and suddenly aware that someone was approaching him, he grabbed his rifle again and, with the gun levelled from his hip and flicking off the safety catch, swung round.

The younger of the two tavli players pulled up sharply three or four yards off from him. He was a man of about Haldane's own age. 'Leandros?' he asked.

Haldane nodded and lowered the barrel of his rifle a little. The man came up to him and pointed in the direction taken by the Noukakis brothers. 'Two, three hours ago,' he said.

Haldane considered the man and then nodded his thanks. Resetting the safety catch, he slung the rifle over his shoulder and started up the slope and into the trees. Spiridakis had been right, he thought. He had said that the news that Leandros of the Andarte was hunting Matheos Noukakis would spread quickly. But then, he reflected grimly that if the people of the mountain villages knew this then surely so must the men he was following. And if that was the case then sooner or later somewhere up there in the rocky wilderness below the snowline they would be waiting for him.

Annika, alone in the chapel, her eyes closed, knelt on the stone floor and prayed.

Then after some minutes, she rose from her knees, crossed to the candle stand, slipped a handful of coins into the box, took a candle, lit it from the guttering flame of one already burning and then wedged it into the sand. For a few seconds she stared at the taper then she turned from it and walked away and out through the chapel door.

She crossed to her car. The sun, an enormous blood red ball, was beginning to sink behind the mountains. Silhouetted against it, Annika stood and gazed at this symbol of mankind's most ancient beliefs and silently she delivered up another prayer to other gods.

As the sun sank and the mountain air around them grew cooler, Noukakis and his brother heard the helicopter and dived for cover.

The chopper came close to their hiding place but then veered off on another course.

From his seat beside the pilot, Krasakis scanned the mountainside below them through binoculars. He could detect nothing moving on the rugged terrain and the light was going fast. He lowered the binoculars and signalled to the pilot to turn back. The pilot nodded and then swung the helicopter on to an easterly heading and a course which took it exactly over the spot where, 200 feet beneath it, Alan Haldane lay, cramped and motionless, in the shelter of a defile in the rocks.

When he judged that the helicopter was too far away for anyone in it to spot him, he got to his feet and slung his haversack and the rifle over his shoulders.

Haldane had known from the very beginning that he was on the right track from the information given to him by the occasional shepherd he had met on the way and by checking, whenever he had been close enough to a village with a telephone, with Spiridakis to whom all the ex-members of the Andarte immediately relayed any sightings of the fugitives.

And less than an hour earlier, from a high peak, he had caught a glimpse of Matheos and Ioannis Noukakis through the powerful field glassed Spiridakis had given him. He had estimated that the two small but identifiable figures were, at most, only four miles ahead of him and, as Major Krasakis had predicted, were heading west towards Sfakia.

Soon it would be dark but while there was still some light he might be able to narrow the gap between them some more. He set off in pursuit.

It was nearly ten o'clock at night but Babis Spiridakis was still in his office. Spread out in front of him and illuminated by the lamp on his desk was a large scale map of the western half of the island.

Spiridakis spoke into the telephone. 'Yes . . . Yes . . .' he acknowledged. And then he checked the map. This latest information confirmed the last sighting he had been given. 'Good,' he said into the phone. 'Thank you.' And he hung up.

As he did so the door of his office, which was still ajar, was gently pushed open and Major Krasakis stepped into the room.

Spiridakis quickly folded the map and got to his feet.

'Forgive me, *Kyrie* Spiridakis,' the Major apologised with a smile. 'But there was no one in the outer office to announce me.'

Spiridakis shook his head. 'No. My secretary is not here.'

Krasakis stood in the doorway and looked at him. He glanced at the folded map on the desk. 'And yet you are still working,' he said, and there was a faint note of surprise in his voice.

'On personal business,' replied Spiridakis.

'And your telephone call?' Krasakis enquired pleasantly.

The lawyer frowned. 'Was in connection with that,' he countered abruptly.

'I see,' smiled the Major. He crossed slowly to the desk and, as he did so, Spiridakis casually picked up the map and put it into a drawer.

'I have been to Leandros' house,' Krasakis went on. 'He was not there.'

'Oh!' The lawyer hoped that he sounded sufficiently surprised.

'No. And I thought that perhaps you might know where he is.'

Spiridakis shook his head and met Krasakis' gaze. 'No, Major. I am afraid that I cannot help you. I have no idea where he is . . .' He paused and then added to give truth to the statement, 'at this moment.'

Again the Major studied him. Then he nodded thoughtfully. 'He was close to the Vassilakis family, was he not?' he asked.

'Yes.'

'More than just a friend would you say?'

'He loved them,' replied Spiridakis. 'All of them. That is no secret.'

'And their deaths will naturally have caused him great pain.'

'Naturally. As they pained all who knew them.'

'But Leandros more than others perhaps?' persisted Krasakis. 'Particularly since he knows they died in his place.'

Spiridakis shrugged. 'Perhaps.'

'And knowing that,' the Major went on, 'and knowing who killed them and who it was who would have killed him, a man like Leandros might be tempted to do something foolish, do you not think?'

Spiridakis gave him a puzzled, questioning look. 'Something foolish, Major?' he asked innocently.

Krasakis nodded. 'Like seeking revenge. Taking the law into his own hands.'

Spiridakis hesitated. Then he made a gesture. 'Who can say?' he said. 'He might.'

'Yes, he might,' Krasakis nodded and he was no longer smiling. 'That is why I went to his house. To advise him against taking any such action.' He turned and moved to the door where he paused and looked back at the lawyer. 'You understand?'

Spiridakis nodded. 'I understand.'

'Good,' said the Major. 'For were he to find Noukakis and kill him in vengeance that would make him a murderer, and put me against him. And I would not want that. Tell him this, will you?'

'Yes, Major,' replied Spiridakis levelly. 'I will tell him.' He shrugged and gave the policeman a faint smile. 'When I next see him.'

Georgios Kaladis yawned widely and scratched himself as he crossed to the front door of his house and opened it to the first light of a new day. He stepped outside, spat and looked around sleepily.

Kaladis' house and the small patch of land which he owned and worked with his wife and family lay on the outer fringes of a small village high in the mountains. Yawning again, he surveyed the scrubland beyond where he stood.

It was then that he saw and recognised Matheos and Ioannis Noukakis.

They were approaching the house along a path which would bring them within twenty feet of it. Matheos was holding his rifle over his shoulder while his brother had his nestled in the crook of his left arm. They were moving quickly but warily. But not warily enough, thought Kaladis. They had obviously not spotted him in the doorway.

He stepped back ino the house took down his shotgun from the pegs on which it rested on the wall beside the fireplace and loaded both barrels.

Matheos and his brother came level with the house and, as they did so, Kaladis appeared in the open doorway. He took two or three paces out of the house and levelled the shotgun.

'You two!' he called out. 'Stop! I know who you are. Do not move.'

Matheos and Ioannis pulled up sharply and slowly turned to the old man. The shotgun was unwavering and the expression on Kaladis' face was uncompromising. Noukakis shot a worried, questioning look at his brother. Ioannis gave him a brief nod and, as Matheos made a sudden, feinting movement as if to make a run for it, Kaladis swung the shotgun round to cover him.

In one swift, fluid movement Ioannis levelled his rifle and fired.

The impact of the bullet hurtled Kaladis back through the open doorway and on to the floor of the house. From inside a woman screamed.

The Noukakis brothers turned and ran.

An hour or so later, Haldane heard the piteous wailing coming from the house when he was still a long way from it. He paused and frowned. He was unshaven, stiff, chilled and very tired despite the few hours' sleep which he had allowed himself, huddled in a crevice in the rocks.

The wailing continued uninterrupted and at times chorussed by other voices. Haldane walked on again and, as he drew nearer, he saw the group of villagers gathered around the front door.

At his approach the group outside the house turned to him, the men among them looking grim and angry. It was clear to Haldane that they knew who he was when he heard the name 'Leandros' whispered among them.

One of the men moved away from the front door and confronted him on the path. 'They killed Georgios,' he said. And he indicated the route which Matheos and Ioannis had taken when they had fled. Without a word, Haldane stepped off the path and headed away from the house.

He had only gone a few yards when a distraught woman in her mid-thirties, her face stained with tears, ran from the house, pushed her way through the villagers outside and caught up with him. Dropping on her knees in front of him, she took his right hand and kissed it. Haldane showed no surprise, his face was expressionless. Then the woman put into his hand a traditional Cretan dagger in a silver sheath.

The Englishman looked at the knife and then at the woman. He nodded. He would carry the knife for her so that his vengeance should also be hers.

Slipping the dagger into his belt, he moved on again.

The old shepherd was building a fire on the mountain-side while his grandson kept a watchful eye on the flock of goats. He looked up from the pile of kindling and out over the natural amphitheatre some way below the slope where his animals were grazing. Without rising, the shepherd shaded his eyes with his hand so as to get a clearer sight of the two men crossing the hollow and making for the mouth of the car on the far side of it.

He frowned and then scowled. Still without moving, he whistled softly to attract the attention of his grandson and, motioning him to keep low, beckoned him over to him. Crouching, the boy hurried to his side and in a low voice the old man whispered his instructions. The boy shot a look of alarm down into the amphitheatre then nodded excitedly and, still crouching, ran off along the track which led to their village.

Noukakis and his brother crossed the hollow, which was littered with outcrops of rock, climbed up the narrow ledge which led to the cave and, exhausted, flopped down on either side of the entrance to it.

Wearily Ioannis unstrapped his rucksack and opened it. From it he took some bread, some olives, a piece of cheese wrapped in a cloth, and a bottle of wine.

At Spiridakis' call they had come from every part of the district. Some of them had travelled with the lawyer from Heraklion. Others had made the journey from places even further away. Now, with their cars and pick-up trucks parked around them, they had gathered together on the open ground in front of the monastery of Arkadhi.

There were more than seventy of them, the majority of them had fought together in the Andarte during the war, the others were their sons. They were all armed, some with shotguns but most carried those same rifles and stenguns which they has used against the Germans so many years ago and kept in their homes ever since. Many of them had bandoliers of ammunition slung over their shoulders or across their chests.

Babis Spiridakis, standing in the back of a pick-up truck parked just outside the gates of the monastery and holding a rifle, addressed them. 'You all know what has happened,' he cried. 'Ioannis Noukakis has shot and killed Georgios Kalakis, a good friend to all of us and a brave and faithful comrade when we were of the Andarte of Crete.'

There was an angry roar from the crowd.

'My brother, Leandros, is already in the mountains seeking vengeance for the great wrong which Matheos Noukakis has done,' Spiridakis continued. 'But now, with the murder of Georgios, we too must act. Or we leave unpaid a debt which we owe to his wife and family.'

This was greeted by a cry of assent from the assembly. One of men called, 'We are with you, Babis Spiridakis. We follow The Eagle.'

'Leandros is no longer alone in his search,' shouted Spiridakis. 'Are we agreed on that?'

There were cries of,'Yes, Yes,' and, 'Avenge Georgios.'

'I have received word that Matheos and Ioannis Nukakis have been seen close to Kalogerado. And Leandros will not be far behind them I think. Come!' He jumped down from the back of the truck and the crowd broke up as the men hurried to their vehicles.

Spiridakis opened the door of his car, put his rifle on to the passenger seat and was about to get in when a police Land-rover and a lorry drove up the road to the monastery.

The lorry, loaded with armed policemen, pulled across the road and blocked it while the Land-rover came to a stop close to Spiridakis' car. Major Krasakis and an armed sergeant got out of it. The ex-members of the Andarte exchanged angry looks. They were not to be put off their hunt. And, if necessary, they were prepared to take on the police should they try to stop them. As if to make this point absolutely clear one of the men standing alongside his pick-up truck pulled back the bolt of the stengun he was holding. The sound echoed menacingly back from the walls of the monastery.

Krasakis looked grimly around the forecourt and then he studied Spiridakis. Slowly the two men advanced on one another and came face to face.

The police and the men of the Andarte watched them and each other anxiously and warily. Spiridakis frowned.

'You were not here, Major. You have not seen us,' he suggested.

'But I am here,' said Krasakis with a shrug. 'And I have seen you.'

'Then do not try to stop us.'

'I have to, the Major told him.'And I will. As you know

275

I must.' He sighed. 'For this way leads to anarchy, and anarchy leads to more Colonels. It has happened before and, sadly, perhaps it will happen again. But I will not contribute to bringing that about.'

He looked around at the faces of the veterans of the Andarte and knew that it would only need a signal from Spiridakis for them to open fire on his men. He looked back at the lawyer again.

'Stay on this course and blood will be shed between us, Babis Spiridakis,' he said. 'For if I must, I will use force to try to prevent you from doing this thing. And that will give hope and comfort to all the barbarians of this world. That is the truth. And you know it. And you, of all people, would not have that.'

Spiridakis considered the Major, turning over in his mind what he had said and knowing him to be right. He nodded. 'The word is that the Noukakis brothers are hiding near Kalogerado,' he said quietly.

'Yes, I know,' said Krasakis. The lawyer gave him a look of surprise. Krasakis smiled. 'You who were the Andarte are not alone in having eyes and ears across Crete,' he said patiently. 'How else do you think I knew of this gathering. But I thank you for telling me.' He turned to move back to his Land-Rover.

'We will come with you,' said Spiridakis. And it was more of a plea than a suggestion.

The Major turned back to him and studied him once more. Then he gazed around again at the faces of the ex-partisans. Looking back at the lawyer he held his gaze for a while and them smiled. 'Is it not the duty of all good citizens to assist the police?' But then he added formally. 'But under my command. Under my orders.'

Spiridakis nodded his acceptance of the terms and called out. 'We go with the Major.'

There was a cheer from the men pledged to him. The Eagle had spoken. Honour was satisfied. The confrontation was over. The police breathed again and wiped the sweat from their faces.

As the Major moved back to his Land-Rover, Spiridakis got into his car and then, with the Land-Rover and the lorry in the lead, the convoy moved off.

From his vantage point on the mountainside the old shepherd sat, squatting on his haunches, keeping watch.

He reacted with a start when he saw Haldane approaching the amphitheatre. His first reaction was to call out a warning but he realised that that would only alert the Noukakis brothers in the mouth of the cave and that, out in open ground, the Englishman would be an easy target for them. If they did not spot him until he was in the hollow then, with so many rocks to shelter behind, he would, at least, stand a better chance. And from what he had heard of the cunning and skill of this Leandros he might just spot the two men first.

The old man looked up at the sun. It was high in the sky and he found comfort in that. If his grandson had followed his instructions the men of the Andarte would be on their way by now. They could even at that moment be on the track beyond the crest of the slope above where he was squatting. They would have to leave their vehicles there and climb up the far side of the ridge for, except along the path which led to the village and on which a large party of men would be too exposed, there was no other way to reach the hollow for a surprise attack.

Standing up, the shepherd turned and, moving as quickly as he could, he started up the steep slope behind him. If the men of the Andarte were close at hand then they must know of the danger that their comrade was in.

Ioannis was dozing. Noukakis put the half-empty bottle of wine and the remains of their meal back into his brother's rucksack, got to his feet and stretched. Then he saw Haldane. The Englishman was not more than thirty yards off from the hollow. Noukakis kicked his brother awake and Ioannis stood up beside him. Noukakis pointed. Ioannis scowled and reached for his rifle.

The policeman and the ex-partisans got out of their

vehicles and awaited orders. Krasakis gazed up the slope of the mountainside to their right and, as he did so, the old man appeared on the ridge and started scrambling down to them, waving excitedly and pointing.

Krasakis shouted a command. 'Spread out!' The policeman and the men of the Andarte did as they were ordered. And then, with the Major and Spiridakis slightly in the lead, they began to advance up the slope. But the going was not easy and they moved slowly.

Haldane entered the amphitheatre, took cover and looked around. If he had to choose a site for an ambush this would certain be the spot he would pick. He saw the cave on the far side of the hollow and checked it through his field glasses. There was no sign of movement. But it offered just the kind of shelter which two tired men on the run would welcome. Cautiously, his rifle at the ready and zigzagging from one outcrop of rock to another, he crossed the hollow. Using all the old skills he had learned in his days with the Commandos and with the partisans, he reached the mouth of the cave convinced that if the Noukakis brothers were hiding in it, then they had not yet sighted him. For a few seconds he stood on the ledge to one side of the entrance, his back pressed against the rock then, with his rifle at the ready, he swung round in a crouching position into the mouth of the cave. It was empty.

Haldane turned and looked back across the amphitheatre. There was no sign of anyone. He had been wrong. If his quarry had stopped here at all then they had moved on before he reached the spot.

He climbed down from the ledge and started back across the hollow and then, as he reached the centre of it, Ioannis Noukakis broke cover to one side of him, took aim and fired. The shot echoed and re-echoed through the mountains.

The bullet missed the Englishman by only a few inches and ricocheted off a rock. Haldane whirled round, dropping on to one knee as he did so. Ioannis was in plain view. Snapping his rifle up to his shoulder, Haldane fired. The bullet slammed into his target's chest and Ioannis Noukakis was thrown backwards by the force.

The police and the Andarte were now half way up the slope on the far side of the ridge. They had heard the sound of the two shots and the echoes of the second were still around them. Spiridakis and the Major exchanged deeply troubled looks.

Krasakis turned to a policeman who had come up beside him and, taking his rifle from him, hurried on up the slope, scrabbling over the stoney ground. Spiridakis and the others followed him.

Ioannis Noukakis writhed for a few seconds and then lay still. Haldane waited for almost a minute but then, when there were no further shots, he edged out from behind the rock where he had taken cover. If Matheos Noukakis was waiting to fire, then Haldane reckoned that he had, by now, exposed enough of himself for the murderer to loose off a shot at him. Nothing happened. There was silence in the hollow and no movement anywhere.

Keeping low and pausing every few feet, Haldane zigzagged across the amphitheatre towards Ioannis. He dived for cover once more and waited. Again he raised his head and peered around the hollow. Of course it was just possible, he thought, that Matheos had gone on ahead leaving his brother to lie in wait for him. If so, then the man with whom he still had a score to settle was gaining a better lead on him with every second that passed.

Haldane broke cover again and crawled the last few feet to Ioannis and crouched by his body. He was dead, his eyes open and staring, his mouth already filling with flies. Sickened and still looking down at the dead man, Haldane slowly straightened up.

'Englishman!' shouted Noukakis. His voice came from

behind Haldane. Knowing that Matheos would have him covered, Haldane turned very slowly.

Noukakis was standing on the top of an outcrop of rock behind and slightly to one side of him. My God, thought Haldane, he could only have been a few feet away from me when I crossed the hollow. Then Noukakis took careful aim and fired.

The bullet punched a hole into Haldane's stomach. He dropped his rifle and cried out in agony as he was pitched back several feet by the blow on to the ground. He clutched at his wound and bleeding badly, he rolled over onto his face and looked up.

Noukakis, his rifle lowered, was still standing on the rock watching him. Very slowly and wracked with pain, Haldane began to crawl to where his gun was lying. It was his only hope and he knew it. Noukakis waited until the Englishman's hand was just a few inches from the fallen rifle and then, smiling, he raised his gun again and took aim to administer the *coup de grace.* Haldane lifted his head, saw the rifle levelled at him and knew that he was only seconds away from death. Noukakis' finger tightened on the trigger.

Haldane heard the shot but it seemed to him to come from far away and then he fell into a deep, dark pit and went on falling.

Major Krasakis, standing on the ridge of the slope overlooking the hollow, slowly lowered the rifle with which he had just killed Matheos Noukakis. And as he did so, Spiridakis and the others came up on to the crest and joined him.

Falling, falling, falling. Haldane fell further and further. 'Alan, Alan, I love you,' cried Lorna Matthews as her face swam before him. And then she was no longer Lorna but Ruth, and she was laughing. And now Ruth was Melina, eighteen and naked, her arms outstretched to him. 'We had to sell,' snapped his brother and Alexis begged him to fly the kite with him again. And then he was on a beach and The

Knot was blazing and people were running. 'Every day,' smiled Elena, 'it is our pleasure. My father would be pleased, do you not think... do you not think... do you not think? Nikos raised his glass to him. 'Yassou,' he cried. He ran towards Melina. 'I wrote to you,' he heard himself shout. 'I wrote to you.' She laughed and ran past him. Spiridakis embraced him. 'Love is a gift... a gift... a gift,' said Annika and Noukakis levelled his rifle and squeezed the trigger. And then he was on beach again but this time by a river and he was no longer falling. Charon, the ferryman, held out his hand to him and Haldane offered him his fee.

The nurse had just given Katerina a drink and she was straightening the bedclothes when Annika came into the room carrying a framed photograph and Haldane's three letters. Her face was expressionless.

She crossed to the chest of drawers opposite the end of the bed and laid the framed photograph on it, face down. Then she turned to the nurse and, with a movement of her head indicated that she would like her to leave the room. The nurse smiled at her, nodded and hurried out, closing the door behind her.

Slowly Annika crossed to the bed and, standing alongside it, looked down at her mother.

Katerina gazed up at her helplessly. Annika raised the three letters into her line of vision. The old woman's eyes widened.

'I should pity you,' said Annika quietly. 'But I do not. I should love you. But I cannot. Leandros lies wounded in the hospital. Dying perhaps. Even now they are operating on him to try to save him. But no one can say for certain that he will live. Already six people are dead, among them your own granddaughter and your great grandson. And you killed them, mother. Oh, it is true that yours was not the hand that took their lives, but you killed them nonetheless. And why? Because of your hatred and bigotry. Because of your own guilt. Born out of the festering sore which you have nursed for more than thirty years. No other reason. Leandros did not dishonour my sister, Melina. You did. By withholding these letters from her. And you did that not out of your love for her but out of your hatred for the foreigner to whom she had given herself. Out of your hatred for all foreigners.

You were the cause of so much misery and unhappiness. Then and in the years which followed, and you knew that. And felt guilty. Oh, such a burden of guilt you carried on your shoulders. And then, when Leandros returned to Crete and you saw that I loved him as Melina had, that you could not bear.'

Katerina struggled to speak but no words came. And she could not move. Annika went on remorselessly. 'Because you knew that if you had come to me with the truth it was you who would stand accused and not him. And that I would see that. And Elena would have turned against you. And rightly so. For you had done her a great wrong. You had robbed her of the joy of knowing her true father. And you knew that also. So you took your guilt and twisted it and placed it as a cloak around Leandros' shoulders. Now his punishment would be your absolution. First you conspired to drive him away and then, when he would not go, you used another man's jealousy and greed in an attempt to kill him.' Annika paused and shook her head. 'Well, are you pleased with the result, mother,' she asked bitterly. 'What is the weight of your guilt now? You are a wicked, evil woman. And a murderess. A stench in the nostrils of God. Remember that when you stand before him. And just as you have alienated and lost the love of your son, so now you have lost me. For you will never see me again. And I take from this house my inheritance. Hatred. And I know how to use it. For am I not your daughter.'

She crossed to the chest of drawers, picked up the framed photograph and set it upright on its stand in a position where, paralysed as she now was, Katerina could not help but look at it.

The photograph was of Elena, Nikos and Alexis, a

282

happy family group in a somewhat stilted and formal pose.
Katerina's eyes widened even further with horror.

'To keep you company,' said Annika. 'To remind you.
Through every waking moment while you still live. Look
at them, mother. Look at them. As you must. As you
cannot help but look at them. And pray. Pray that you die
soon.'

She crossed to the bedroom door, opened it and
beckoned to the nurse. As she re-entered Annika pointed
to the photograph.

'Do not move that,' she said in a conversational tone.
'Leave it exactly as it is, always. It comforts her so.'

The nurse looked at Katerina and gave her a warm,
sympathetic and understanding smile and then she nodded
to Annika.

Annika looked at her mother for the last time and then
turned and walked out of the room.

The nurse studied the photograph, looked at Katerina
again and gave her another smile. Then she sat down on
the chair beside the bed and picked up her embroidery.

Katerina stared at the photograph and then, unable to
bear the sight of it, closed her eyes. But she knew that she
would have to open them again and that it would still be
there; that it would always be there while she lay in that
bed in a very special kind of hell from which there was
only one escape — if then.

Soundlessly, the old woman screamed.

Haldane, pale, his eyes closed, lay in the hospital bed, a
blood drip connected to his arm.

Annika stood by the window gazing out through the
slats of the shutters which were closed. She turned to the
door as it was opened and Spiridakis came into the room.
He glanced at her and then crossed to the bed and gazed
down at Haldane. Annika moved to his side. The lawyer
looked at her questioningly.

'Has he regained consciousness yet?' he asked.

Annika shook her head. 'No. And he is very sick. But

the operation was a success. The doctor says that he will recover.'

Spiridakis nodded. 'And you?' he asked. 'How are you?'

'I am free,' she replied fervently. 'As never before.'

Spiridakis studied her and then frowned. 'Have you been here all night?'

'Most of the night.'

'Then you should get some rest.'

'No,' said Annika quietly. 'I will stay. I want to be here when he wakes. And later, when he is strong enough, there is much we have to say to each other, Leandros and I.'

She moved a chair close to the bed and sat down on it.

Spiridakis looked at her and then turned and left the room, closing the door quietly behind him.

Annika reached out, took Haldane's hand, kissed it and then held it to her cheek.

BY THE SAME PUBLISHER

Crete 1941 the battle at sea by David A. Thomas in English.

Der Kampf um Kreta by Franz Kurowski in German.

GREEK LITERATURE

The Mermaid Madonna by Stratis Myrivilis in English.

The Schoolmistress with the Golden Eyes by Stratis Myrivilis in English.

CRETE
Gramvousa
Pondikonisi
KASTELLI
KHANIA
Sternai
SOUDHA
RETHIMNON
IRAKLION
Amnisos
Áyios Nikolaos
Pakhia Ámmos
Itanos
Sitia
Plaka
Koufonisi
Gaïdouronisi
Gavdo
N
Kándanos
Palaiokhora
ELYROS
LISSOS
Khóra Sfakion
Spilion
Amárion
Pérama
ELEUTHERNA
M. ARKADHIOU
IDAEAN CAVE
AXOS
TYLISSOS
SKLAVOKAMBOS
KNOSSOS
Anóyia
Krousón
Áyios Miron
VATHYPETRO
Kastéllion
CHERSONESOS
MALLIA
DREROS
Neápolis
KARPHI
Tzermiádhon
DICTAEAN CAVE
LATO
Kritsá
Kalamávka
Ierápetra
Vóri
PHAISTOS
Miraï
GORTYN
Pirgos
LEBENA
Anu Viannos
Sémbronas
Voukolia
Alikianos
Varipetron
Galatas
Meskla
Lakkoi
Omalos
Armenoi
Koumas
Kirianna
Khoumeri
Zoniana
Livadhia
Episkopi
Fourfouras
Kamares
Akoumia
Zaros
Avdhou
Kera
Vrisai
Maronia
Pevkoi
Ziros
Skinias
Sikologos
Kharakas

Greece